A Breath Before Drowning

Kate Church

1

       I was seventeen and just like any other teen growing up in a small town. There wasn't much to do except hangout with friends or stroll around in the great outdoors. As recent immigrates from our native Ireland my family stood out despite our efforts to blend in. I was the youngest of three children, born to parents who had been together for the better part of three decades by this time. My folks were university sweethearts and met one dreary afternoon in the university's library. Considering their love of literature, it's easy to picture them colliding into one another as their focus was heavily drawn to the books they were reading. They seemed like the perfect parents, and we were nearlythe perfect family, nearly.

       We arrived in the town of Warwick just shy of a year ago. My parents almost immediately found comfort in their positions at the university, but our new surroundings were not as kind to my brothers and I. As the offspring of professors in language and literature, speaking out of turn or improper grammar was simply unacceptable. This alone made us stand out like lepers among fellow members of the student body. In addition to our nearly perfect grammar, we were a strict Catholic family. Under my parent's ever watchful eyes there would be no philandering, shenanigans or ill-mannered behavior of any sort or one would risk being cast out. I am greatly comforted by my faith, but when dealing in absolutes it rarely, if ever, leaves room for deviation.

While the relocation was sudden my eldest brother, Rhys, and I made short work of putting our mark on our new environment. He quickly found a position at a local warehouse slugging boxes and enrolled at a university where he could work towards the engineering degree he started back home. He has always been an overachiever and I expected nothing less when we relocated here. I was nothing if not a bookworm, so excelling academically was my top priority. I chose to participate in a few societies at school and focused heavily on my studies. My other brother, Liam, did not take well to the transition and from the moment we arrived he has progressively slide further down the rabbit hole. While his behavior was challenged for several months by our folks, I believe even they have relaxed hoping his behavior would one day divert back to the young man he once was. I was not so hopeful and did what I could to avoid him.

Starting off my junior year, I told myself this year things would be different. I was anxious shed my wallflower reputation and to step into the limelight even if it was just for a moment. This and my family's finances were the two biggest obstacles in my way. While my parents were educated what was considered a substantial salary in Ireland appeared to be petty cash here. I mostly wore name-brand knockoffs those were not going to win me any popularity contests. However, I was fortunate to have a few friends that didn't seem to mind our finances or what I wore. Those two ladies were the same friends that I had since we arrived in Warwick. Those type of friends are what keep you grounded, remind you what matters and can be there for you when you feel like your world is falling apart, which for most juniors that can occur on a daily basis.

On a cool, crisp Friday night my friends and I decided to head out to a varsity football game. There was nothing particularly different about this night just something to do. The game started off in the usual fashion and since I wasn't a football fan that meant it was time to mingle. Snacks were in order along with bogarting a small nook near the edge of the field where the gossip could commence uninterrupted.

As the temperature dropped so did the game clock and I took a much-needed restroom break. I went alone figuring I could catch up on the gossip upon my return. On my way to the ladies' locker room, I ran into one of our school's most desirable bachelors. Derek was stunning in appearance; hair was the color of wheat in the fall and his near perfect skin appeared to glow in nearly any light. Tonight, was no exception. I may have been lower on the social ladder, but my flirtatious behavior accompanied by his charisma managed to draw him if only for a moment. He may have been highly flirtatious and notoriously unobtainable, but our brief encounters and mild flirtation upon my arrival in Warwick had left me wanting.

I can hardly recall what words he spoke only that he seemed insistent that we speak. Unlike our previous encounters this time we were entirely alone and out of earshot for the majority which certainly set tongue's wagging. We walked toward the school while making small talk when he casually veered towards the backside of the high school where I followed him without question. Based on rumor alone, moments alone with him were coveted and rarely given so publicly as to not taint his father's political standing as the town's mayor. I would notbe so careless as to refuse the opportunity laid before me.

In the dark the area looks hauntingly abandoned compared to the hustle and bustle that would be found during the day. As the awkwardness of the small talk dwindled away, he revealed his attraction to me despite what his previous behavior may have led me to believe. I'm sure my face was mirroring the perplexing thoughts in my head, but nevertheless I was intrigued by his newfound interest in me. However, not all interests and desires expressed in the dark are genuine.

We maneuvered our way through a labyrinth of buses and stopped between two buses parked against the stone wall that was the backside of the high school. He turned to face me, placed his hands on my shoulders and leaned in to kiss me. To my surprise, my words were lost, but there was no denying I wanted his kiss. I felt his warm breath dancing across my cheek right before his lips touched mine. His lips were warm, and his breath was that of sweet cherry cola. He pulled his body closer to mine forcing me to step back in surprise where I was pinned to the cold metal of a sleeping bus. His breathing became labored and his hands anxious. Warmth rushed over me a like a wave of comfort and ecstasy followed by a bone chilling cold that set my teeth on edge. Everything seemed to go into slow motion as if I were watching my life on instant replay.

While his hands were smooth and warm, his touch became aggressive and rushed. I bit his lower lip hoping to make my point right before I pushed him away. Blood slowly began to run down his chin and those once so welcoming eyes were now ignited in anger. While his breath may have tasted of sweet cherries, his blood was like poison and burned in my mouth. Before I could speak, he grabbed me by my neck and arm forcing what breath I had been holding to burst out in a gasp.

He turned me around and pressed my face against the metal paneling of the bus. I could feel his forearm pressed against the back of my neck as tears began to stream down my cheeks. He leaned in towards my ear and began to whisper something. I got my chance. With a violent shove I pushed against the bus enough to startle him and break free, all the while hoping I was only steps away from the light of the field. My luck would not hold out on this night. As I turned to flee, he was able to secure his grip on my belt. I was thrown off balance and all my weight slammed onto the ground below. A brief flicker of light from the stadium caught my eye as the once so charming bachelor laid his weight on top of me and all went dark.

I awoke several minutes later alone, bitter cold and afraid. My head was pounding from the fall and my body was on edge. As I struggled to get up, I struggled to piece back together the moments I had lost while trying to find something to clean myself off with, but of course there was nothing. I did my best to pull myself together as I made my way to the back entrance to our school. Luckily, I got therewith only a few awkward glances along the way. Once inside I made my way to the ladies' locker room wheremuch to my amazement no one was inside.

As I turned the lights on and locked the door, I slowly walked toward the mirror to see the results of the trauma I had just endured. I looked at myself in horror. My lips were swollen and there was blood in my hair and running down my cheek. This is not the lady I once was, there was something different about her. I quickly grabbed some paper towels and turned the faucet on. As they slowly dampened, I looked downward. My pants were as dirty and bloody as my face. There was a knock at the door. I ran to the nearest stall, locked the door, and cowered in fear. I waited there for several minutes until I was sure they were gone before I walked back out to the sink where the water was still running. I couldn't stay.

Every fiber of my being told me to run and hide. May the Lord forgive me for what I'm about to do. In a panic, I wiped the dirt off my shirt and took off my pants. I had to work quickly if I were going to pretend nothing happened, but that would be a part worthy of an Oscar if I could pull it off. Minutes dragged on like hours in my panicked fury when I turned to face the last of my clean up. My favorite knickers were now tainted and with them my innocence lost. Why did this happen to me? The idea of reliving the trauma only made me nauseated and it rapidly overcame me.

Exiting the locker room, I was able to see that enough dim light remained to hide what I could not at least until the swelling would start to subside. I returned to the nook by the edge of the field where the night began in hopes that we could continue with no mention of my absence, but again I would not be so lucky. Concern was expressed over my absence, and I couldn't help but think any day the Academy would be calling to deliver my Oscar as I continued to evade any and all questions that were thrown at me. Reluctantly, they accepted my answers.

Then they noticed a certain bachelor staring at me from across the field. Before I turned and brought him into view, I could feel it. His steady gaze watching my every move. A part of me wanted to expose the monster within him, but I felt frozen in time as if the world stopped in that very moment to remind me of my choice and I couldn't catch my breath. I closed my eyes and tried to think of anything I could do to make him stop. Unfortunately, the more I tried to think of anything else the more I felt like he was breathing down the back of my neck. When I opened my eyes again, he was gone.

I rushed over to a portion of the bleachers for cover and said a silent prayer before I began to scan the crowd. I knew he was there somewhere, and I refused to let myself be caught off guard twice in one evening. Searching for him was both agonizing and reassuring at the same time. I felt I needed to find him. I excused myself once again explaining I was not feeling well. I started walking towards home but was drawn back towards the faces in the crowd. I began to walk along the field's exterior fence carefully keeping to the shadows.

I've been afraid of the dark since I was little, but

something about getting lost in the shadows seemed to comfort me at this particular moment. Monsters and prey can both be sheltered in the dark and he clearly knew thisas well as I did. After searching three sides of the field only the parking lot remained and just the thought of going out there alone made the hairs on the back of my neck standup. I was beginning to hope that his presence would continue to elude me and decided to call off the search.

After all, what was I going to do if I found him anyway? With that thought in mind, I headed back over to my friends.

I arrived at their sides just in time to watch the final touchdown of the evening and the game was over. Rather than wait for the crowd to die down I pressed them for a quick exit. We made our way swiftly through the crowd and before I knew it, we were at the car. Dozens of people were still fleeing the packed stadium, but at least I knew that other than terrorists most criminals do not attack in a crowd. I was safe, for now. The ride home seemed quieter than normal, but that could be due to my very own silence. I was lost in my own thoughts and as much as I wanted to pretend, I just couldn't play along any longer. My house came into view, and I noticed all the lights were off. Thankfully, it appeared everyone was either in bed or still out. I didn't want to be alone, but I knew I needed time to process.

I crept in through the back door hoping this would cause less of a disturbance than coming through the front and tonight my gamble paid off. I didn't bother to drop off my bag or jacket but continued to creep through the kitchen then upstairs to my bedroom. Unfortunately, my parents are old fashioned and insisted on buying a home built in the late 1800s versus a new build which means stairs that creek with each step. Good news is they are sound sleepers, and I couldn't be more thankful for that tonight. Last thing I needed right now are more questions when I haven't even answered my own questions. I reached the top of the stairs and dashed towards my room as quickly as I could making sure to turn and lock the door behind me. My legs gave way and I collapsed from exhaustion. I was home and I was safe, but this was far from over. His gaze still haunts me and little did I know what transpired that night wouldn't be so easily forgotten.

2

I awoke to the sound of my mum bagging on my door in a panic as my door is rarely, if ever locked. As my room slowly came into view, I realized I was still lying on the floor where I collapsed the night before. It was not a dream and sooner rather than later I would have to deal with the mystery of my behavior from the night before.

"Mum I'm alright, just not feeling quite myself," I explained as I slowly peeled myself off the hardwood floor.

"Isolde, why is your door locked?" The bagging stopped, but her voice was just as insistent.

"Must have locked it by mistake, my apologies Mum."

"Open this door," she demanded.

"Mum, please leave me be, I'm not well!" I insisted.

She scoffed just before stepping in closer to the door to inquire, "Are you alright my dear?"

"Of course, just under the weather I suppose, my apologies once more," I persisted with my lies hoping to she would let the matter rest.

She let out a sigh and turned to walk down the hallway stopping after only a few steps. Something made her hesitate but ultimately, she continued on her path, and Iwas left to my own devices. In our home, doors were generally not locked, not even the bathroom door, but I would rather get questioned about locking my door later than about the secret I was really hiding. No one could know how foolish I had been. Truthfully, I wasn't feeling well, but there was no cure for the illness that ailed me.

I got my bearings and finally stood up. My muscles ached and my stomach was weak. I needed to rest. I needed to eat. I stood briefly in the sunlight as it shown through my window allowing me to just breathe for a moment without a thought or care to what would come next. I closed my eyes and tried to remember how it felt to have the sun on my body during our vacation the previous year. In a flash he invaded my memory once more and jolted me back to reality. I stepped out of the light and headed towards my dresser to find clean clothes. However, I couldn't focus on the task long enough to put two and two together, so I opted for my bathrobe before reluctantly unlocking my door.

I peered around the door looking for anyone I may encounter on my way to the family bath down the hall. All clear. I tiptoed out into the hallway and slowly shut my door behind me. The bath was just around the corner and from the sounds of it everyone was downstairs watching the game. A typical Saturday afternoon for our family and as much as that might alarm most people in my position it was relief. With the lads of the house distracted meant my absence could go unnoticed. I nearly reached the corner when I glanced back towards the stairs just for peace of mind. Still no change. I let out a sigh of relief and turned to press on. To my surprise, Rhys came around the corner causing me to stumble backwards slightly and let out a shriek.

"Whoa Izz. You alright? You look like you justsaw a ghost," he said.

"I'm fine Rhys, just not feeling well and you surprised me. I thought everyone was downstairs, so," my voice trailed off and I was doing my best not to look directly at him.

He was always good at telling when I was lying, andthat pressure was not helpful right now. He didn't move.

"If you would please just let me pass," I insisted.

"Izz, what happened to you? You're filthy and it looks like you just crawled out of a dumpster," he snickered.

"That's ridiculous. I fell at the game last night and just hadn't had a moment to clean up," I snapped.

"Please don't tell me you went to bed dressed like that. Mum will be beside herself if you did."

I tried to push past him, but his 6 ft. and 180 lb. frame made that difficult. Even if I had a running start, I don't believe I could knock him over or out of my way.

"Please Rhys, I really don't feel well, and I just would like to take a bath."

I looked up at him and pleaded with my eyes. I needed him to let me pass or I was going to collapse under the pressure. He finally stepped aside, and I quickly shuffled past him. I already knew that I was different, but I didn't want other people to see or feel it too. I rounded the corner when I heard him speak once more.

"Make sure to take care of those scrapes. You're too young and pretty to have scars."

I did not turn or make a sound, only opened the door,

and closed it softly behind me. I was alone and safe again. I turned on the water and allowed the bath to fill slowly in hopes the sound of running water would mask thesound of my pain and the tears that followed. Each article of clothing felt so heavy it was almost a relief to remove it, but as each piece fell to the floor, I could see more and more of what really happened. It was time. I stepped in front of the full-length mirror. The swelling that was once my biggest concern no longer troubled me. There were bite marks on my neck and shoulder. Bruises on my arms, ribs, back and thighs. There were blood smears on my thighs and stomach. I fell to my knees and cried out in horror without any thought or care regarding my surroundings. It wasn't long before my cry was heard and there was a knock on the door. It was Rhys once again.

"Izz, are you alright?" he whispered.

I covered my mouth in hopes of silencing my cries, but it merely muffled them. I prayed for the strength to calm myself and for a guiding hand to lead him away from the door. While my cries softened, I did not have a strength to reply.

"Do you need me to get Mum? Is it a, um, womanly issue?" his voice cracked at the awkwardness of his question.

"No! I just have a large bruise from my fall last night and I bumped it while undressing, I'm alright, really!" I shouted.

The thought of our mum becoming involved was too much to bear, but I knew I was bordering on risky behavior by being so dismissive of his concern. Not to mention growing up with two older brothers does not prep you for potential conversations like this one and I could still hear him by the door. He did not say another word, but part of me will never know whether he remained to listen or to make sure I was not disturbed. Regardless of my feelings, I didn't have the strength to fight the pain and my family at the same time. I crawled across the floor, stood briefly and I stepped into the warm bath. As I lowered my body into the warm water and winced as each scrap was touched by the heat, I knew what I had to do.

With a soft washcloth I began to clean each mark, each wound until no sign remained. Most of my memory from the night before was blurred, but with each passing moment a little more came back to me. Since memory lane wasn't a road I wanted to go down again so soon, I drained the bath. The water was filled with trails of crimson, but as I watched the last of it circle the drain, I felt a little better. Not in the sense that I was truly feeling better, but more like I was one step closer to sealing my secret away forever or so I would hope. I didn't bother drying off since most of my skin I either nearly rubbed off or was already maimed, so I decided to just don my robe and head back to my room. Carefully, I picked up my clothes from the night before and wrapped them in a towel until I could figure out what to do with them. Then I grabbed the handle and said a silent prayer. When I opened the door, my prayer was answered. Rhys was no longer there.

I headed back to my room in a more casual fashion trying not to draw attention to myself and upon my arrival locked the door behind me. I attempted to put something on, but the irritation seemed to be too much for me. My knickers and robe would have to do for now. I knew before I could rest, I would need to hide the clothes I was wearing, so, I tucked them into an old shoe box and stuffed the box onto a shelf at the top of my closet. I will have to dispose of those later, but it would have to be after nightfall when no one would notice me carrying a small box out or maybe the next time I take out the trash. Anything just to appear normal.

Finally, I could rest. I fell back onto my bed and curled up on top of the comforter. Just as I was closing my eyes, I noticed a note on my nightstand.

We need to talk.

I held the note in my hands for several moments while I read the words repeatedly. What did Rhys mean by those words? What does he know? How much did he hear? My mind raced over the possibilities, and all went black once again.

3

This time when I woke night had fallen and the house was quiet. My bedside lamp was lit even though I don't remember turning it on, but I really don't remember anything that happened in the last several hours. I don't even recall dreaming. I was looking at the note Rhys wrote and now I'm awake, but nothing in between. What time was it even? I scanned the room in search of the time when I noticed a figure sitting in my corner chair carefully hidden from the light. The sight of a stranger in my room made me jump.

I slowly shifted my weight to the side of the bed and let me toes lightly touch the floor before taking a stand. Carefully watching my footing, I worked my way over toward the closet in hopes of reaching the baseball bat that was housed within. As I opened my closet door the figure shifted its weight in the chair, it was a man, but how? I locked the door; I was certain I locked the door. I wanted to scream for someone to help me, but I just couldn't. I could feel my body trembling as I reached for the bat. Then he spoke.

"Ahhh!!"

I lounged forward in bed gasping for air when I realized it was all a dream. I did my best to slow my breathing and sat on the edge of the bed. My head was pounding and I decided I've punished myself long enough. I desperately needed some aspirin for this headache. I sat up quickly and got on feet, apparently a bit too quickly since my sea legs caught up with me and I toppled to the floor with a thud.

"Well, that was graceful," I muttered trying to pick myself up off the floor.

Finally, I was back on my feet. I pulled my robe closed and walked towards the door. It was dimly lit outside, but I didn't have the slightest inkling as to what time it could be, nor did I care at this point. I was so thirsty, and my head was throbbing for any numbers of reasons I assume, but no time to dwell on the pain I just needed to move. I opened my door and began to head downstairs as quietly as the stairs would allow, which wasn't as quiet as I would hope, but here I am.

As I reached the bottom of the stairs the kitchen was in sight and just the thought of a cold drink made my mouth water. I sprung over to the fridge with enthusiasm and reached for the first thing that sounded refreshing, orange juice. Didn't even bother with a glass, just tipped the carton up and began to take in that refreshing goodness. It was just what I needed, and I could feel my body relax as the cool liquid coated the dry emptiness of my stomach. I was already feeling a bit better but decided to rifle through the cupboards to find Mum's aspirin just to be on the safe side. I tossed back a couple and decided to take what was left of the orange juice and headed outside for some fresh air.

I watched the magnificence of the dawn as it began to radiate across the horizon and onto the trees below. I've never really been a morning person, but something about this moment captured my attention. I remained there on our back porch for several minutes just starring out onto the horizon, thinking of all the possibilities that lay before me when the thought entered my mind once more, what do I do now? It was the question that entered my mind the moment he began to speak to me the night before and continually came into my mind periodically over the last 24 hours. The answer still alluded me. I know that over time we all are faced with life altering questions and situations (or so my parents tell me), but I've barely learned how to complete my calculus homework on time let alone tackle a situation like this. Part of me wanted to tell someone, anyone, but deep within me something pulled at me persuading me not to do it. I needed a distraction.

After finishing what was left of the orange juice I journeyed back inside and up to the family bath this time avoiding any and all mirrors when I could. The throbbing that once nearly overcame me was subsiding and while I was still sore, I was at least feeling a bit more perked up. I didn't realize how desperately I needed to use the bathroom until I was there, but better to go now than later when I must fight several others for the one bath we had.

I quietly closed the door behind me and sat down. I've never been burned before, but I'm confident this was the equivalent of what lighting my insides on fire would feel like. The discomfort and pain took my breath away and even after I had finished my insides still felt scorched, something else they never teach you in health class. I braced myself as the pain continued as once more said a prayer for the strength to restrain my discomfort from the world. I got my bearings together and stood up, but quickly decided that the icy feel of the ceramic tile might be a wise choice to put out this fire. This time the gamble paid off and the coolness of the tile comforted me beyond measure if only for a few moments.

In the stillness of the early morning, I now saw myself in a different light. In darkness we see darkness and as the sun rose above the horizon, I was able to see myself for the first time in the light. Gazing down towards the opening in my robe I observed some minor bruising around my knees and some heavy bruising on my thighs. I brought my hands up and across my cheeks to find that the swelling was truly subsided much to my relief.

As my hands came down and into view, I noticed thechipped amber polish from several of the tips and a few broken nails. Little burn marks were noted near the cuticles and along several knuckles as well. You'd think I was some sort of ape dragging my knuckles on the ground or an auto mechanic by the looks of my hands, but not in the least. I began to open and close my hands in hopes this would alleviate some of the stiffness that I was feeling, but I think it could take more than a few squeezes on the imaginary stress ball I was holding to make that happen. I could feel my stomach start to turn, so decided to lean my head back against the wall and close my eyes for a bit.

It was dark again and I was lying on my back starring up at the stars. There is a dark figure pressing his body against mine and breathing heavily upon my neck while kissing me softly. The smell of cherries and cola once again brought me to my senses. My arms were being held down above my head and I was weeping in fear. I attempted to flail about, but I just couldn't budge from my current predicament. I could feel pressure between my legs as he continued to push himself inside of me. I began to cry once more. His pace slowed as he tilted his head back enough so I could see his face. His golden hair fell onto his forehead with a look of sadness on his face. His mouth opened as if to speak, but I cannot recall the words.

There was a knock at the door. I was dreaming. This time it was my mum and she sounded in a bit of a rush. By the look of it outside, we were most likely late for mass, so best not to delay her further. I quickly scrambled to my feet and scurried to open the door.

"Isolde, my dear, are you alright? You've been in there for hours and we didn't see you at all yesterday," she said concerned.

"I'm just a little under the weather, that's all," I mumbled quietly.

"Well, I wish you would have said something. You know how I worry. Would you like me to stay with you today and we can send the lads off?" she said as she smiled hopefully.

"Maybe another time. I think I need a little more rest and I'll be skipping again in no time," I said with an awkward smile.

"Alright, if that's what you really want. I'll make sure to bring you something lite back for lunch, you're looking terribly pale. Kiss, kiss," she said in a somber tone.

This time as I made my way down the hall toward my bedroom it was brightly lit, and I could feel the warmthof the sun on the hardwood floor under my feet. My home was once again filled with the sounds of laughter and the bustle of a family. That happiness would be their distraction as I navigated the second floor of our home.

I reached my bedroom and quietly closed the door. While I could still hear sounds of the family scurrying about downstairs they seemed far away. We could sense the presence of one another, but generally you would have to really be paying attention to follow someone's every move, one of the many benefits to living in a large house. I sat down on my bed and picked up the note once more. I toggled the note about for several minutes pondering what it could mean but came up empty. For now, whatever it was would have to wait.

As the last of my family headed off to mass, I was alone once more. I decided to put on some sweats and dispose of the clothes I had tucked away. Not sure why, but I decided to double check that the door was fully shut and locked before getting undressed. Maybe I was being paranoid. I walked over to my full-length mirror and dropped my robe to the floor. I'm not sure why I thought today would be better, but it was further from anything I could have imagined. The once reddened areas have developed into plum and maroon patches covering a sizable portion of my torso and trailing down my legs. The bite marks and scraps have a tinge of blood blistering to them, but overall, they were the least of my concern. If I didn't know any better, I would have assumed I was beaten with a bat, but in actuality that would have been a welcomed alternative to the truth.

As I went to touch one of the bite marks my hands began to shake and my stomach began to turn. I was going

to be sick. In a panic, I unlocked my door and ran towards
the family bath. I arrived just in time. A moment later and
I would have had a mess to clean up. My body emptied of
everything it could until only air was left. I was in pain, and
I was weak, but there was little I could do to ease my
troubled mind. I always have considered myself pious and
chose to display my virtue like a badge of honor. There was
no making sense of the events leading up to my current
state and others having knowledge of what happened would
only bring shame upon myself and my family. No one can
know.

I cleaned up and headed back to my room. Without
a second thought I covered up my mirror and began to get
dressed. I donned my favorite set of fuzzy gray sweats and
tied my hair back in a ponytail allowing my dark curls to
fall down my back in hopes of looking normal. Normal I
believe is a relative term but, in this case, this is as close to
normal as I may ever get again. I headed down to the den
and searched for a good book to read. We are not much of
a cinema family, but books we love. We pride ourselves on
possessing a vast collection of books in the den and I take
every opportunity I can to work my way through the
growing collection. One with an old leather-bound spine
spoke to me and I popped over to the sofa to be begin my
escape.

I must have dozed off because when I woke, I was
covered with a blanket and the book I was reading was now
set on the coffee table. I couldn't guess the time, but I
could hear my mum humming in the kitchen. She usually
does that on Sunday afternoons while baking special treats
for the family. The smell of sugar and fruit lifted me off

the sofa and floated me into the kitchen. My mum's face lit up as I stepped into the room.

"Good morning, Mum?" I inquired as I moved towards the counter and rested my elbows on the edge.

"Isolde, you're awake...how are you feeling my dear?" she smiled with excitement and delight.

"Still not feeling all that well, but I'm glad to see you," I said and gave her a bit of a smile.

"I'm glad to see you too, sweetie. Would you like something to eat? I haven't seen you eat in ages it seems. How was the game on Friday? I heard Liam did well, but I haven't had a moment to ask you about your night," she said as she turned around to cut the dessert and began humming once more.

She slid a slice of fresh fruit torte in front of me. The smell was intoxicating, and I could feel my stomach rumble with excitement at the smell of the freshly baked sweet treat. It could have been the thought of food in general that caused the rumble, but at this point I believe determining that would be like splitting hairs.

"It was fine! Nothing worth talking about. Really!" I blurted out.

Her head snapped in my direction before saying, "Are you alright? I'm not trying to pry sweetie. Just wanted to make sure you and the ladies had a good time."

"We did. Sorry Mum," I said while trying to calm myself and spinning my unused fork on the counter.

"I'm not feeling well...I'm going to go lie down." I stood up and walked out of the kitchen.

"Isolde come back! You didn't even take a bite!" she shouted, followed by a scoff.

I continued through the living room followed by what I can only assume was a disapproving stare of my father and brothers. It's amazing really, in two days I've gone from kind and helpful daughter to neglectful recluse, but clearly not all change is for the better. I arrived back at my sanctuary where I decided the best thing to do right now was to just fall face first into my bed and pretend this week never happened, but clearly someone had other plans for me. There was a knock at my door, and I didn't even wait for someone to speak.

"Go away! I just want to be left alone!" I demanded.

My demand was muffled as my face had already been planted in my comforter, so breathing was challenging let alone speaking. I heard silence for a moment followed by the sound of footsteps walking away from my door. I was left to my own devices once more and all I wanted was to rest. I don't recall dreaming this time either, however by the looks of my bed and the surrounding area when I awoke clearly something stirred the pot during slumber time. It was exceptionally early Monday morning and since there was no escaping attending classes today, I had to get up and get on with it.

4

I rolled out of bed and hit the floor without any grace or pause before heading off to take a shower. The house was quiet in the wee morning hours which allowed me to slip into the shower and back out without any interruption. The sun hadn't even started to rise after what felt like a lifetime in the shower. I put in some extra effort this morning and picked out something particularly nice considering I was just going to class, but I needed something to take the edge off my glum attitude. I curled my long dark hair and added a bit of makeup to brighten up my drab skin. It's not something I usually found the need to put on, but something told me I needed to shed this dark cloud and really put my best foot forward, or face in this case.

I tiptoed down the steps and swung myself around the banister in the usual fashion only to be greeted by Rhys coming in from work. He's an ambitious guy that goes to university during the day and works most nights just to get ahead. In all honesty, Rhys is the epitome of the perfect guy and best of all I have the privilege of being younger and only sister. He's extremely kindhearted, intelligent, loyal to a fault and is tall, dark and handsome. He's the type when he smiles, you smile no matter your state of mind or how you feel. I gave an awkward smile and strolled into the kitchen. As long as I could get through the next hour and a half, I may be alright. Rhys did an about-face turned and followed me into the kitchen.

"You're up early. To what do I owe this undue pleasure?" he said softly as he walked over to the coffee pot and poured us both a cup.

"Too much sleep I believe, and it finally caught up with me. Thanks for the coffee," I said as I propped my hip against the kitchen sink.

"My pleasure. You really had us all worried this weekend," he glanced over and gave a little smirk before saying, "but I have to say by the way you look this morning I'm thinking my sweet sister passed on this weekend and gave birth to the stunning beauty before me."

"You flatter me so, please never change. I don't know what I would do without you," I said while shaking my head and of course with a smirk on my face now.

"Are you ready to tell me what really happened?" His tone was firm, and his gaze fixed on me.

"Um uh, I'm not sure what you mean," I muttered.

"You're a terrible liar Izz and for now, keep your secrets, but if there's ever anything..."

He started to say before I cut him off by reaching over and hugging him tightly. He was surprised and caught off guard, but he's still getting used to dealing with the mood swings of a seventeen-year-old sister, so I forgive him.

"I'm not ready to say just yet but know that when I'm ready to you'll be the first to hear."

Tears began to well up in my eyes as I struggled through the words.

His grip tightened around me, "I'm always here."

He pulled away and wiped the newly fallen tears from my cheeks before kissing me on the forehead. As I turned to face the window, I could hear him let out a sigh right before walking out of the kitchen.

In what felt like no time I was off to class with makeup refreshed and hair as perfect as can be. Unfortunately, I was still distracted. Barely a few steps off the beaten path and there they were my two best friends, Jade and Emma. Jade was unusually lighthearted this morning, so either things went extremely well with Ethan (the boyfriend to be) this weekend or she added something Irish to her coffee this morning. Either way, watching her jet-black hair waft from side to side while she frolicked towards the main doors was hard to resist. Just when I thought I was the only one to take notice of her delight I look over and observed a vast portion of the student body with eyes like a Margaret Keane painting just staring at her. All I can say is life is never dull with these two around.

They always seem to know how to make my day better. Between Jade's giddiness and Emma's consistency their smiling faces made the past few days melt away. As we made our way towards the entry doors, I listened to them rehash over their weekends and give thoughts on the impending lessons for today. I did my best to play along. Considering I cannot recall much from this past weekend playing along was my only option.

The buzzing halls seemed typical for a Monday morning and were quite mind numbing. Trying to decipher what materials I needed for class seemed a bit more challenging than usual, but I needed this to be my escape.

Our mind at times can be a source of comfort and solace, but now mine felt more like a prison with my nightmare on repeat. I was determined to overcome this, but I was still struggling to find the tools.

I turned to walk towards my first class and there he was watching me from down the hall. I took a few deep breaths and glanced towards the floor hoping when I raised my gaze and focused it would have all been an illusion. It was not. I glanced upwards quickly trying not to be obvious who or what I was looking at and when I did, I noticed something, he was walking towards me. He had a habit of strutting down the halls making sure to take notice of the ladies swooning over his ample biceps and luscious lips and today he looked particularly delectable. I, personally, cannot share in their delight now that I've seen and felt the monster within, but I did take notice as he progressed towards me. I tried not to give more than a second glance, but with each glance he was moving closer and closer. By the time my nerves settled enough for me to feel the urge to run he was standing before me. I could feel his eyes upon me burning my flesh as the anticipation began to boil over. He stepped towards me once more forcing me to a take step back where once again my back was against a wall.

He dared to lean in close and whisper in my ear, "Isolde, you are looking particularly scrumptious this morning. Good enough to eat."

His hand landed softly on my waist just below were the books I so desperately clung to stopped and I recoiled from the pain of his touch. I refused to give him the satisfaction of seeing the tears slowly start to resurface at the sound of his voice or the fact that I still trembled uncontrollably at his touch. Unfortunately, at this stage neither one could be controlled and as I closed my eyes, I could feel him brush my hair back away from my face.

"Don't cry love. I want to think about this face all day," he said before caressing my cheek with his lips then kissing me softly.

By the time I opened my eyes again he was gone, and the bell was ringing. While the overwhelming nausea had returned at least this time I was able to keep that sensation suppressed. I scurried towards my first class and slid into my assigned seat. While I could vaguely process the lesson plan the teacher was working through, I just sat scribbling on my paper book cover reliving the events of this morning. What was he doing? Why would he kiss me? I felt like I had been enlisted as a personal concubine but was not let in on the secret. My plan to uplift my spirits had clearly backfired since the one person I did not want to take notice did and he did so with gusto.

The day continued to drag on as one tedious and monotonous lesson was followed by another until at last it was time for lunch. My chance to discuss something other than the weekend or what was really on my mind had arrived. My friends and I fetched our lunch before heading out to the patio to peruse some new fashion magazines. Homecoming was just around the corner and like most juniors we were all dying to be asked to go. Well, in truth they were dying to go, I no longer seemed to have the drive to do or go anywhere besides to bed. We were giggling at the prospects when out of nowhere I felt like I was hit by a bus.

"So, what gives with you and Derek?" Jade inquired with her usual raised eyebrows and devilish grin.

"Ahhh, I'm not sure what you're talking about. In case you slipped and cracked your head over the weekend he is virtually untouchable by anyone of my status," I scoffed and rolled my eyes.

"Oh, come on Izzy. It's not like you two were standing in some secret corridor this morning. Everyone saw you two and it's now becoming quite the source of gossip. And the football game, what the heck was that about?!?!" Jade raised an eyebrow of disapproval at the idea that there could ever be secrets between us.

"I agree, so spill it. We want all the details," Emma chimed in.

"Nothing is going on, really. He mentioned he liked the way I looked today and that's the end of the story. I don't have the faintest idea what the football game was about, if he's not careful I will label him as a disturber of the peace. The entire thing is just a bit too eccentric for me." Trying to shrug everything off I quickly changed the subject. "So, what do you think of this dress?"

I pointed to a cerulean off the shoulder number on page 27 of the latest Cosmo.

They both looked at each other with a disapproving look and then back at me before saying in unison, "It's a great dress, but you're in denial."

"He's into you and you need to acknowledge and capitalize on that," Emma added with a smirk as she twirled on a few of her long sandy blonde locks. "Besides he's the mayor's son and being seen publicly with him means something. You know Mr. Strom wouldn't allow his son to be seen with some tramp for fear of ruining the election."

"In all seriousness, if he'd pinned me to my locker like that, I would have let him strip me down right then and there. I mean, seriously, look at him, is there any doubt that the man can plow?" Jade added clearly feeling a little hot and bothered by just the thought of him taking her in the hall like she was in some racy romance novel.

"I just remembered I need to get something from my locker. I'll catch you ladies later."

I grabbed my belongings and rushed towards the nearest entrance which gladly led me into a very quiet and vacant part of the school's library. Rushing over to our reader's nook I was relieved to see that I was one of the few bodies housed within. I sat back in disgust at the perilous situation I somehow lodged myself into by one haphazard mistake. It's a perplexing conundrum really. How is it that one evening can take a relatively sweet and innocent young woman and twist her into *She-Ra, Mistress of the Underworld*? Last week I would have never uttered a lie, but now I can't seem to stop myself from telling them. This must end.

The bell rang softly in confines of the library and that meant my time for solitary confinement was over. Only a few classes left in the day and then I would be home free. What I didn't count on was having to partake in gym class today. I arrived at the ladies' locker room where I sought asylum in only a few days before and I stopped at the door. I could hear locker doors being jerked open and the chatter from the ladies within. I had to go in, but I needed a moment to gather my strength. With a deep breath I opened the door and hurried to the back of the locker room where my locker was and sat down on the bench. The whispering began when I came in the door and the other girls did little to hide who they were talking about. I gathered my things and headed towards one of the dressing rooms to get suited up for class. Generally, I would have just changed in front of my locker, but I am already getting enough stares and my body right now would only fuel the fire. A few deep breaths later I began to undress, but a sound from across the locker room drew my attention.

"Ewww, what the hell is wrong with some people!?!? This is disgusting!!" one of them exclaimed.

"I agree! This chick needs to learn to use a tampon instead of the stall door. Someone should let coach know," another added.

The clothes I previously removed I placed back on my body and exited the dressing room. I was afraid if I stayed hidden that would be even more suspicious than coming out to take a peek. I crept towards that end of the locker room to see what the commotion was about. The stall that kept me hidden and safe during my hour of need was in full view for the world to see. In my state of panic, I must have forgotten to wipe down the stall walls and door. As luck would have it, the barbies made it out to be worse than it was, but fingers crossed the janitor would be summoned and matter dropped. Well, here's hoping.

Taking a deep breath, I turned to walk away when the nausea that earlier seemed suppressed overcame me and I vomited all over one of the barbie's shoes. Clearly, I'm not making any friends today and now there is one livid barbie heading in my direction. Like most sensible ladies in this situation, I ran for cover and waited until they were all into the gym for class before making my exit. Of course, this took several minutes of her shrieking and cursing at the stall door, but it was worth it to get away from her. I don't think my body, or my mind could take anymore trauma right now.

With a quick glance around the stall door and the adjacent lockers I decided to make a break for it. I quickly gathered my belongings and through two doors later I was out the side of the building and on my way to the bleachers. I've never been the type to skip class, but I believe the events of today warranted an exception to my usual behavior. Not to mention it's better to ask for forgiveness than permission. I should have just stayed home.

The sun was still perched high in the sky, so for now I would just have to hide in what little shade I could find under the bleachers until it was closer to dismissal. I didn't really know what I was going to do there, but the thought of being alone presented endless possibilities. I tried to just sit and let the sun warm my face, but my legs were restless. Pacing under the bleachers was not my idea of a good time, but at least it gave me time to decompress. Here there were no questions, no second glances or gossip, only comfort to be found in the silence. I could hear the wind rustling through the leaves and pushing the stranded leaves across the ground. While most of the birds started to fly south for the winter, I could still hear some in the distance rejoicing over the beautiful afternoon we were having. It's a shame it was wasted on me.

I heard the afternoon bell ring and that was my cue to make myself scarce. As my classmates poured out onto the doorsteps, I circled around to the front of the bleachers hoping to bypass the football team as they headed over for practice. Last thing I need right now would be for Liam to catch me shirking off classes. Once I was sure they all were hidden inside the locker room I made my way to the forest for cover. Whether it was luck or nothing short of a miracle I managed to remain out of sight until the darkness of the forest cloaked my presence and down the path I went.

5

Due to the enormous branches overhead the narrow dirt path could rarely capture light from above, but that is part of what makes this path so unique. During the warmth of summer and early autumn months it can shade you, and during the bitterness of the winter months it can shield you from the elements and provide the most basic form of protection. For me, this is just simply my form of commute to and from school. I believe it belongs to an old man down the way that just didn't have the heart to sell it off to developers. He and my parents believe not all advancements have been to our benefit. I would have to agree with them on that.

I was nearing the end of my journey when I decided to veer off course. I don't believe I was ready to go home yet. I just needed more time to process everything and determine a more appropriate course of action. Avoiding class and becoming unhinged at the sight of blood or football games was not going to go unnoticed for long, so I needed to think fast.

For a lady of seventeen, I believed I was smarter than the average junior and I was a problem solver by nature. Having university professors for parents meant there was little room for laziness and puzzle solving was one of their favorite hobbies. I, too, love locating all the pieces to a puzzle and figuring out how they go together. However, this wasn't your typical Sunday afternoon puzzle and there were clearly several missing pieces. There are still too many 'Why' questions in the picture and I'm starting to think I'm not supposed to solve this mystery. Perhaps I'm just supposed find a way through the darkness and back into the light.

Finally, I decided to concede to the questions for the day and head for home. I was over two hours late and I could already feel my father's anger brewing in the den. He's the type that is not truly angry because I'm late it's because I made my mum worry and when she worries it becomes everyone's problem. I didn't even bother this time with entering the back door, just waltzed in through the front door like nothing out of the ordinary. My brother, Liam, was lounging on the couch in his usual fashion snickering at some cockamamie television show. I decided to simply ignore him and begin my ascent up the staircase.

Liam was a high school senior this year and the opposite of my brother, Rhys. His manner was cantankerous, curmudgeonly, and often caustic resulting in his fists finishing whatever his mouth started. Back in Ireland he was an avid rugby player and when that didn't translate here, he took to the football fields only fueling his already aggressive behavior. With little regard for academic performance, he excelled on the field and when hedid it added to his already challenging personality by making him egotistical as well. If it wasn't for the fact, he was easy on the eyes members of the opposite sex would avoid him like the plague.

"I'd tread lightly if I were you. You're late and they're fuming about it," he whispered while shaking his head with disapproval. "Not to mention skipping class is not your style."

I scurried over to him and knelt next to him.

"How do they know about that? Did someone call?"

"That place call? Oh, come on, they have their hands full keeping up with guys like me," he smirked. "And it wasn't anyone there that told them, it was me. You forget we go to the same school and when I didn't see you in the hall or leaving the building, I assumed you were still sick and went home. So, you can imagine their surprise when I inquired after your well-being, and they had no idea what I was talking about."

Without pause or consideration I punched him as hard as I could in the chest causing an actual squeal to exit his body. If I wouldn't have already been so ticked myself, I might have actually giggled at the sound.

He leaned forward bringing his face within inches of mine and demanded, "What the heck is wrong with you?! Have you gone insane!?"

"Have you?! Since when do you care about my well-being?!?" I spat back.

"Since I heard rumors you're with Derek Strom." His voice trailed off. "I mean," he started to add.

I cut him off by my putting my hand over his mouth and shaking my head from side to side. Clearly, gossip travels faster than the speed of light in this town, but I also know that now is not the time to clarify. I'm supposed to be trying to be unseen and right now I'm painfully aware that our voices rose significantly above a whisper. Our parents were standing under the archway to our kitchen. I'm not sure how long they had been standing there but based on the looks on their faces it had been long enough.

"Is that what has been going on?" my mum uttered, but despite her effort it only came out a strained whisper.

"It's not what you think I swear. I...I... just can't explain it right now," I pleaded.

"Answer your mum," my father demanded with his booming voice.

"We are not together! He only spoke to me in the hallway and said I looked nice," I insisted.

"Well, that's not what he claims," Liam uttered under his breath.

"Nothing is going on! I can't believe all of you would rather listen to gossip than to me. I'm out of here," I growled and then stormed off to my room.

I slammed my door in disgust at the situation, but secretly hoping this would end the speculation at least for the time being. I flopped down in my armchair and just stared out the window trying to make sense of a senseless situation. Nothing came to mind unfortunately and before I could get too comfortable there was a knock at the door. I didn't even make a sound in response, but the door opened regardless. I couldn't determine who was the intruder, but I could hear Liam bantering with my father over the rumors swirling around the school. Clearly, those two weren't bothering me, so who was.

"Please leave me be. I really do not want to discuss my day or the rumor mill that is apparently my high school," I muttered before crossing my arms in disapproval.

"I brought you some tea. You seem tense." My mum slowly stepped across the threshold and came into sight.

"Mind if I sit for a moment? I think we need to talk."

"There's nothing to talk about. I'm just not feeling like myself and I need everyone to give me a break," I sighed.

"Well, I don't think that quite covers it. Your behavior has been erratic and unruly. While I understand you weren't feeling well after the game on Friday is one thing but skipping class and disappearing without telling us will not be tolerated."

"I understand Mum and I'm sorry. It won't happen again."

I took a sip of tea and closed my eyes. She was right, I was tense and could really use this, but I wasn't ready to admit she knows me better than I know myself most days or that I was defeated just yet.

"When you're ready to talk about Derek or anything else that is bothering you, please know I'm here for you."

Before I had time to present a rebuttal, she stood up and walked towards the door and turned to smile at me briefly before closing it. I sat there completely puzzled for a moment at how calm my mum was and then I remembered the lads in this house are hot heads not the ladies. The only instance when my mum has been angered that I can recall was when Liam was brought up on assault charges for retaliating against some ruffians at school. She is serene by nature and to top it off always impeccably dressed, constantly smiling and stunning in appearance.

It's rare in my opinion to be that happy and gorgeous, but who am I to judge our creator in his infinite wisdom. If one day I end up only a fraction of who she is I would consider myself quite fortunate.

I finished my tea and decided to tuck in for the night. Normally I'm very clean and organized, but suddenly those parts of me didn't seem to take priority anymore just by a quick pan of my room. Regardless, now was not the time to dwell on it, so I opted in for a quick shower and a few chapters in the book I had started the day before. I could have said another silent prayer for a pain-free shower, but I'm sure it goes without saying that this was one prayer that wasn't going to be answered. Woefully, the damages showed no signs of improvement. At least from the few quick glances I took getting in and out of the shower I was able to deduce that at least they were not worse. Most people equate becoming blind to a curse, but truthfully, I would greet it with open arms right now. Showering along with changing my clothing with my eyes firmly shut the first time was difficult, but I think I've got a firm handle on it now.

I quickly finished dressing and then hurried off to my bedroom in hopes of bypassing any unwanted communication. Once back to my sanctuary I firmly closed the door and locked it. I may not be able to escape what was happening to me, but I could at least keep the world at bay for a while longer until I was a bit more like my usual self. If in fact that lady would ever return...I really hope she does. I curled up in bed and grabbed my book. I may have lost the majority of myself in one weekend, but this was the one thing I still loved and needed. When a good book finds you it allows you to get lost in the story and become part of it rather than just sitting on the outside looking in, a true escape from reality when done right. I quickly dove in and before I knew it, I was transported to a land of hope and mystery followed quickly by dreamland.

The night came and went in a flash and once again it was morning. Following suit with the previous morning I woke up before the sun and began debating even the simplest of decisions only to conclude I was determined not to look how I felt. I picked out of pair of skinny blue jeans, boots and one of my favorite pumpkin-colored sweaters. At least with me wearing a sweater I didn't feel the need to keep my hair down, but I did at least try to style it a bit before pulling it up into a typical ponytail. Made a quick pit stop in the family bath to double check my makeup then I headed down for breakfast. I didn't particularly feel hungry but in all seriousness, I couldn't remember the last time I ate. During lunch the day before I recall picking up a sandwich and fries in the lunch queue, but not eating them.

I must have arrived in the kitchen later than yesterday since Rhys was already home and cooking breakfast. The smell alone made my mouth water, and, in that moment, I knew I really was starving.

"Morning Izz, feeling famished yet? I'd be happy to fetch you a plate if you're up for it," he said slightly glancing over his left shoulder. "There's fresh coffee or tea if you'd prefer."

"Morning Rhys, that would be lovely. Thank you," I smiled.

"How was work?" I pretended to be interested.

"You don't want to hear about work," he snickered. "However, I heard you caused quite a stir on the home front last night."

"Oh no, not you too." I sighed as I clasped my hands in front of my face.

"You should know me better than that Izz. Gossip is gossip and I have never listened to that nonsense."

He placed breakfast down before both of us and began eating. I began eating as well and to my surprise I devoured everything on my plate and then some. When I finally finished, I looked up and was about to speak when my brother's eyes came into full view, and they were the size of cue balls.

"I guess I was hungrier than I thought," I said grinning.

"Guess so," he chuckled and shook his head. "Now that is the lady I'm used to having breakfast with."

"Sorry about everything lately. I just—" he waved a hand in front of me cutting me off.

"No need to apologize or say anything. When you are ready, I will be here. Just make sure to put forth a better effort with the folks or there will be no living with them," he winked at me and then began cleaning the kitchen up in his usual fashion before Mum came down.

I picked up my things and trotted off to school. The path from the previous day was even darker in the morning light, but I welcomed the comfort of its shadows and the silence it provided versus the typical sidewalk most teens take. The day began like any other day and the stress to perform was mounting. I arrived at the front of the school just in time to meet Jade and Emma as they were stepping off the bus. I greeted them with a giddy smile and hug in hopes of shaking off the awkwardness of the afternoon before. If there is one thing worse than not being popular in high school, it's having to go it alone because you either didn't bother to make friends or you were a lousy one. I refuse to fall into that category over that monster.

"So, where did you go yesterday? I mean, you disappeared during lunch and then skipped out on the last few classes of the day." Jade looked concerned.

"I haven't been feeling well and all this unwanted attention from the whole Strom drama pushed me over the edge. That's all, no need to worry," I shrugged. "Besides, I think someone needs to fill me in on how things went with Ethan."

My devilish grin was showing, so I was probably overselling it, but better to oversell than seem uninterested.

"Beyond amazing!! He actually sneaked out after he got home from the game just to see me," Jade said smiling.

"Oh, and they got caught making out on the porch at like one in the morning!!" Emma interjected followed by uncontrollable giggles.

"Emma!! You could at least let *me* tell the story. Ugh!" Jade sighed, but you could tell by her blushed cheeks she placed the memory on rewind and was reliving it over and over again. That right there is what I wanted for myself. A chance to look back with a fond memory of my first real crush and it would still make me blush. I could tell she was completely lost in the moment when Ethan found us in the crowd and escorted her away. I don't recall him saying much of anything to Emma or myself, but he did whisper something to Jade prior to their departure. They went strolling off hand in hand and grinning ear to ear. Emma and I were completely frozen in place with our jaws hitting the pavement. In what twisted universe were we the type of friends to just dismiss each other over a guy? In truth, this is high school and the games that we once played as children were over. She was happy and Emma and I were just going to have to adjust to functioning more as a two-some.

"What the hell just happened here?" Emma spat. "I mean, seriously, no hi, bye, kiss my tush or nothing."

She was clearly upset.

"Well, I guess this means they're dating now and it's our turn to play second fiddle."

I gave a little scowl and started walking towards the school doors hoping she would follow. She did. We didn't really say much on the way in or on our way to first period. I think we were both lost in thought or at the very least trying to handle the equivalent of a trigonometry question on an algebra-based education. Either way, I wasn't ready to ignore the situation I was in, but I'm not sure how much more time and energy I could devote to this paranoia I was feeling. This time, however, the whispers and stares were directly on me by fellow classmates and Derek was nowhere to be found this morning. I didn't want to encounter him, but I was terrified to my core of what would happen if he caught me off guard again.

Seeing how I live in a small town, this type of gossip would not go away quickly, but once his attention passed on to someone else then so would everyone else. I was counting on it. Other than being the most eligible bachelor, he was notorious for being highly flirtatious but never obtainable, at least not by anyone here. He's one of those guys that are extremely casual about dating. Always available, but never willing to be publicly tied down to someone long term. It would ruin his reputation if women thought he was obtainable let alone a true wolf in sheep's clothing. It would ruin the game for both sides.

As I pressed through the day and my emotions the final bell rang and it was time to be released once more from my physical prison into the far more restraining prison of my mind. In there it is dark and unforgiving. Despite my best efforts I couldn't find a way to shut him out. I thought by closing my eyes to sleep I could escape, but even there he is able to find me. Out the side doors to the path hidden among the trees where I could have a few moments to myself and truly feel my pain without anyone there to witness or ask questions. I found myself only a few steps inside when I dropped to my knees and began to weep. I'm not even sure where the tears were coming from, but once inside the forest I could feel my body relax and the pain I was holding inside could finally be released. I was trying desperately to hide my secret, but I now know that this may not be possible.

A twig snapped a few feet from behind me and without thinking I rose to my feet and ran. I did not look back and I didn't say a word. In what only seemed like a matter of seconds my feet had carried me hundreds of yards away where I slid behind a tree and held what breath I could. I'm not sure what I was running from, but when I heard that twig snap it's like I couldn't stop myself from running. Over the years in the public education system I can recall several times when the discussion of fight versus flight has come up, but up until this point I don't think I really understood the concept. I felt like I was being hunted. The possibility of escaping unharmed is minuscule but given the chance I had to flee.

My breathing finally slowed just as I began to say a quiet prayer that I was not pursued and for the courage to look back. I leaned around the tree's large trunk to peek at what might have disturbed my very private moment. It took me time to focus but when I did, I could see a figure stepping out of the forest with a backpack on. To be more specific, it was my backpack. I must have left it when I got up to run, but why would someone take it? Who was that anyway? From the sheer distance in between us and the haze over my eyes from hyperventilating I couldn't focus on the details. The figure appeared too large to be female, but from the sheer distance alone I couldn't divulge the simplest of details. Were they tall or short? Light or dark hair? What were they wearing? I wasn't sure of the answers, but just like that night at the football game I was frozen in place. I could see something, and my mind wouldn't let me take my eyes off it and despite my want I couldn't force my body to move either.

Minutes turned into hours and once again I was late. I sat in the woods staring at the opening to the forest for so long the sky was already blackening and there was a chill in the air. I ran home as fast as I could hoping I could sneak into the house unseen. Through the side windows I could see everyone migrating to the kitchen table for dinner, so that meant the back door was off limits. I could try the front door or the tree near my brother's bedroom window. I know he has used it once or twice to sneak in and out, but between my fear of heights and risk of his window being locked it was another coin toss decision. I know I could reach my window from the same tree, but my windows are generally locked up tight. I'm going to have to go for his and hope for the best. If I get caught coming in late again, I will be walloped for sure.

I began my journey on wobbly legs, but rapidly found my footing to ascend the large tree. At last, I was within arm's length of the window ledge, and I reached for it. For a few moments, I recall my brother's childhood Stretch Armstrong doll and couldn't help feeling sympathy for him at that moment as I probably was the human equivalent. Thankfully, the window was unlatched, and I was able to slide it open just enough to get at least part of my upper body in. It took some work and a considerable amount of pain to pull myself inside, but I was in. To my knowledge so far, my late and awkward entrance had gone unnoticed. With a deep breath I tiptoed across the floor taking note not to move or step on any of Liam's dirty laundry, sneakers, or football gear. I never understood why he was so disheveled all the time. Thankfully, the room didn't reek, or I'd probably have fainted from the smell. I reached the door and carefully peeked into the hall. The coast was clear, and I needed to move fast. Continuing to tiptoe down the hall I could hear the family rustling downstairs. It was time to eat and soon they would be looking for me if they weren't already.

"Don't worry, I'll go get her. She needs to eat anyway," my father's voice resonated up the long staircase as he rounded the banister.

I hurried inside my room trying not to make too much noise and covered myself up on my bed. Pretending to take a nap seemed a bit more logical than trying to explain what I was really doing ten minutes ago or two hours ago for that matter. There was a soft knock on the door before the knob turned and my father entered.

"Isolde, it's time to eat. Please come down to dinner," he spoke in a soft, but firm tone.

"Alright father. Be there in just a moment," I spoke softly as if I was speaking through a yawn.

He turned and left my room without closing the door behind him. Once I was sure I heard his footsteps making their way down the stairs I flung back the covers and I got out of bed. I glanced down for a quick check of my clothes, knocked off a bit of dirt and debris before quickly slipping out of my boots and into my fuzzy slippers. I made my way down to the kitchen where I was greeted by my family patiently waiting for me to arrive so the blessing could be said.

Grace was said in the usual fashion, short and sweet, followed by me rapidly devouring the fixings of my mum's hard labor. We were raised in the presence of manners, so as long as my mouth was full and I finished quickly there would be no time for questions, well that was the hope.

Mum leaned over and whispered to me.

"Are you feeling alright my dear?"

"Just tired that's all. Thanks Mum," I whispered back.

"Go on up to bed. I'll bring you some tea a bit later," she smiled and shooed me away with her hands.

I nodded and quietly got up from the table making sure to place my dishes near the sink before heading upstairs. I could feel Liam glaring at me from the other side of the table as I walked towards the stairs. He wasn't as perceptive as Rhys, but I suspected he knew more than he was saying. Based on his comment the night before, I knew he not only was hearing bits and pieces of the rumors that were going around he was believing them. Liam was well liked despite his ill-mannered behavior and being on the football team awarded him special insider's information when it came to certain A-list classmates. While I know and understand that all gossip stems from a bit of truth not all of us know how to determine what portion of the gossip is fact is which is false. Clearly, he was focusing on the false a bit too much, but as this moment attempting to reason with him wasn't going to benefit me unless I desired to unveil the whole truth.

Instead of returning to bed I decided to take a quick shower and ponder the events from earlier. I've been taught through religious studies that water is a means to purify the soul and cleanse the spirit within, so I figure this can only help. Granted the water hasn't been blessed and a priest is not presiding over me, but you get the idea. This time I didn't cover the mirrors or close my eyes and I'm not sure why. I strongly believe there was a part of me holding onto a hope that I'd been dreaming this entire time and I'd wake up only find this nightmare was a product of my own imagination. However, what my eyes were seeing wasn't something that could be imagined or wished away. As children we all witness the products of violence either through first-hand experience or through alternate sources such as television or books. The vast majority of us will never be able to relate to such violence, so it's hard to imagine what it would be like to see such trauma on our own bodies.

I cannot say I was pleased at my findings, but at least my injuries appeared to sort of be healing. The bruising was mostly still a deep maroon and plum color, but this time with a faint hint of yellow peering around the edges. The scrap marks and torn knuckles appeared to be sealed over apart from the new scraps caused from my ascent up the tree earlier this evening and the blood blistering from the bite marks were slowly shrinking. Nothing I couldn't explain or cover up and that was all I was really worried about at this point. I didn't feel the overwhelming nausea that once consumed me, but my stomach was uneasy. I stepped into the shower to let my sudden weariness wash off and to my surprise it did.

As I leaned my head against the cool tile I began to think once more about my encounter in the woods. I tried to focus on the moments just after I heard the twig snap. Could I smell anything? See anything? Did they say anything? I clenched my eyes shut tighter struggling to relive that afternoon, but my mind failed me. Only more and more questions plagued an already desperate and over encumbered mind. I tried once more pushing my mind further back in time. Was I being followed or was this person simply taking a casual stroll and happened to stumble upon me in that terribly vulnerable state? I cannot recall being followed, but with so many students fleeing the school grounds it would be difficult to tell. If that had been the case, who would be following me and why? Regardless of the answer, it would only create more questions. I needed to focus. I attempted to stretch my mind once more but came up empty. I decided to reprieve myself for the evening and finish getting cleaned up.

Upon exiting the shower, I realized what a terrible headache I had given myself and decided I really did need to lay down. Without giving it another thought, I donned my night clothes and quickly fell asleep.

6

I opened my eyes and blinked several times. I was distraught and weeping once again on the ground floor of the forest and this time I wasn't alone. I could hear someone stepping onto the trail of loose leaves and branches from the soft grass of the school grounds. They did not speak, but the more I listened, the more I could hear them walking toward me. They did not appear to be hiding their presence, but carefully choosing when or how they were going to announce themselves. The gap between us was disappearing and soon they would be on me. I just needed to hold out for another moment. My mind and body were both anxious and I could feel my hands clammy with anticipation. Just as I started to turn my head slightly, I could see a man's hand reaching out to grab me out of the corner of my eye. I fell back and screamed for help.

"Someone help me please! I'm being attacked! Please help!"

"Isolde wake up! You're safe!" my mum was shouting at me while shaking me vigorously.

"What happened? Where is he?" I blurted out.

"By the sound of it you were having a terribly violent nightmare and threw yourself on the floor. Liam and I rushed in here as soon as we could," Mum stated with a look of distress still on her face. "Where's who my dear?"

Taking in a quick glance of my surroundings I realized I was at home in my bedroom. Liam was looking upon me in horror and by the amount of blood that had accumulated on the towel he was holding I didn't need to imagine why. I must have fallen onto the floor and hit my head. I was home and safe, but why didn't it feel safe? I reached up and wiped the sweat from my brow and in turn smeared the blood into my hair and eyebrows.

"I'm not sure, just a nightmare I guess."

I grabbed the towel from Liam and began pressing it against the gash near my temple.

"Just let me get this cleaned off and I'll pop right back into bed. Sorry for waking both of you."

I tried to stand up, but quickly lowered myself back down. My legs felt like rubber and my head was throbbing.

"You've hit your head pretty hard. I don't think you should go back to bed just yet," Liam mentioned. "Let me walk you to the bathroom and I'll help you get cleaned up. Mum, can you meet us downstairs?"

"Of course," she replied.

Mum looked upon us with concern, but ultimately headed downstairs to make some tea and toast. I think this is something that her grandmother must have taught her because it's her standard go to for any problem. I let Liam help me up and off we hobbled to the family bathroom. He had me sit on the side of the bath while he rinsed the towel and began to gently wipe away what remained of the blood and sweat on my brow. We both had the appearance of wanting to speak up, but ultimately failed to do so. It was one of the most uncomfortable silences I've ever had, but this was a side of him I'd never seen before. Calm, collected, and caring. Liam was more the loose cannon or reckless type. I don't believe he ever intends to cause trouble, but he believes in taking the path less traveled even if that road means trouble. I admired his courage in that manner.

He finished cleaning me up in only a matter of minutes and even applied some ointment to help prevent scarring prior to escorting me downstairs. I sat down for some tea and toast at the kitchen counter where Mum was waiting for me. She nodded Liam off to bed and slid a cup of tea towards my hand. I politely began to sip the warm tea, but I could feel the room spinning. I needed to lay down, but I know at this point my mum would never allow it. I looked up at her with tears in my eyes and attempted to not only meet but hold her gaze. I could not. I placed my face in my folded hands and began to weep.

"I don't know what to say. It was so real to me," I whimpered.

"It may have felt real, but it was only a dream I assure you. You're safe here always."

She nodded as if to visually reassure me of what she was saying, I wanted to believe her. My dreams were no longer just a figment of my imagination, they were memories tucked away trying to come into the light. I wanted to let them. I did my best to finish what I could of my tea then I took a bite of toast, but I quickly felt ill. With the room spinning and now my stomach in knots I felt like I was fighting a losing battle.

"Mum, I really don't feel well. Please let me lay down," I placed my cheek down on the table and closed my eyes.

"My dear, you cannot lay down just yet. You could have a concussion."

She brushed my hair back off my face and gave a slight smile. I could see her face out of the corner of my eye. If she was worried it wasn't written on her face any longer. She actually appeared happy in a strange sort of way.

"Sometimes we just have to let others help us and when we can't God will be there to show us the way."

She did her best to help me up and brought me into the living room where I collapsed onto the couch. She turned on the television in hopes that something there would keep me occupied for a bit. However, her attempts to keep me awake all failed and I closed my eyes to the light and my mind fell into darkness. I was once again lost and running through the dark chambers. Nights like these I don't dream at all, but then there are others that become so vivid they couldn't be dreams. At this point, I no longer felt safe when I was awake or in my dreams.

I awoke what felt like a lifetime later only to note the afternoon sun setting. The day has come and nearly gone without my eyes even opening. I sat up ever so slightly and glanced around the room. My mum was nowhere to be found, but I could hear some commotion coming from within the kitchen.

"Mum? Are you there?" I attempted to shout towards the kitchen.

"Everyone's out Izz. Mum needed an afternoon off, so Father took her out and Liam is out with the guys. Can I get you anything?" Rhys shouted from within the kitchen.

"Oh, how long was I asleep? I feel like I've been hit by a bus," I groaned.

"Wait till you look in the mirror. It almost looks like you have been. Well, at least part of you has been."

I could hear a deep sigh followed by a long pause. "You've been out most of the night and all day if I understand everything correctly. Mum nearly took you to the hospital because she was so worried, but Father persuaded her against it. Make sure to hug him for that later."

He leaned around the corner and winked.

"If you think waking up this late in the day is strange, imagine waking up in a brightly lit room with IVs in and no idea how you got there," he snickered at the idea.

The rooms fell silent for several moments causing my mind to race about what he was really thinking. Just as I was about to speak, I could hear slight muttering escaping from the confines of the kitchen walls. Rhys was rarely at a loss for words, but he was clearly struggling to find them now.

"So, I know I said I wouldn't ask, but..."

"Inquiring minds must know?" I added.

"Something like that. You know I would never pry, but Liam saw something last night."

He walked over and knelt next to me.

"He said you were tender when he helped you up. More so than would be expected from a head injury."

"I told you I fell at the football game last week. I've never been particularly graceful as you know." I smiled and attempted to shrug his curiosity off.

"But these wouldn't have been caused from a fall."

He brushed my hair back and ran his fingers across the blood blistering that was clear evidence of the bite marks that once resided there. When I awoke moments ago his eyes were filled with joy and now, they were terribly dark and cold.

"So, you mentioned you and Derek are not an item and I believe you, but is there someone else?"

I quickly pulled my shirt up around my neck and turned away. I could feel tears welling up in my eyes and I didn't want him to see that again.

"There is no one else. I'm just working through something that I can't explain."

I brushed a few tears off my cheek and sniffled.

"Izz, did someone hurt you?"

I couldn't answer the question. I wasn't hurt. I was broken on an emotional, spiritual, and physical level.

"Well, I can't fight the battle for you, but I can listen," he leaned in and kissed my forehead before getting up and heading back towards the kitchen.

"Just do us all a favor and be safe. You don't need to take unnecessary risks."

I sat there focusing on those words for several minutes and dwelled on the irony of the situation. Those particular words seemed to hold more meaning than they used to. Kind of like when a parent tells their child to drive safely, and later they are found paralyzed from a car accident. You'd give anything to go back to truly hear those words, but for some reason until the worst has already happened, we tend to disregard the warnings and advice of others. The young believe they are immortal and that the troubles of this world will never find them, but in truth I believe it already has. It's just waiting for the opportune moment to present itself.

I headed into the kitchen for some refreshment and a couple of aspirin to ease the throbbing sensation in my head. Rhys handed me a glass of orange juice and two aspirin along with an approving nod. He was pleased to see I was up and moving, I'm sure. I finished what I could of the juice and was able to keep the aspirin down much to my surprise. My stomach was no longer groaning or grumbling for nourishment every few moments, only an occasional ache to remind me I'm still human. I walked outside and sat on the back porch just staring off at the slowly setting sun. I've never thought of sleep as a possible solution to a problem, but it does pass the time. When time is what you truly need to heal, sleep offers a kind of fast forward option if you will.

7

When my parents arrived home awhile later, I didn't have to try hard to get their permission to stay home another day. While I knew this wouldn't be a long-term solution it would at least keep my mind and body relaxed a bit longer. I found that the things I was once so easily amused by no longer held any luster. All teenagers at one time or another feel the passage of time in high school moves at a snail's pace and I was no exception. Minutes felt like hours and the days felt like months to pass. I could feel the broken shell of the lady I used to be wrapped around me, butthere wasn't a way to repair the mold. I had been transformed or reborn if you will as someone else.

Soon nightfall was upon us and all in the house were sleeping. I retreated to my bedroom hours before to ponder my next move. I was determined to keep my secret, but after recent events I'm starting to wonder if my subconscious is unwilling for my secret to be kept. I'm not sure how much more my mind and body were willing to bend, but something told me I had to risk it. I was willing to take the risk because my family and my friends were worth it. This is a secret that would hurt everyone around me and cause a ripple effect. This part of me was only to be given to my husband when the time had come and not before. Without it I would be considered damaged and not worthy of a proper match. I was determined to conceal my shame and my secret.

Unfortunately, no matter how exhausted I felt I couldn't bring myself to close my eyes. Rather than see his face again in that terrible light I opted in for staying awake until the break of dawn. My father would be pleased at the amount of literature I was able to devour in one day, but at the expense of my beauty rest I'm not sure he would be so pleased. I waited for most of the house to clear out before stepping out of my room. In the last week between the sleepless nights and the need for a distraction I had read the majority of the books on my bookcase. While there was homework that could have been conquered, every thought that led me back to school led me to him and I wasn't strong enough to face him again. I needed the distraction of escaping mentally to a new world. I decided it was time to raid the den and pick up a few novels for the impending weekend ahead. My intent was to not only skip the football game, but the homecoming dress shopping with Jade and Emma that Saturday afternoon as well. So, if I was going to make it through I would at the very least need mental nourishment.

I scurried down to the den and began raiding the shelves of any decent distraction material. I stumbled upon one of my favorites, *Anna Karenina*. Most people know the story but fail to find the true meaning behind her tragic tale. It's a warning to those who believe the grass is greener on the other side. I used to believe that as well, but I just learned that the man who most ladies, including myself, greatly desired at some point has now cost me a part of my soul I may not be able to recover. There might be some pearls of wisdom held within and if not, it's an excellent read regardless. I've read it on several occasions, but I found my own tragic tale has led me to understand the grass is greener myth more than the novel ever could.

Once my stack was complete, I trudged my way back upstairs. I placed the stack next to my armchair and propped my feet up in preparation for my escape to the world of fantasy and fiction. I started making my way through the stack when I just couldn't take it anymore. I was exhausted and collapsed in the chair, but collapsing wasthe key word. My bouts of sleep were the equivalent of a black out drunk experience at least to my knowledge. When I'm not having nightmares, the sleep I am able to acquire comes and goes in a flash. I blink and entire days disappear. It's the strangest thing.

I jerked myself awake from another nightmare after nearly falling out of my armchair only to find that time had barely passed me by. It was barely lunch time, and I was already in need of another distraction. As much as I loved to read it just wasn't cutting it anymore. Since I'm already going to hell in a hand basket for my behavior in the past week I might as well be *really* naughty. I decided to sneak into Liam's room again and look for his secret stash. Liam was the unruly wild child and most likely to misbehave. The crazy part is my parents must know about everything he does, but they don't seem to be overly concerned about it. Interesting really.

Once inside I was careful not to disturb things just in case he recently became the type to notice. It's amazing what a person is able to learn about someone by simply perusing through a few drawers and nightstand. Aside from a few disturbing yet typical items most guys have hidden away, I found all sorts of drawings. I never knew my brother to be an artist, but then again if the guys on the football team found that out, I'm not sure how much longer he would be considered one of the guys. In my opinion, being an artist is a talent that is grossly underrated, but in a town such as this one that would be more of a point of humiliation than something to boast about. Regardless of my other findings I was able to locate the bottle of liquor he carefully kept stashed away. Other than his disgust regarding our recent relocation I'm not sure why he felt the need to climb in the bottle, but I know I definitely have a need for it.

My plan was to have my first drink in the confines of my bedroom, but as fate would have it that was not to be. I heard the front door open, and slam closed followed by footsteps quickly rushing upstairs. I made a mad dash for my bedroom and thankfully whoever was rushing upstairs not only had their back to me they seemed to be very preoccupied. So preoccupied in fact that they didn't notice the sound of my feet thudding across the floor or the clang the bottle made as it accidentally nicked my doorknob. I did my best to stay hidden, but I had to know who was rushing into our home in the middle of the day and why.

I wouldn't have to wait long for the answer, however. Just when I thought my life couldn't get any stranger the person in question became persons and one of those persons happened to be Liam. I'm surprised the thud of my chin hitting the floor didn't alert them to my presence, but they were clearly involved. They barely cleared the stairs before he began stripping her clothes off and nearly falling onto his bedroom floor. I was trying to focus on who the lady was, but unfortunately, I couldn't get over the fact that Liam left school during lunch to bed someone. I mean, seriously, did I enter the twilight zone when I wasn't looking.

When I was sure the coast was clear and they were in the throes of passion I got dressed quickly, tucked the bottle in the nook of my arm and ran out the back door. If there was one thing that could push me over the edge it was the thought of my brother bedding someone in the next room. Part of me wanted to admire his ambition and his guile, but the other part was just disappointed. We may not have been the wealthiest family in the neighborhood, but we had morals and stood for something or so I thought.

I arrived in the woods after a short jaunt and plopped myself down next to a fallen tree in a secluded part of the forest. I'm sure I looked like at absolute lunatic sitting there drinking and talking to myself, but at this point I felt like I was out of options. I've never drank before and part of me wondered what the appeal was, but after several sips and then several sips more I was beginning to understand. A week ago, my life seemed completely normal and now, my life is a train wreck. To be clear, a train wreck in slow motion and the hits keep on coming. Maybe that is why people drink. When your life is falling apart you drink and your life may still be falling apart, but you don't care as much. You become numb to your surroundings and then you can learn to cope or start the healing process. They say time heals all wounds, but I believe that time is not what heals our wounds. It allows our minds and our bodies to scar over the wounds, so they don't hurt as much anymore. I had figuratively been branded and that would take time to overcome if I was even able to.

From where I was sitting, I couldn't hear the bell ring signaling the end of another class, but I was able to hear some chatter from across the forest, which means the majority had returned to class after lunch or were on their way. My assumption would be that Liam and his mystery lady would be finished and returning to class by now, but I had no intention of going back just yet. There was more than one lunch period and who's to say they didn't intend on staying between the sheets for the remainder of the afternoon. Granted I slept without dreams or nightmares this time, but with the overwhelming nausea I'm not sure I could even stand up just yet. Worse-case scenario, I would just have to shimmy up the tree like the last time I crept my way back into the house. Well, that is if I can get my bearings together enough to walk back to the house.

I staggered to my feet and attempted to gather my bearings by walking around the forest prior to making the walk of shame home. I stumbled more than I expected, but I was going to try to work through it. Just because I had a moment of weakness and needed some help doesn't mean I was going to make a habit of it. While I know I was a bit more inebriated than was customary I could have sworn I heard someone walking toward me. I stopped briefly to see if I could hear the sound growing louder and when I stopped the sound stopped. Either I was being paranoid and the sound I was hearing was my own or my stalker was in near perfect synchronization with me. I decided to chalk it up to paranoia and kept walking.

Someone from behind me grabbed the partially drank bottle of liquor out of my hand and the shock of it forced me to turn suddenly and stumble over a fallen tree limb. For a moment I had begun to free fall towards the ground. Before I had time to fully react, I could feel this person's arm slide behind my back and pull me towards them in a sudden and swift motion. This save felt smooth, effortless, and yet controlled. Almost like this mysterious stranger showed up prepared for me to fall and embraced the chance to briefly dance with me in the afternoon light.

In my intoxicated haze I was having trouble focusing on the person before me, but I could clearly decipher that it was a young man and possible athlete based on his sheer size and firm grip he had on me. At this particular moment, I was not focused on who he was only the fact that I felt like he saved me. As he pulled me in closer to his chest and wrapped his arms around me, I couldn't resist wrapping my arms around him. I desperately wanted someone to hold me and let me be vulnerable with them. Not because I needed someone to tell my woes to, but just someone to hold me and be there for me while I powered through my troubles. I had decided this was a dream and nothing more. My subconscious knew that I needed to see and feel that beauty was still in this world and in the spirit of that this young man was brought to me. I could have stayed in this moment forever.

I glanced up in hopes to get a glimpse of the mysterious stranger, but still could not fully see the man due to the sun's position in the sky behind him. After nearly a week of pure paranoia and exhaustion I realized I didn't care who he was. I just wanted to remain in the illusion of his loving arms. If I only had him for a few more moments that would be enough. I think a part of me needed to know that not all men were monsters and that what happened to me was tragic, but not the end of my story.

Raising myself up onto my tiptoes I leaned in and kissed his neck ever so softly. Again and again, I kissed his neck until he accepted my invitation and pulled my lips towards his. He was interested. He brought his hands down and gripped my thighs in order to lift me up and onto his waist. As I tightened my grip on his waist, I could feel his enthusiasm and I wanted more. It was only a dream after all and if it wasn't then it was a remarkable hallucination. What harm could come from getting carried away? I let him carry me over to a large maple tree where he stood holding me. Our bodies were interlocked and in the throes of such a lustful encounter I wouldn't have believed my imagination was capable of such even if you told me.

I closed my eyes as he began to kiss my neck, then my collarbone and then the tuft of skin on my chest right below my collarbone. Lacking experience in this area I never realized it could feel so passionate and all encompassing, but it did. I now understand how men and women alike can fall prey to this powerful feeling and lose sight of all their morals and beliefs in the throes of a few passionate kisses. Other than Derek, I've never been intimate with anyone and while it was a memorable experience it left much to be desired. This young man felt completely different. He was patient and gentle, not anxious, or aggressive, he just appeared to be relishing every second of our encounter and every inch of me his hands or lips could touch.

We did not speak, but as I opened my eyes to gaze upon the man my body wanted so desperately. The sunlight had shifted through the trees and his face became clear. The monster had found me, and I had invited him in oemore. I jerked myself back against the trunk of the tree and my body became tense.

"What's the matter love? Don't you want me anymore?"

He pressed his hips deeper between my legs closing the gap between our bodies that I had created when I jerked myself away from him.

"Clearly, this part of you not only wants me, but desperately needs me."

He raised an eyebrow and gave a quick smirk before adding, "I must admit I'm surprised at how willing you've become. It turns me on."

While he held me tightly, he didn't appear to be trying to restrain me only to support me and entice me. He started to pull his one arm from around my waist and I winced in pain. He accidentally brushed against my bruised torso, and I looked away in hopes of hiding my discomfort. I continued to brace myself against the tree in case I needed to use my legs for leverage or a sneak attack, but to my surprise he lowered my legs to the ground for me and placed his hands on my waist. Making sure to casually run his fingers along the rim of my blue jeans. I don't believe he was trying to seduce me any longer, but he was clearly getting under my skin, and he could tell.

"Derek, please don't. I'm not your toy."

I could hear my voice trembling and I'm sure my body would not be far behind. I continued to look away before closing my eyes and beginning to silently pray. He leaned his upper body back to have a better view while keeping his hips firmly pressed against mine and raised my shirt enough to see what was causing my sudden discomfort. He glanced at the bruising and then back towards my face. He stared at my face so long that I couldn't help but look in his direction. When I did, he pressed his lips against mine and began kissing me once more. Not overpowering or aggressive, but soft and tender.

"This will heal love, but until it does let me help you forget it." He pulled me in closer and placed my hands on his chest. "Do you feel this?"

"Feel what?" I mumbled as I lowered my head and turned away.

"My passion for you, our chemistry," he said while dropping his gaze to meet mine.

"Look at me," he insisted.

"Derek please." I gave in and looked at him as tears started to stream down my cheeks. "Please let me go."

"I can't do that. I've had a taste of you and now I want more. You can understand, I'm sure."

"Derek, you attacked me! I'm not sure what game you are trying to play, but you could have killed me!" I shouted at him and began pounding on his chest with my fists.

He grabbed my wrists and pulled me in toward his chest. He may not have been trying to restrain me before, but he surely was now. After a few minutes of struggling, Igave up and collapsed into his arms. Wrapping one of his arms around my shoulders he kept the one free to wipe the tears from my eyes and the hair from my face.

"I didn't mean to hurt you," he paused to kiss my forehead before continuing, "but after our brief tryst this afternoon I can't say I'm entirely sorry. There is so much passion in you that my body is still on fire for you."

"It was a mistake. I wasn't myself. In all honesty, I thought all of this was a dream," I sniffled.

"I don't believe that and I'm going to prove that to you." He took a step back and pulled his shirt off revealing a perfectly chiseled body. Before I even had a moment to process what just happened, he stepped towards me and attempted to lift my shirt. I could feel panic setting in, so I grabbed the bottom of my shirt and held it firmly in place.

"Please don't, I... I... I don't think my body can take anymore..trauma," I pleaded with him.

"I don't want to hurt you," he said as his eyes narrowed.

I closed my eyes. I'm not sure where this was going, but I was too afraid to oppose him. I knew that I could not overpower him, and he already has me at a disadvantage. His hands slid under my shirt and slowly lifted it off my body allowing my long locks to free fall onto my chest and back. My hair was being brushed bdk when I slowly opened my eyes to see him staring at the marks that covered a good portion of my stomach and chest. I could see his breathing change and his eyes began to dart back and forth between marks. I couldn't tell if he was admiring his handy work or if he actually felt sorry for what he did. I felt exposed and self-conscious. I wanted to cover up and shelter my body not only from the elements, but from his gaze. I crossed my arms and started rubbing my arms for warmth.

"You're shivering. Let me warm you up," he said after clearing his throat.

He extended his arms out assuming I would once again fall into his warm embrace, but I couldn't. We were playing a game and I didn't understand the rules, but I had to try. Only two options were left on the board, and both came with consequences: resist and risk being beaten or brutalized again; submit to his volition and desire and leave physically unscathed, but emotionally shattered. This was a game I wasn't going to win, so I mustered what strength I could and went to him. Wrapping his arms around me gave me a false sense of comfort and security. There was a monster lurking within and to keep the monster dormant I needed to appease the man.

I brought my arms up and wrapped them around his neck forcing me to fully close the gap and press my body firmly against his. I ran my fingers through his soft golden locks and watched as his eye lashes fluttered with each passing stroke. His eyes were the color of a long-lost blue only found in deep oceans and appeared to be softening with my touch. His grip was weakening, and I could feel his skin burning up. As his breathing deepened his pulse continued to climb.

He wanted me to kiss him and provide him with that most basic form of intimacy, but I couldn't bring myself to kiss him. In truth, I was afraid I would become ill and that would upset him. So, I compromised and laid kisses across his cheek and trailed them down onto his well-defined chest. I lowered my hands onto his chest and ever so gently started to dig my fingernails in. His body began to quiver. His eyes were open, and they were yearning for me. I could feel his breath dance across my skin once more. He leaned in to bring his lips to mine, but I promptly turned forcing his lips to graze my cheek. He was not pleased. The hands that were once so gently stroking my back and waist had now tightened putting pressure on my already fragile body.

"Please...let me...," I started to say before my voice cracked.

"Why tease me? Can't you see how desperately I want you?" his voice raised slightly.

I raised my hands up from his chest as a way to signal my potential surrender. Surprise was not a reaction I expected, but it was written all over his face. I reached up and slid the straps of my bra off my shoulders while controlling my unfaltering gaze into his eyes. He accepted my offer and leaned down to kiss my now naked shoulders. With each kiss I closed my eyes even tighter and pretended I was somewhere else or with someone else. I would have given anything to be the equivalent of black-out drunk at this point, so when I would wake from this terrible nightmare, I wouldn't be able to recall how far gone my mind must have been to let this charade go on.

Multiple attempts were made to kiss my lips, but I continued to brush off his attempts. The thought just nauseated me beyond words. As I continued to refuse his affections, he proceeded to stop trying to kiss my lips and decided removing my bra would better suit his desires. He pressed his body fully against mine, so I couldn't get away and reached for the clasp in the back. I couldn't let this happen.

I turned my head and brushed my cheek against his cheek in hopes that he would try to kiss me once more. When he did, I let him and then I bit his tongue as he attempted to put it in my mouth. That was taking it too far as I'd soon find out. He pulled away quickly and touched his mouth in surprise. Within a few seconds, multiple blows of crushing pain overwhelmed my abdomen, and I doubled over out of breath. I was gasping for air when I noticed Derek had picked my body up off the ground and was carrying me.

"You have a beautiful body love and I just want to fully enjoy it." A mischievous grin appeared on his face. "I didn't want to hurt you, but then you had to go ahead and do that."

"Derek, I... can't...breathe...help...me," I gasped for air between each word and clutched my sides.

"Relax love. The pain won't last." He looked down towards my face and kissed my forehead.

As long as I was cooperating, he was willing to be gentle with me, but biting him was a mistake and I knew it. I bit his lip at the football game, and I still can't remember everything that happened. Now I think something is seriously wrong with my body and I can hardly breathe. Several steps later I felt him kneel to the ground and lay me down on something soft. The smell was sweet and floral. The more I inhaled the scent I realized that's how Derek smelled. He had laid me down on a blanket by the feel of it or possibly multiple. This was planned. How could he have possibly known I'd be here unless I was being watched? In between labored breaths I noticed his eyes were focused on me with an intensity I hadn't quite seem before.

"Let me go…I don't want you to hurt me anymore," I pushed the words out of my lungs with speed and ferocity.

He pressed his hand against my chest.

"Are you talking about here?"

He lowered his hand and placed it between my legs slightly stroking my inner thigh.

"Or are you talking about here?"

A gasp escaped my body and goosebumps rose all over my body like a cool breeze rushing over you on a hot day.

"Ah, there's were your concern truly lies. Don't worry my love. A little pain is worth the pleasure I'm going to give you."

A diabolical grin washed over his face and while I closed my eyes trying to block out the pain. I could feel one of his hands slide up my legs and start rubbing my inner thigh. While I was laboring just to breathe, I started to feel my pulse pounding as my heart rate continued to rise. I was frightened and now I was injured to the point I don't believe I could get away.

"You're focusing too much on the pain. Close your eyes," he whispered.

I felt his hands on my knees pulling them apart before he slid his pelvis in between my legs. His lower body was firmly pressed against mine and I could feel his enthusiasm even more than I could before. He refrained from lowering his body onto his forearms to spare me the torture of his full weight on my delicate torso. I could feel his breath dance across my skin and the beat of his heart. He preceded to run one of his hands down my side touching just slightly with his fingertips before returning once again to the rim of my blue jeans. While I was in a great deal of pain, the slight touch of his fingers on my bare skin tickled and caused a smile, though brief, to appear on my face.

"See, no pain," he whispered as he glanced towards my face and then back again at my stomach.

My breathing deepened and I could feel his touch awaken the woman that captivated him earlier today. While I was afraid, I shamefully found pleasure in the kisses he placed upon my skin and I'm certain that is exactly what he wanted me to feel. This wasn't me. He started kissing my skin just above the rim of my blue jeans and slowly made his way up my body paying extra attention to any sensitivity he could find along the way. My skin was soft, youthful and it allowed his fingers and his lips to slide across it with minimal effort.

"No pain?" I whispered to him more as a question of what was to come.

"No pain," he nodded hoping to end the debate.

I swallowed and nodded to show I understood. He smiled and he leaned in to kiss my lips. I closed my eyes and let him kiss me but did not reciprocate the kiss. I did what I could to try and tolerate my unease of the situation, but by no means did I want to appear willing or accepting of his coercion. Since he hit me, I felt nauseated, but thankfully, I was able to suppress the sickness within and focus my energy on just breathing. If I thought biting him would anger him, I can only imagine what vomiting on him would do.

He didn't need to say anything, but I could tell he was not pleased about me refusing his affections. The kisses became forceful and invading. He began biting me and placing one arm around me pulling our bodies together causing what little breath I could muster to escape my body. He was becoming insistent and, without stating his desires, his grip on me was an attempt to persuade me into bending to his will. If I didn't soon, he would surely hurt me again. I placed my hands on the sides of his neck and brushed my thumbs across his swollen lips.

"I'm sorry. I don't think I can," I whispered.

"Then show me you're sorry," he said as his eyes narrowed.

I closed my eyes to prevent him from seeing how glassy they were becoming before placing my lips upon his. Again and again, I kissed him, and I could feel his excitement grow. I could feel him start to tug at my jeans and panic overcame me. I started to thrash about in hopes of breaking free and for a brief moment, the grip on my waist relaxed, but it was followed by his hand clasping my throat almost to the point of cutting my circulation off. I had infuriated the beast within.

"I don't want to hurt you, but I will if you don't learn to behave," his eyes narrowed emphasizing his anger and frustration with me.

I nodded as best as I could. Anything to appease him and allow me to breathe again. He took pity on me and removed his hand from my throat. I coughed and regained what breath I could. In an act of desperation, I wrapped my legs around his waist and pulled him towards me showing I was willing to give him what he wanted. Through the tears and shortness of breath I reached for him and started kissing his lips ever so softly. He was pleased and began rubbing my thighs and grinding his pelvis against mine. Creating the sensation of our bodies being engulfed in flames.

"Give yourself to me," he uttered in between our kisses.

I placed my hands upon his chest and pushed him back slightly to sit up. He grabbed my arm as if to remind me he was in control here. I gave an awkward smile in his direction, and he lifted his hand off me. I reached down and attempted to unbutton my blue jeans, but my hands were shaking something terrible. Derek took my hands and kissed them and then kissed my stomach as I slowly lowered my body back onto the blanket. I recall my legs starting to tremble as he began to remove my jeans, but my mind was currently heavily focused on the fear even more so than the pain I was experiencing. I laid there exposed and frightened. I closed my eyes and let him cover my body with his. I have no memory of him removing his clothing, but I could feel the warmth of his skin against mine as he laid down on top of me.

"Love, just breathe," he smirked, "it will get easier and more pleasurable each time. Just breathe."

"Derek, I..," I started to say.

He held his fingers up to my mouth cutting me off.

"Behave yourself," he insisted. "You have nothing to fear. I know how to please a woman."

I kissed them softly before pulling them away.

"Do you want me?" he asked.

He may have posed it as a question, but I don't believe he was truly asking. He just needed the satisfaction of hearing a woman say they wanted him. I denied him that satisfaction and when I did not respond I noticed his head dropped. My assumption was that he was leaning down to kiss me once more, but seconds later I could feel his teeth clamped down on my neck hard. I let out a cry and I began to squirm once more. He relaxed his grip and began kissing the surrounding tissue as if to prove he was not entirely a monster. I couldn't take another moment of the pain.

"I'm yours," I whispered.

I regretted the words the second they passed through my lips, but my response clearly pleased him. He did not hesitate in grabbing my thighs and pulling me onto him. The action took my breath away. After the first few minutes I wasn't in any pain just as he promised and the tears that were once falling had disappeared.

8

Hours later, I awoke to the sound of my parents arguing. I could tell the hour was late, but the journey home remained a mystery to me. As I started to look around the room, I realized I wasn't home at all. I was in an isolation room at our local hospital. The washed-out white walls and smell of bleach gave it away. I've never been known to see the inside of hospital walls with any kind of frequency but, based on those two things, I knew this was a room in the closest hospital to our home. A few years ago, my brother Liam was brought here after getting into a knock down drag out fight with one of his many rivals. A few hours were spent here while both parties recovered or at the very least had their wounds addressed. This was, also, the same time he was brought up on assault charges, but later the rival dropped the charges.

I attempted to sit up but was met with resistance. There were pillows on both sides of my body and I noticed tubing running from my body to two IV pumps very near my bedside. I glanced around the room for any additional clues as to my condition or to at the very least divulge the time. Unfortunately, I couldn't locate either, but the door was open just enough that I could see a glimpse of my parents standing by what I can only assume was the nurse's station. The nurse seemed to be taking notes, but when my open eyes were brought into her view she quickly rose and rushed over to me.

"You're awake. My name is Karen. How are you feeling? Any pain?" she leaned slightly over the railing for me to get a better view of her.

"What happened? Why am I here?"

"Miss are you in any pain?" she repeated with an insistence in her voice.

"What happened to me?!?!" I shouted at her.

As soon as the words left my body, I felt a stabbing pain on my abdomen, and I couldn't seem to catch my breath. When I woke, I do not recall being in any pain, but raising my voice provoked something from inside of me causing me tremendous and unrelenting pain. I could not ask for help because I was blinded by the pain, so I did what I could and reached for the nurse at my bedside. She met my reach and held my hand as I slipped into darkness once more.

As I slowly came back to consciousness, I could see someone sitting on the end of my hospital bed. Their face had fallen into their cupped hands and all I could see was dark curls falling forward onto their hands. As my eyes began to focus, I could see it was my brother, Rhys. His head began to rise from his hands while slowly turning in my direction. His eyes were surrounded by dark circles, but they briefly lit up at the sight of my open eyes. He grabbed my hand and gave it a gentle squeeze before kissing it.

"Izz, I'm so glad you're awake," his voice sounded strained.

"What happened?" I spoke softly.

"Let me get you some help," he replied.

Regardless of the cryptic nature in his response it was not like my brother to shy away from me in that manner. It wasn't long before two strangers entered the room and closed the door behind themselves. Rhys did not accompany them back into the room.

"Good morning, Isolde, I'm Dr. Burgess. How are you feeling?"

"What happened to me?" I did my best to keep my voice low, but I believe I was firm in my request.

"Do you remember anything before waking up here?" Dr. Burgess evaded my questions and presented another one of his own.

"Why am I here?" I persisted.

"Miss Walsh, you were found unconscious in the forest near your home when a fellow student discovered you. Based on your injuries we have not been able to determine the exact event that caused you to lose consciousness."

Dr. Burgess pulled a chair closer to my bedside and sat down. The nurse that originally entered the room with him was taking notes of the encounter only a few steps behind him. As my eyes darted around the room and between the two strangers standing before me, I noticed that while Dr. Burgess clearly looked concerned the nurse accompanying him looked upon me with suspicion.

"Am I being accused of something?"

"No, not at all," Dr. Burgess tried to reassure me before continuing. "Based on the injuries we were able to observe and their various stages of healing, we need to know if someone has been hurting you? Unintentional or otherwise."

He folded his hands and patiently waited for a reply. When I didn't respond he added, "In addition, we found evidence that leads us to believe you may have been sexually assaulted."

I could see my hands trembling at the sound of it, sexually assaulted. I had temporarily forgotten about the events of that afternoon, but with those two words my mind became flooded with the memory of it.

"Where's my mum?" I mumbled.

"She's waiting outside with your family. I told her we needed to speak privately for a few moments."

"Who found me?" I uttered under my breath while keeping my head down to avoid his gaze.

"I'm sorry?" he replied.

"The classmate who found me. Who was it?" I insisted.

"Derek Strom," he paused briefly, most likely to observe my response, but when all he received was a sudden upward glance he continued. "To my knowledge he hasn't left the hospital for more than a few moments since he brought you to us. Would you like to see him?"

I didn't know how to respond. Not only did that name give me an instant headache, but it turned my stomach into knots just thinking about him.

"When can I go home?" I urged.

"We are not sure yet. Please think about what we discussed. I will be in to check on you later."

He stood without effort in one swift motion and gave me a smile before exiting the room along with his nurse and the door was closed behind them. I laid there for several moments trying to wrap my head around Dr. Burgess's questions. He seemed to be on a fishing expedition but was determined not to reveal his hand. I was left to ponder this, but I quickly abandoned my quest out of sheer exhaustion. I was about to push the call button when I heard the door click open. It was my mum.

"You're awake my dear. I'm so pleased."

She was smiling, but her eyes were filled with tears. She did not say anything more, but she quickly scurried over to my bedside. She clasped my one hand in hers and leaned in to kiss my forehead. The light that normally radiated from her skin was nowhere to be found. Her face was blotchy and reddened from what must have been hours of tears and strain accompanied by a shuddering sound that exited her body with every breath she took. In a week, the consequences of my actions have nearly destroyed all the beauty that I once found in my mum.

"Mum, please forgive me," I whispered. "I need to tell you something."

"What is it my dear?" she took a moment to wipe her eyes but looked at me intently.

"Derek isn't..."

I stopped suddenly as I heard the door latch click once more. I held my breath until I fully see the person behind the uninvited intrusion. As the intruder began to step around the door, I could see the familiar golden locks of Derek Strom. I could feel my body grow tense as he approached my bedside.

"I thought my ears were burning," he bowed his head towards my mum as means of acknowledging her presence. "Mrs. Walsh always a pleasure. I'm not interrupting, am I?"

"Of course not, Derek. Please come in," she said politely with a smile as she walked over to hug him.

It took a moment for me to fully see it, but I recognized the look on her face. It was the same look she gave me the first time I went to a school formal, the first time I won the school spelling bee, the first time I read a book on my own. She was elated and proud. I was completely befuddled at the thought and at the sudden prosperous reunion they were having. I mean, why were they hugging?

"Um, Mum...what's going on?"

She took his hand in hers and brought him over to me and place his hand on mine.

"My dear, Derek and I have gotten to know each other a bit and he explained so much of what has been going on. While you and I have much to talk about this is something to celebrate."

She gave her best smile and with a twinkle in her eyes she walked towards the door. She stopped briefly to glance back, but only for a moment. Then she made her exit, and I was alone with him once more. He took my hand inhis and leaned in to kiss me, but before his lips could connect with mine, I spoke.

"You won't get away with it," I whispered.

"I already have," he whispered back.

He winked and then pressed his lips firmly to mine. I attempted to evade his attempt but was met with resistance. In my current condition along with bed rails and body pillows there was nowhere for me to go and he was determined to make his point. By not bending to his will and returning his affection he decided that some persuasion would be required, and he took little time to capitalize on that thought. I could feel his hand slide up my side and when he reached my rib cage, he began to add pressure. I tried to hold my breath and brace myself, but the pressure was too great. I began to weep into his kiss, just before he removed his hand and broke off the kiss.

"You gave yourself to me and we made love, or have you forgotten?"

His voice was still a whisper, but those words cut me deeply. While I know I was not displaying a well-rehearsed poker face I cannot presume why his expression had fallen into a form of surprise and sadness. There is part of myself that still cannot determine if this was just an elaborate game to him or if he really truly believed what he has done was without consequence. It begged me to focus on whether I was the one that was delusional or was he.

There was a knock at the door just before it clicked open once more and it couldn't have come at a better time. However, the man who entered I didn't recognize, and he wasn't dressed like any hospital employee I'd ever seen. He was tall with dark features and wore a dark suit. He did not say anything at first, I can only assume he was observing the situation. We all know things are not always what they seem, and I was counting on this dark stranger to see the writing on the wall.

"Please don't let me interrupt. Take your time," he stated.

The tone of his voice never faltered, but he appeared to have an agenda. While projecting a persona of patience towards us I could tell he had no intention of waiting. Derek glanced in the stranger's direction.

"Hello again Officer Chaney. Always a pleasure."

He nodded in the officer's direction before leaning in to kiss my cheek.

"I'm yours," he whispered to me.

He rubbed his cheek against mine allowing the warmth of his skin to warm my very own. Much like the way he touched me the Monday after the attack, was he really becoming fond of me or was this just a front to avoid suspicion. I'm not sure how I could have been so ignorant, but in just two words I produced the illusion of consent he needed making this a near perfect crime. I turned my attention back towards Officer Chaney as Derek made his way towards the door.

"Miss Walsh, I'm Officer Chaney. I've been assigned to your case. Do you mind if I ask you some questions?" he stated in the same monotone voice he projected when he first entered my room.

"Of course not," I stated not meaning a word of it.

I very much minded, but sometimes you need to break a few eggs to get the recipe right.

"Thank you. Can you tell me what you made you venture into the woods last Thursday?"

Last Thursday, why did he say last Thursday? Wasn't that just yesterday? I must have been pondering the thought longer than he cared to wait since the next thing I knew he was snapping his fingers in front of my face jolting me back to reality.

"I was feeling under the weather and needed some fresh air."

"Under the weather...how so?"

"I've been having trouble sleeping."

"Do you usually drink Irish whiskey while you're getting fresh air?"

My eyes widened. Clearly, I was asleep longer than I was aware, and Officer Chaney had done his homework.

"No, not usually," I blurted out in surprise. "Actually, I'd never drank before, but I thought it might help."

"Yes, your mother mentioned you've been troubled by something lately, but alcohol at such a young age is no solution. Are you positive that you only went to the woods for *fresh air*?"

"Yes." I glanced down at my hands that were starting to shake from the anxiety of this situation and continued. "I take sanctuary in the forest."

"Tell me about your relationship with Derek Strom."

"Relationship?" I could feel my eyes widen and my cheeks start to flush. "Umm, we are classmates, that's all."

I did my best to struggle through the words without faulting in my tone, but I fear I was unsuccessful.

"Hmm, interesting," he uttered under his breath. "Now is not the time to be coy Miss Walsh."

"I'm not sure what you mean."

I closed my eyes trying to hide from him, but I knew there was no hiding from his gaze. I could feel it burning my skin and the tighter I closed my eyes I could feel my blood pressure rise.

"Are you a harlot Miss Walsh?"

My eyes burst open, and I became livid at such anaccusation.

"How dare you?!?!" I shouted at him. "I would never be so careless with my body!!

I grimaced and began clinching my side once more. He stepped over to my bedside in such a rapid fashion before I knew he was moving he was there and when he arrived, he slammed both hands down on the railing.

"Then why lie about the man who you were sleeping with?!" he shouted back at me.

The door opened suddenly and there stood Dr. Burgess.

"Officer Chaney, that's enough. This child is not on trial here and she needs her rest."

Office Chaney glanced in Dr. Burgess's direction and gave a scowl of disapproval. He knew he had taken it too far and while I couldn't do anything to stop him, he could. It took him a moment to admit defeat, but when he did, he tore his hands from the bed rail and stormed out. When I let out the air I was holding in I felt like my lungs were going to explode. My eyes focused on Dr. Burgess and without saying any words at all I think he knew I was grateful for him bursting in when he did.

"What's wrong with me?" I implored.

He turned toward what I can assume was the nurse's station and signaled for assistance. A male orderly appeared a few moments later and took a stand only a few steps behind him making sure to close the door. He couldn't have been more than a couple of years older than I was with very short dark hair and bright eyes. At first, I barely gave him a second glance, but as I watched his eyes work tirelessly to avoid mine, I wanted to know more.

"Miss Walsh, you came to us severely dehydrated, malnourished, and unconscious. In addition to those ailments, you have multiple contusions and scraps at various stages of healing and multiple fractured ribs."

He strolled over and sat in the chair beside me and folded his hands in his lap.

"I don't understand," I said confused.

My eyes rapidly bouncing between Dr. Burgess and the orderly now standing towards the foot of my bed. Before he was attempting to avoid eye contact and just merely appear to be present, but as he stepped forward his head dropped a bit. I'm not sure if he knew what was going on or just that the conversation was a bit uncomfortable for him. I thought staring at him for a few moments would bring his attention back to reality, but my attempt fell short.

"Your parents have made it known they would like these injuries recorded and someone charged if given the chance. We would like to examine you for sexual assault with your permission as this may provide a valuable piece of the puzzle that Officer Chaney needs to pursue a suspect. Will you let us do the exam?" his eyes were intent.

"If I do agree to it, how could that possibly help?" I added.

"Any evidence found could help link the suspect to you. Without it, Officer Chaney can still work the case, but this would be extremely helpful."

"Then I'll do it," I blurted out, "but I would like someone else to do it. I hope you understand."

"Alright. I will have an associate of mine paged and made aware of the situation."

He pursed his lips as if displeased but nodded reflecting his understanding.

"Please get some rest. I'll make sure Officer Chaney is kept on a tight leash as long as I can."

He mustered a polite smile before standing and exiting the room. The orderly proceeded to follow him shortly thereafter, but he didn't smile or attempt to look at me. He kept his head low and for a moment it felt like sadness radiating from his body. It didn't feel like pity, but the strength he came in the room with had abandoned him. I leaned forward slightly and held my hand out. I reached out in an attempt to grab his attention and it worked. He paused at the sight of my sudden movement and turned slowly in my direction.

"Wait, you there. May I speak with you a moment?" I called to him.

"Yes Ma'am. How can I help you?" his head lifted and the sadness that once was secreting from his pores had temporarily receded.

"Um," I blanked on what to say next since I didn't expect him to answer me let alone be so polite. "Who are you?" I inquired.

"I'm Tyler, an orderly at this hospital."

"Why were you called in here?"

"Just in case you or Dr. Burgess would have needed any assistance."

"Oh, it's nice to meet you," I paused trying to think of something that would keep him here for a bit longer. I needed answers, "I'm really uncomfortable. Could you help me get settled in a bit better?" I gave a brief smile hoping that's all it would take.

"Most certainly. Are you in any pain?"

He rushed over to my bedside and reached behind me in order to support my torso. His large arms wrapped around me tighter than one's true love in hopes of providing better support for my broken ribs. As he leaned me forward, I grabbed his forearm with my right hand. The reaction caused him to jerk as if he had been bitten and if his head would have turned any quicker in my direction it could have potentially caused him a touch of whiplash.

"What do they know that they're not telling?" I insisted in a whisper.

"I'm not sure what you mean," he appeared perplexed at my sudden behavior change.

"I'm being questioned like a criminal and as I'm being questioned, they appear to already have knowledge of my answers before they have even been uttered," I whispered.

He used one of his hands to loosen the hold I had on his arm and carefully placed another pillow behind my back.

"Ma'am, it's been nearly three days since you were brought to us and this is the first time anyone has seen you alert," he whispered back to me. "There has been a lot of talk regarding your situation and Officer Chaney has wasted no time in starting the investigation."

He slowly laid me back against the newly positioned pillows and began checking my vitals. More than likely, he was attempting to wind the clock down, but I refused to let him go without squeezing every ounce of information I could out of him.

"But why question me?"

"Whatever happened to you that afternoon in the woods remains a mystery. The man who brought you in was initially a suspect but has since become a key witness in your case."

As the words exited his mouth and entered my body, I felt like I couldn't catch my breath. When I did attempt to speak it felt like there was thistle in my throat and with each breath it cut deeper and deeper.

"By key witness you mean Derek?"

"Yes, ma'am. They were suspicious of him at first due to the circumstances, but after he explained they were able to corroborate a great deal of his statement."

I laid my cold hand down upon his as the tears began to well up in my eyes.

"He's not who you think he is," I whispered, "he's a monster."

"I don't understand," he looked genuinely surprised and concerned.

"There are few in this town that will. Please believe me when I say I can't be alone with him."

"Should I get Officer Chaney?" he turned slightly as if he was about to head for the door.

"No, please don't. Could you just stay with me for a bit? At least until I fall asleep."

I squeezed his hand gently. Anything to stop me from feeling alone in this world. After a moment of suspense, I felt his hand gently squeeze mine and a smile appeared on his face. He turned and closed the door before taking a seat next to me at my bedside. He placed his hand on mine and grasped my hand once more. I closed my eyes and before I knew it, I was off to sleep.

9

I awoke awhile later to someone lightly tapping my shoulder. It was a woman I didn't recognize, but she appeared to be another hospital employee based on the garb she was wearing. As I opened my eyes and glanced around the room, I could hear the woman speaking to me, but I was more concerned with where the man from earlier had gone. I didn't have to look far. He wasn't sitting in the chair next to me any longer, but he appeared to be bringing fresh linens into my room along with a few other bagged items. I turned my attention back to the woman who woke me from my slumber.

"Forgive me, what did you say?" I mumbled in my groggy state.

"Ms. Walsh, I'm Dr. Jordan and I'm here with my nurse, Merida, to perform the requested examination by Dr. Burgess and Officer Chaney. Do you understand?"

I nodded.

Tyler was laying out some items onto a blue sterile field that was now covering what appeared to be a bedside table. I wasn't entirely sure what was going to happen, but in the strangest way I was glad to see him. I turned my face in his direction and I could feel my strength slowly melt away as it was replaced by fear.

"It will be over before you know it. I promise," he whispered and was soon ushered out of the room.

The nurse made sure all the windows and doors were covered or shut and did her best to keep what dignity I had left intact. Merida was kind enough to provide a basic explanation of the steps involved, but before she could finish, I simply waved her away. Hearing details of the examination process only makes the examination more difficult. I laid there exposed and vulnerable as they continued to take samples and photos of my body from all angles. The room fell into silence and all that was left were the sounds of my IV pump and my heart monitor as those two women efficiently did their work. As much as I hoped for some kind words or a comforting touch, there was none to be found.

As Tyler assured me, it was over sooner than I anticipated, and while I hoped a sigh of relief would come over me it failed to do so. Dr. Jordan and Merida were kind and politely collected their things before stepping out the room leaving me once again to my own devices. I began to weep once more and even though it hurt, my anguish had nowhere to go but out my eyes. Whether I wept like that for minutes or hours I cannot say, but the only comfort I found that night was in the absence of all others. I did not ponder my next move or struggle to find the hidden meaning in the events that led up to this moment. I just wept. When I couldn't weep anymore, I allowed myself to sleep and do what I could to heal my broken body and shattered mind.

I continued in and out of consciousness for several hours or maybe even days until I finally awoke. To my astonishment with each breath I took the pain that previously consumed me seemed to significantly subside. Either they increased my pain medication enough that I couldn't feel it anymore or I was on the mend. Unfortunately, with the blinds covering the windows to the outside world I couldn't tell what day or time it was now either, and for the first time in days I wanted to get out of bed. I reached for the side rails and strained to pull myself up into a sitting position. Surprisingly, this simple action exhausted me. You'd think I was waking up from a coma with the way I felt. Either way, powering through the exhaustion seemed like the only way to go.

As I began shifting my weight, I could hear a slight beeping over my shoulder as I began to pull myself towards the edge. With each inch I moved closer the beeping became louder and louder. I carefully slid both legs over and let them hang over the edge. Just as the tips of my toes barely touched the floor there was a knock at the door. A look of disgust came over my face followed by a louder than expected sigh as the door crept open.

"Good afternoon Ms. Walsh, may I come in?" A woman's voice came through the small opening.

"Of course," I chirped.

It appeared to be another nurse either designed to poke and prod me somewhere or antagonize me with more questions. She swung the door open wide only to find me sitting and that apparently is not what she was expecting.

"Oh no, you shouldn't be trying to get up on your own," she rushed over to my bedside and quickly grabbed one of my arms and part of my shoulder trying to stop me from sliding off the edge.

"Why are you trying to get up on your own darling?" she spoke in a soft yet sweet voice, almost like the way my mum speaks to me. Makes me wonder if she talks to everyone like that or if she's like a radio personality htonly turns on that tone at work.

"I can't remember the last time I stood. I didn't realize I wasn't permitted to stand on my own."

"Doctor's orders darling. Here let me give you a hand."

She bent down slightly and pushed one of the buttons located the bedside rail. Moments later there he was. I turned my head in his direction and while I was exhausted, I could feel my cheeks flush. He was more handsome than I remember and with a smile that truly lit up the room. He ran his fingers through his dark chocolate locks allowing me to see the light sitting perfectly on his high cheekbones. Seeing the light shine off his face in such a way made me smile. He was beautiful and even though I felt as if I had been terribly rude to him during our initial encounter, I was pleased to see him.

"Hello, Jean, need a hand?" he said cheerfully.

"Thank you, Tyler. I would really appreciate that," she nodded in his direction and then leaned her face down towards mine. "Are you ready?"

"Yes Ma'am," I nodded.

She nudged Tyler towards my left side, "You take that side, and we will stand on three."

He lifted my left arm over his shoulder and wrapped one arm around my waist helping to support my torso and she mirrored his positioning. Their warmth was better than any blanket that could have been wrapped around me and while I didn't know them, I took comfort in their careful embrace. As they counted upward, I could feel their grips tighten before I took one final breath and stood. At first, I felt relief at finally standing upward, but I soon felt my legs give way.

"You can do this. Close your eyes and focus on my voice," he spoke softly, and I listened to his words.

Pressing my toes onto the floor I attempted to stand once more. After a moment of hesitation, I was up.

"Very good. Now when you're ready step forward." He spoke again with strength and encouragement in his voice. Standing was not without difficulty. The parts of my legs that were tingling and half asleep before standing were now regaining life. My breathing while once rapid has now slowed to short shallow breaths. Each breath felt like I was being squeezed tighter and my body growing heavier. The longer I attempted to stand still, however, made my legs weak and I could feel my head begin to throb as the blood dropped to my legs. It was now or never. I exhaled and nudged my foot forward.

"I don't feel so well. Is that normal?" I asked.

"Yes darling. It will take time to get your strength back," Jean responded.

Again, I stepped forward and again. I could feel their arms relax allowing my breathing to become more natural.

"Thank you both for helping me," I said softly.

"You're welcome darling. We're just glad you're getting better."

I could see her smiling out of my peripheral, but I told myself I needed to keep my attention on an object in front of me in order not to lose sight of what I was trying to accomplish. I must keep moving. As I continued to move forward each step got easier and easier. Soon enough my legs grasped the concept, and my motions were once again stable, well sort of. I was far from moving like my old self, but at least I was walking again even if it wasn't entirely on my own. We continued to walk until we reached the other side of the room where I was able to briefly stop to catch what breath I could before turning and returning to my bed.

"You did great darling. Now let's have you lay back down, and we'll take a look at everything."

Both helped me back into bed before beginning to run my vitals again. Jean signaled with her arms for Tyler to leave and as soon as I noticed her signal I objected.

"Please. Let Tyler stay. Please," I pleaded.

I wasn't sure what came over me or why I was so insistent he remain, but I was. Odd really, being charismatic has always drawn people to me with minimal effort, but for me to be drawn to him in such a way it felt unnatural.

"Alright Ms. Walsh. I need to remove your dressing and perform a wound check. Would that be alright?" she asked.

I nodded.

"Tyler, please give me a hand."

She reached into the bedside table and pulled out a cover that she laid over my lower torso before lifting my gown just shy of my breasts. I didn't particularly want to look at her, so I drew my attention to one of the ceiling tiles above me. I could feel her applying pressure to different points on my abdomen while discussing her findings with

Tyler. Due to my lack of medical knowledge and terminology it was difficult for me to determine what they were referring to. Knowing that, I did my best to block them out and try to just pass the time. I felt a cool metal object slide across my skin and the sudden sensation made me jump a little. Tyler laid his hand upon my shoulder.

"Sorry, the scissors we are using to cut your dressing off are a bit cold," he said.

They continued and when they reached the other side of the dressing, I could feel the dressing pop. I didn't realize how tight the dressing was wrapped until it broke loose, and while I was uncomfortable breathing with it on, this was much worse.

"How does that feel darling?" Jean piped up with some enthusiasm.

"I think I preferred it on. I feel like I'm being crushed."

"Won't be too much longer and we will have you wrapped up again. Just hold on for us if you can," Jean sounded reassuring.

She slid her fingers across my ribs stopping periodically to check for sensitivity. While there was some unpleasantness, it appeared to be light years away from what it felt like previously. Jean seemed pleased with my progress. She lowered my gown back down and moved the covering up over my breasts while she took the top part of my gown down. The two of them fell back into the heaves of their complex medical discussion and once again I did what I could to block them out. Their behavior reminded me of how a coroner would behave when performing an autopsy. They spoke as if I wasn't in the room, but they were touching my warm body.

"Everything alright?" I inquired, not meaning to interrupt.

"You're healing quite nicely," Tyler stated with a rather boyish grin on his face.

Just seeing him grin made me grin and reminded me of Rhys. Much like Rhys, there was a comfort to Tyler's presence that would like to embrace. Like when you first meet someone, and you just have this feeling the two of you are going to be close in some way. He and Jean continued with their work and began charting notes on what I can only assume what observations of the time they were in my presence when there was a knock at the door.

"Just a moment, we are nearly finished," Jean raised her voice to be heard.

The knocking stopped and the room fell silent.

"Would it be possible for me to take a short walk? I feel like I've slept for ages and the walk would perhaps do me good."

"I suppose that would be alright." Jean nodded before turning her head back towards her paperwork. "Just give me a moment and we will get you up once more."

"Would Tyler be permitted to take me?" I blurted out.

She paused at my sudden request and raised one eyebrow clearly displaying her curiosity. It only lasted a moment and then it was as if a switch inside her flipped and she was back to her old self.

"Alright darling. Let us get you covered up."

She pulled my gown back onto my shoulders and removed the privacy covering that was used before the exam started. They worked quickly to get the room back in order and finish their notes. By the time they were finished I was more than willing to try again. With their help I was able to sit up in one swift motion before dangling my legs off the edge of the bed. Jean stepped away for a moment to the side of the room that I could not see and when she returned, she had a soft sage robe with her. It was my robe, but where did it come from.

"Where did you..."

"Your mother thought you might like to have it here. Just in case," she interrupted.

I don't know why that didn't occur to me that my mum would have been so thoughtful. That is very much like her and while for days all I could see was my pain as I glanced around the room, now I see I was surrounded by the love of my friends and family. There were fresh flowers among stacks of fresh baked treats and well-wishing cards. I've never been one to take in the essence of fresh blooms, but their sweet smell just now made the rest of the world disappear. If I closed my eyes, I would have mistaken the room for a sunny meadow where I was just a humble traveler who had fallen asleep.

"Pardon me Jean, have I had any visitors other than my family and," I hesitated, "the lad who found me?"

"Unfortunately, your care team determined it was not in your best interest to have too many visitors under the circumstances," she smiled, "but they bring well wishes and fresh flowers nearly every day."

I dropped my head in disappointment. It felt like ages since I had seen Jade or Emma and now more than ever, I wish to see their smiling faces. In my moment of reflection, I heard Jean's voice once more.

"Are you ready to try again?" Jean spoke softly perhaps not to startle me.

"Yes Ma'am, I'm ready."

With those words I was up and on my way with Tyler by my side. It took me a few moments to get that natural motion down again, but each time was getting easier. We made our way slowly out the door and around the nurse's station before setting out on a course down a barren hall. At first, he did not say much other than some words of encouragement, but I was hopeful that this desolate hall would change all of that. Despite my better judgment, I felt a desperation, desire if you will, to know more about this handsome stranger that was brought into my life.

"Thank you for the other night and for escorting me now. It's very kind of you," I spoke softly in hopes of avoiding an echo situation.

"My pleasure Ms. Walsh."

"Please call me Isolde. Ms. Walsh just seems so formal."

"Isolde it is," he nodded. "How are you feeling?"

"Much better actually. How long have I been here?"

"Four or Five days now, but you're recovering nicely."

We continued down the hall stopping every five to ten steps for me to catch my breath, but I was relieved to have Tyler by my side. He wasn't family and he wasn't quite a friend but talking to him helped me to unburden my soul. We were nearing the end of the hall and I could see the sun shining through some windows down the next hall.

"It's so quiet here. Where are we going?"

"Just a few more steps and we should be there," he said followed by a smile.

We rounded another corner and stepped into a dead-end hall where the sun light was free flowing into the space warming the cold tile and myself. There was an old wooden chair sitting against the wall next to an ornate looking door with stained glass in it. This space doesn't appear to be used often, but I could see the beauty that was once housed within. To think that something so beautiful could be forgotten just appalls me, but it really wasn't forgotten by all. Tyler knew it was here.

"Did you know about this?!" I squealed.

I could feel my face light up like a Christmas tree and clearly, it wasn't just a feeling. The look on my face was mirrored on his. He looked so happy, and the look wasn't like he was proud of himself more that he was overjoyed at seeing my reaction.

"I thought you deserved to see something as beautiful as you are."

I could feel my jaw drop moments after the words passed his lips and I clasped my hands up and over my mouth in shock. Without even trying, I had drawn him in and left part of him wanting. I couldn't believe how thoughtful he had been, and I wanted to take a moment to imprint the memory of his face at that moment in my mind. His face was smooth and pale with a 5 o'clock shadow appearing over a strong jaw. He was beautiful and while part of me was strongly attracted to him I was afraid of what it all meant. I think the silence went on for too long because he started to bite his lower lip as his gaze fell towards the floor.

"My apologies, I didn't mean to stare," I started blinking rapidly. "I just wasn't expecting…"

"Please don't apologize. I shouldn't have said that."

He dropped his head and closed his eyes. I placed my hands under his jaw and cupped his face ever so gently.

"Thank you for being kind to me."

I whispered while staring into his bright eyes. Upon closer inspection his eyes weren't just bright. They were this magnificent shade of jade I've never seen before in human eyes. They captivated me so and even as he continued to blink it only enticed my curiosity over them. He was blinking slowly, and I could feel his pulse start to race ever so slightly. I brushed my thumbs across his cheeks and then across his lips. They were slightly dry, but still soft to the touch. I'm not sure what I was feeling. For a moment, I wanted to kiss him and then the next I wanted to run from him. It's a perplexing thing, the human heart. I believed mine might have been shattered forever, but clearly a piece remained of the original Isolde. I brought him closer to me and hugged him gently.

"I don't know or understand what you're going through, but I wanted to show you something beautiful to help light your candle," he whispered in my ear.

I wiped a tear from my eye and pulled away before more started to fall. When I turned, I was able to view the central gardens the hospital was built around. While the blooms from earlier in the spring had all but gone, the colors of the trees and bushes were beautiful and just what I needed to see. He was around me for only a matter of days and already knew what my soul needed to heal. Remarkable really. He laid a hand on my shoulder as if to provide reassurance that I was not alone, and we stood there for several minutes just in silence.

"They used to bring patients here toward the end of their lives to help them make peace. Unfortunately, no one really comes back here anymore except for me, but as long as you're here consider this your space. No one will bother you here."

I don't know how long we stood there surveying the land, but my body was growing weaker and weaker by the minute. I was beginning to slouch when I noticed Tyler set the chair carefully behind me. It's hard to explain the inner battle that was waging within. In a sense, I had never felt so much indifference in my life, but in another I was completely conflicted. Was this guy just really good at his job or was there more to it? I have never been the perceptive type and that has caused me great distress on more than one occasion, but it's hard to know and understand everyone's intentions.

Eventually the silence was broken by some unexpected commotion down the main hall, and it providedus with a valuable starting point. At first, we continued with the small talk we started earlier, but the more we spoke the more I knew I liked him. I learned he was a sophomore at the university the next town over and from asmall family. His mother passed away from cancer when he was just a boy leaving him and his father to fend for themselves. This pontiff moment fueled his passion to study medicine and could potentially explain the caring nature he displayed towards patients. He was soft spoken, but not monotone by any means. Listening to him speak about his mother was one of the most touching sentiments I had ever heard. Before we could dive in further, I heard him being paged and I knew our time was up.

"Better be getting back soon. I wouldn't want them to think I ran away with you or anything." The sound of it clearly made him snicker a bit.

"Would you if I asked you to?"

I looked towards him with eyes wide but focused on his. His cheeks were becoming flushed with color, and I could tell just the suggestion of it appealed to him.

"Forgive me, I shouldn't have suggested it. I just," I turned and looked towards the garden once more.

"Just what?" he added.

"Don't want to leave."

"It will take time to heal from all this. Physically and emotionally, but you will get better."

"I meant I don't want to leave you."

"I'm not going anywhere," he said with a smile.

I smiled in return. It was now time to say my goodbyes to the hidden nook, at least for now. With a renewed spirit and a glimpse of hope in my heart I was able to return to my room with a bit more gusto than when we left earlier.

10

When we returned to my room, I found my mum and Rhys waiting for me. I was relieved to see them, and I felt myself perk up at the sight of them. Both came to my side and hugged me before talking with Tyler about where we'd been and how I was doing. He filled them in while continuing to walk me towards my bed. We reached the bedside and while the conversation continued, I was more focused on what was going to happen when Tyler left the room. For a moment, I felt liberated and relaxed, and I could quickly feel the tension starting to build once again. The majority of their questions were clearly not directed at me, but even so there seemed to be a mountain of them. Tyler was kind enough to answer what he could, but just smiled and nodded the others off. Unfortunately for families that do not enter hospitals much, they are not exactly familiar with the fact that not every staff member knows everything about everyone and, even if they did, they may not be permitted to share that information openly.

I did my best to listen to the conversation, but I was just counting the minutes before all of that concern and worry would fall upon my shoulders. Tyler was kind enough to turn the covers down for me before helping me remove my robe. He made sure not to rush his way through it, but he did his utmost to not appear overly attentive. His touch sent goosebumps down my skin and made me relieved I was getting back in bed where I could cover them up. I slid myself under the covers to enjoy the warmth they provided while Tyler worked to get me hooked back up to all the monitors.

I was curiously and admirably watching him work when we heard a soft knock at the door before it clicked open. As the door slid open everyone's attention fell on the door and who was entering. Seconds tend to feel like eternity in moments like this, but we didn't have to ponder long. The shriek of joy from our mum followed by a glimpse of that golden blond hair told me who had come. She actually had the nerve to get up and give him a hug. A hug! Seriously? How did this monster work his way into my mum's heart so easily? My blood pressure was clearly rising, and I could now feel and hear my heart beating. The monitors were starting to beep at an increasing rate and Tyler took notice.

The monster shook hands with Rhys before focusing his attention on me. He stepped towards me and as the space between us closed my hands lay firmly down at my sides and I began gripping the blankets tightly. I closed my eyes in hopes this was another nightmare and any moment now I would wake up. Unfortunately, before I had the chance, I felt the softness and warmth of his lips upon mine. The sensation instantly nauseated me, and it wasn't until I tasted him again when I felt like I was being pushed over the edge. Physically, I was in a hospital room, but mentally I was transported back to that night. I could hear the fans cheering and the cool breeze washing over me. I began to jerk and thrash violently in an attempt to pull myself away from him. This can't be happening. He can't have me. I opened my eyes and attempted to crawl away from him.

"Love, we don't have to hide anymore. They know everything." A look of concern washed over his face. "I've been so worried about you."

I didn't have a reply for him but recoiled from his very touch. I felt trapped and frightened.

"Ms. Walsh, are you feeling alright?"

Tyler interrupted what I can only assume would have been a magnificent performance and placed his hand on my shoulder. The beeping of my monitors continued to increase and the door to my room quickly opened just as two additional medical personnel rushed in.

"Sorry folks, but we will need everyone out!"

They shouted as they pulled the monster away from me. Rhys insisted on staying and Mum appeared to be relieved at his will to stay.

"I will stay out of your way, but I'm not leaving!" he demanded in response to their request.

The two nodded as if they had come to an understanding before pushing the monster and our Mum out of the room. Once again, I was surrounded by medical jargon and uncertainty. I could tell they were completely perplexed by the state of affairs I had come to in a matter of moments. It was reflected in the shouting and bickering that followed. I did my best to keep up, but it was all happening so fast. At first, they leapt to placing blame on Tyler and then on my family. Just thinking of that along with all the shouting I could feel my blood pressure rising higher and higher. I was starting to feel light-headed, and I couldn't take it anymore.

"STOP IT! ALL OF YOU!" I bellowed.

The sound of my voice echoing through the room drew all their attention to me and for a brief moment the room was silent again except for my monitors.

"Tyler and my brother are not to blame, so please stop it!" I added. "I need a moment alone if you please."

I panned the room taking a moment to stop and focus on the faces of each one of them. I didn't have the strength to shout again as I was already struggling to breathe. I just needed them to respect my wishes and give me a few moments to collect myself before I didn't have any other choice than to tell my secret and watch my mum's heart break. The two strangers left without too much of a struggle, but now remained my two white knights, Rhys and Tyler. I was struggling to find a common ground with them and while I believe both would understand what was happening, the moment I unveiled my secret, both came with risks. Tyler works for the hospital and may be obligated to tell them anything and everything that transpires between us. Meanwhile, Rhys is family and has always protected me. I don't know if he could protect himself from the rage that may become ignited from stoking a fire such as this one.

"Ms. Walsh, please call me if you need me. I will be right outside your door."

Tyler touched my shoulder softly with a little squeeze as his form of reassurance I'm sure and then he stepped out of the room. Rhys stayed. Locked in place and standing tall like a formidable stone wall designed to guard me when I could not.

"Wish me away all you want Izz, but I'm not going. So, either you can start talking or welcome the idea of having a new shadow with you," he said firmly.

"Rhys, I just can't. Life is hard enough on everyone already and I don't want to make it worse."

"Then tell me and unburden yourself," he insisted. "I love you, so I'm trying to protect you from yourself."

"I'm not sure what you mean," he scowled.

"Just trust me, this wouldn't just break Mum's heart," I tried to smile, but it just came off awkward.

"Alright, so, what's with Derek?"

I was impressed at how quickly he switched gears, but in doing so he had put me back in a no-win situation. While I know he wasn't intentionally trying to hurt me the question stung and left a burning sensation that lingered. I looked away from him in hopes that he would drop it, but I could feel the tears welling up.

"That's the part I can't tell you," I choked on the words.

"Then I think you need to tell someone because until you do, we only know his side of the story and his side of the story doesn't become you."

I could hear the disappointment in his voice, and it broke my heart. I don't think I've ever disappointed him before, but while there is a first time for everything, this is not a first I wanted to share with him. I turned to face him, and I noticed his posture had changed. He had leaned back in the chair and folded his arms, but his eyes were still on me. He was never the type to pry or interrogate, so I'm not sure if he was just that upset or if someone prompted him to act in this way.

"Please believe me. It's not what you think."

"Then tell me and we can fix this. Help me, help you. I'm begging you. Before this gets any worse."

I could hear the strain in his voice. He was on the edge and needed to be brought back before it was too late. When he realized, I wasn't going to tell him anymore he slammed his hands down on the arms of the chair before standing and stormed out. What was wrong with me? Rhys was my eldest brother, my protector. He has always been there for me, but when asked my words fell short. While I know my folks would take action if they were given the whole truth, I believe Rhys would become my avenger and in turn destroy any and all chances he had created for a better life for himself. I couldn't allow that to happen. I was conflicted. I thought I had made a decision, but now I feel like I was losing more than just my dignity and self-respect.

I hit the call button on my bedside and a nurse quickly answered.

"May I help you?"

"Yes, is Tyler available?" I responded.

"He's in with another patient. Is there something I can help you with?"

"No, no thank you," I sighed.

I wasn't entirely sure why I wanted to see him. Maybe I was ready to talk or maybe I just needed to see his smiling face again. My behavior earlier put me on thin ice, and I needed to try and mend what bridges I could before it was too late. I tried to think of a way to tell Rhys without needing to tell him the whole story, but that didn't seem feasible at the present moment. I was trying to do what I believed was the right thing to do, but even the right thing didn't seem right anymore. I paged the nurse again.

"May I help you?" A pleasant voice came through the speaker.

"Would it be possible for someone to find my brother? I need to speak to him."

"Of course. We will locate him and let him know."

I was overwhelmed by thoughts of fear and anxiety. My palms were sweaty, and I could feel my stomach start to flip. What was I supposed to say to him? Family is supposed to love you and forgive you no matter what, but I've been lying to them and keeping secrets. I was raised better than that or so I thought. I'm sure my folks would agree. Good news was I didn't have long to contemplate the situation or beat myself up. One of my knights has returned to me.

"Hello again, I heard you called for me. Are you alright?" Tyler spoke cheerfully.

"Yes, but what happened before, my reaction..."

"It's causing a great deal of concern among the staff and well, I'm worried about you Isolde. You seemed blissful moments before we returned to your room and then..."

His voice trailed off and his face turned sharply towards the door. It only took a moment, but I think he was starting to put things together. His eyes widened and his skin grew pale. He covered his mouth with his hand as a gasp was escaping his body and then I knew he had figured it out.

"It's him, isn't it?"

His voice strained and dry as if he hadn't had a drink in days. He attempted to clear his throat in hopes that whatever might have been caught there would soon be gone. He turned his face back towards mine and I could tell he was clinching his teeth. I reached for his hand and squeezed it gently. I nodded to confirm his suspicion.

"I must go. He can't be allowed near you under any circumstances."

"Tyler, I'm afraid."

"I know, but you need to tell someone," he squeezed my hand tightly. "Based on what I've seen I'm not sure how much longer you can continue on this way."

"Am I really in that terrible of a state?"

"Well, you are better now, but if you fall into the state you were in a week ago the outcome may not be favorable."

He leaned before brushing my hair away from my eyes.

"Give me just a moment and I will be back at your side. Security needs to be notified that he is not to enter your room under any circumstances."

"Please hurry back."

"I will."

He headed out the door clearly on a mission. I heard him briefly exchange words with a woman at the nurse's station before heading down the hall. Moments later that same woman placed a call into Officer Chaney's office. I really hope Rhys will get my message before he gets hers. I'm not sure I can handle another encounter with him alone, but I had no way of knowing how much my family already had heard. However, as long as I had faith on my side and was honest, I should have nothing to fear.

I attempted to wait patiently for either Rhys or Tyler to return, but patience is virtue that I was still working on. With the door being cracked open even slightly I was able to hear conversations at the nurse's station that I normally wouldn't have even reached my ears. While there was a great deal of discussion regarding my episode from earlier today there was more than enough gossip to go around about my alleged relationship with the town's most eligible bachelor. I had become the latest scandal and it made me wish I were once again invisible.

At one point or another, we are all searching for something that makes us stand out, makes us unique. In truth, we are already unique, but the desires to be well liked or part of the A-list crowd are great. With Derek, I was pulled in by his beauty, but continued to entertain wild thoughts of him because I was weak. While there was a time I would have given anything to be with Derek, I wish I would have known the cost. The cost for my desire was too great and I paid it without even being asked.

11

In my state of panic and exhaustion I laid back and fell into a deep sleep. This was the first time in what felt like weeks that my slumber was not interrupted by some terrible nightmare. I don't believe I slept long, but it was long enough to calm my nerves and rest my body. As my sleepy eyes slowly fluttered awake, I could see Rhys resting in a recliner near the foot of my bed. He seemed so peaceful I couldn't bear to wake him. Looking at him in this way made me regret how I treated him earlier. He was doing everything he could to be there for me and I was pushing him away. I think he could sense my movement for he woke up moments later.

"Hello beautiful, you're awake," he said softly.

"Yes, I am, and you came."

"Of course, I did. You're my sister."

"Listen, please forgive me for how I've been acting. I haven't been myself."

"No apology necessary Izz. We all know you are going through something, and I was wrong to push."

"I'm ready. That is if you are ready to listen."

Honor be damned along with my pride. He was clearly taken back by my sudden willingness to talk, but I think among the shock was a bit of relief flowing through. He rushed over and sat sidesaddle on the bed next to me.

Taking my hands in his he waited patiently for me to elaborate.

"It's alright. Take a deep breath and tell me when you're ready," he said reassuringly.

"That afternoon I wasn't alone in the forest. There was someone else with me and what happened was no accident."

He nodded.

"I was attacked, and this wasn't the first time this person hurt me."

Tears had started streaming down my face and I had to stop and sniffle about every third or fourth word, but I was able to finish the sentence. When I stopped, I noticed his eyes grew wide with astonishment, and his grip tightened.

"Attacked, Izz, what do you mean you were attacked?" he asked as his eyes narrowed.

I pulled my hands from his grip and used them to lower the top of my gown revealing what was left of the bite marks and the scrapes from in the forest. To add insult to injury I pulled up my gown and showed him my abdomen that was still covered in contusions along with my recently broken ribs.

"These are only part of what he did to me."

I closed my eyes because I simply couldn't look at him. I felt ashamed and embarrassed.

"Did this man force himself on you?"

I couldn't look at him. Looking at him would only confirm that my worries were validated. I didn't want anything to change between us, but it may be too late for that.

"Izz, answer me," he insisted.

"He did," I uttered under my breath.

"Do you happen to know who the man was?" he asked.

"I do and that's the part I've been afraid to tell you."

"I don't understand Izz. Someone assaulted you, why are you protecting this man?" he stood up and protested.

"Because once I tell you who it is, it will change everything, and I don't want it to change you."

"It's already changed me. You were sexually assaulted; someone should have known. Who did this to you?!"

"Rhys, please just let this go," I said softly.

"You know I can't do that, so just tell me," he growled.

"Derek Strom."

My eyes went from staring at random objects around the room to looking straight at him. He was livid and it reminded me of those childhood cartoons where smoke starts coming out of the character's ears accompanied by boiling red eyes. He didn't say anything, but I could sense his gears were turning.

"Rhys, please forgive me. I should have told you."

"Izz, you have nothing to apologize for, but mayor's son or not he won't get away with it." He kissed my forehead before uttering, "I love you."

He rushed out of the room before I could get another word in. I quickly pressed the call button and rather than wait I just started shouting. Someone quickly rushed in.

"Is everything alright?!" the nurse shouted.

"No, the man who just left my room someone needs to go get him. It's very important that he doesn't leave the hospital," I insisted.

"I'm not sure what you mean Ma'am."

"Please just do it! Something bad is going to happen if you don't. Please it's important!" I demanded.

She rushed back out of the room and headed down the hall from the sounds of it. I took a deep breath and realized I couldn't wait to find out. I lowered my bed and did my best to quickly slide to the side. I felt like I needed a boost up, but I really don't believe I had the time. It was now or never. I placed my hands beside me and with one good push I was up. I got caught up trying to unhook the IV when I heard shouting down the hall.

After a few failed attempts at unhooking my IV I decided to just unplug it from the wall and move on. When I turned towards the open door, I saw two guards rush past pushing my body back into panic mode. I quickly rounded the doorway to my room and headed in the direction of the commotion. I felt like I could barely breathe and while grasping my side helped, I may not last long. I couldn't see exactly what was happening, but there were several staff members heading in that direction.

I leaned against the wall and used the handrail to pull myself along. I'm sure I wasn't going to get far before someone noticed, but I had to make sure it wasn't Rhys. Please let it not be him. I wanted to be dreaming, but then I heard it. The sound of my brother's voice echoed down the hall. He was arguing with someone, but I didn't recognize the other man's voice. As I ventured closer, I realized he was arguing with one of the guards and they now had him restrained. There was blood dripping down his chin most likely from a split lip, but from the splatter and droplets on the floor someone else had been there. Clearly Rhys had gotten the best of him. I was close enough to see, but not close enough for anyone to think much of it. I watched Rhys be dragged away like a common criminal. This is exactly what I wanted to avoid.

I fell to my knees as the tears poured from my eyes and I covered my face with my hands. What have I done? My brother is a good man, the best in fact. Now he's gotten into a fight and possibly soiled his good name. He deserved better than this. I don't recall seeing someone walk up to me, but when I took my hands down to wipe my eyes, there they were. A pair of worn white sneakers and I knew I'd been caught. I glanced up to find Tyler staring down at me with an outstretched hand. I took his hand, and he lifted me up. He held me in his arms where I sobbed uncontrollably. He didn't try to stop me; he just held me. There was a failed attempt by one of the nurses to separate us, but Tyler stuck it out with me and let the pieces fall as they may. When they attempted a second time he snapped.

"Her brother has just been taken away and she's in extreme pain. Please give her a moment," he snapped at her.

"Fine, then please make sure to escort her back to her room where she can grieve in private," she snapped back.

The same nurse brought over a wheelchair, but he waved it away. He reached up and grabbed my IV bag before placing it on his shoulder and picked me up. He carried me all the way back to my room where he carefully set me down on the side of the bed. He attempted to fully stand, but my arms wouldn't let him go. I just couldn't and thankfully, he didn't try to resist me. He gave into me and sat down beside me. I could feel myself start to calm down and the tears that were once so uncontrollable had nearly subsided. He didn't say a word just rubbed his hands over my back in hopes of alleviating some of my discomfort.

"I can't believe this is happening," I whispered through the tears, "this is all my fault."

"Shh, you did nothing to deserve this," I felt him lightly kiss my forehead and whisper, "You're safe now."

"But he wouldn't have been taken away if it wasn't for me."

"He was upset and let's just say Derek is lucky that your brother found him before I did. I might not have been as kind."

Hearing his name made me tense up and with how close I was to him it was impossible for him not to notice my unease at just hearing his name.

"What happened?" I mumbled.

"He was strutting down the hall when he saw your brother. I'm sure he was hoping for a friendly face to greet him, but apparently your brother had something else in mind. Rhys grabbed him and slammed him against one of the walls before proceeding to pummel him. Your brother may have some bruises and a split lip, but the other guy has quite a bit more than just a bruised ego."

"Do you think they will press charges?"

"I'm not sure."

I buried my face in his chest and let out a sigh.

"I should let you get back to work. I wouldn't want to get you in trouble," I mumbled into his chest.

"I was off work an hour ago."

I looked up at him and met his gaze as he was already looking down at me.

"And you stayed?"

"You needed me," he said with a smile.

These are the moments I wished would last forever. Aside from my brother, Rhys, I didn't believe perfect men existed, but Tyler was remarkably close. I turned my body slightly and brought my legs up on top of his. I wasn't trying to seduce him, nor had I even thought about it, but as he placed one of his hands on my knee, I knew that we were crossing a line. Even though I knew I wasn't ready to entertain the idea of being with someone, I was afraid of what would happen if he wasn't in my life. He had been there for me in ways that no one else could be and I didn't want to lose sight of that. Everything about him drew me in. I just needed to relax and stop thinking so much. He ran his fingers along my jaw line, and it drew my attention this face.

"Would you like me to stay with you?" he whispered. "If only for tonight."

I nodded. Anything to keep him close. We laid back onto the small hospital bed where I fell asleep tightly wrapped in his arms and our legs intertwined. When I was a little girl, I dreamed of what the perfect evening would be with the man of my dreams and, while tonight was one of the furthest things from that dream, I couldn't have been happier. We met under the direst of circumstances and still he managed to give me hope. He protected me even when it could have meant trouble for him and, most importantly, he knew how to help me even when I didn't know how to help myself.

The arms that tenderly held me that night were the arms that I awoke to in the wee hours of the morning. A nurse was hovering just shy of the head of the bed and when I turned slightly to bring her into view, she did not look pleased. I'm not sure this moment isn't going to add to my credibility, but it was the first decent night's sleep I had gotten since this all began. Tyler was laying behind me and I could feel his breath graze my neck each time he exhaled. As close as our bodies were to each other they felt as one. When he moved, I moved. When he took a breath, I took a breath. It was a thing of beauty really. I attempted to turn over towards him as gently as possible, so I could look at him once more. It appears that I was successful in not waking him as I worked through the awkwardness of it in such a small and restricted space. I was pleased with myself. I found that part of me was terrified that he was just a figment of my imagination and at any moment he would just vanish, but the other part of me had hope for a better tomorrow. He could have gone home or turned away from me, but he didn't.

The nurse had left us for now and I was pleased to be alone with him once more. Hopefully, the nurse would understand and keep this very private moment as such for both of our sakes. As I laid there, I did my best to memorize his face and immortalize his beauty in my memory. From the little scar on his chin to the five o'clock shadow still on his face. I wanted to remember it all. I brushed my fingers along his dark hair before placing one of my hands on his neck. He seemed so peaceful. I felt his breathing change ever so slightly and I worried that my want to take him in had woken him. Unfortunately, I was correct in that assumption.

"You're awake," he said with a slight smile.

"Only for a few moments now," I whispered with a smile.

His eyes opened ever so slightly revealing his bright eyes and they quickly found mine.

"How are you feeling Isolde?"

"Blissful, if that's possible. I never imagined you'd stay."

"I needed to know you were alright."

"I'm feeling a bit better now, thank you. I wish you didn't have to go."

"Not just yet, but even when I do, I'm never far."

He leaned in and kissed my forehead before pulling me closer where I was able to nestle against his chest. He was running his fingers through my hair and down my back almost like a gentle massage. His touch melted my heart and the nightmares of weeks past had all been forgotten at least for a moment. I placed my hands on his chest allowing his pounding heart to be clearly felt in each of my fingertips, the equivalent of throwing a stone in a pool of water. Even though the stone could no longer be seen the ripple effect couldn't be missed. I couldn't bring myself to kiss his lips for fear my subconscious would step in and

make a mockery of my new-found hope, so I did the only
 thing I knew wouldn't break my heart, I kissed his chest.

While thoughts of the impending day were slowly
creeping into my mind, I tried to focus on my blessings: the
smell of flowers in my room, the cards brought by my
friends and loved ones, Rhys, the brother who clearly
would do anything for me, the man at my side, and above
all my life. While the monster may have wounded me,
Tyler spared my life and I need to do my best to never lose
sight of that. No one likes to hear that everything happens
for a reason, but what if it really does?

"Why don't you lay down and rest a bit longer. I'm
going to check on things and get you some breakfast. I
won't be long," he said softly.

I nodded and watched him slowly get up. The bed
that once felt so small now felt too big for my little body,
but his warmth remained with me at least for now. I
watched him straighten himself up and cover me up with a
fresh blanket from the closet before heading to the door.
He placed his hand on the door and hesitated for just a
moment before pulling the handle back. I'm not sure what
prompted his sudden stop, but it gave me a brief moment of
concern. When he turned to blow me a kiss, I knew that
my concern wasn't needed and perhaps the hesitation was
just a moment of reflection versus a sign of trouble ahead.

As the door closed behind him, I could only hope
that our time apart would be short lived, but as the bed
began to cool and the hands of the clock turned onward, I
knew that it may be a bit longer than I'd hoped for. As I
laid there, I slid my hand back and forth across where he
was laying and tried to relive the moment in my mind. I've

been happy in my life, but nothing like this. In the middle of my bliss however there was a knock at the door and Jean stepped inside.

"Good morning darling, did you sleep well?"

"I did. Thank you."

"I noticed you had some company last night," she tilted her chin down and raised an eyebrow at me.

I could feel myself start to blush as just the thought of where she was going with this. Either she witnessed this event with her own two eyes, or the other nurse vocalized her displeasure. I didn't want to become defensive or deny her findings as this would only make it seem more suspicious than it already was. If I've learned anything, it's better to be honest than deceitful especially when someone has already made you.

"Yes, I did. He's someone I feel comfortable talking to and right now there aren't many of those."

"I understand. You're going to have a busy day today. Would you like to get cleaned up?"

"Yes ma'am, but what exactly do you mean by busy?"

"Well, they are thinking about letting you go home soon, but before they do, Officer Chaney will be by to ask you some questions."

She pulled out some fresh towels and helped me up. I wasn't thrilled with the idea of more questions from Officer Chaney, but I think my grace period for avoiding people was over and it was time to set the record straight. Since my sea legs were gone and I was no longer a fall risk, she wasn't required to accompany me to into the bathroom and I was thankful for that. The thought of someone

126

needing to help me bathe was something I didn't want to entertain at this present moment. She provided me with instructions on how to use the shower and what to do if I needed help before sending me on my way.

I was anxious to really look at myself in the mirror since it had felt like a lifetime since I did and, once the door closed behind me, I wasted no time in removing my gown to do so. To my surprise there wasn't much there to see. Nearly everything from the attacks were gone. There were still several noticeably discolored parts of my abdomen, neck, and legs. However, overall, I was starting to look like my old self. To my surprise my hair and face were well taken care of even though I cannot recall tending to either of them in days, but who would have taken the time? I didn't ponder on the thought too long and ultimately vetoed thinking on the matter further. As I stepped into the shower, I braced myself for the pain that usually had followed. To my surprise, I didn't feel a thing other than the warmth of the water. My physical recovery was nearly complete.

I finished getting cleaned up and stepped out of the shower. I noticed that Jean didn't lay out a gown for me, so I crossed my fingers and opened the bathroom door. Thank goodness I was wrapped in a towel, or my mum mayhave gotten more than she bargained for. She was primping the flowers that were brought over the last week. I couldn't see her face, but I could hear her sniffles and knew she had been crying. While there were times I found her humming and blissful attitude too much, this was the first day I missed hearing it.

"Mum...are you alright?" I said softly in hopes of not startling her.

"My dear, I'm so glad to see you."

As she turned around quickly, I watched her face light up right before she rushed over to me. At first, she grabbed me swiftly and intensely. Hugging me so tightly I nearly lost my breath, but as I gave out a gasp for air her grip loosened.

"Sorry dear, didn't know my own strength, I guess. I've missed you so."

"I've missed you too, Mum."

She glanced down and realized I was still in a towel and gave a face of disapproval before stepping back towards the closet. She opened the door and brought over a small bag full of clothes from home. I was relieved to see some comforts of home and knew that these comforts meant that my time here was almost over. The smile that appeared on my face when I first saw the bag she was holding was now falling into a frown.

"What's the matter dear? I thought you'd be happy to go home."

"I am. I just think that I will miss some of the staff here. They've been incredibly kind to me," I shrugged.

"I understand," she nodded.

I headed back to the bathroom and proceeded to don the clothing my mum brought me. In only a matter of hours I would be walking out of the hospital doors and may never see any of these people again. While the majority of the staff I would not miss, Tyler crossed my mind. Would I ever see him again? I hoped the answer would be yes, but I had to be realistic. He was studying to be a physician with a job and a family of his own. What were the chances that we would even cross paths again let alone stay in touch on purpose? I could feel doubt creeping in again and I needed to force myself to believe. Have faith. He gave me hope when I had none, and he showed me beauty in a world that had all gone dark to me. I needed to believe that if nothing else he would remain someone close to my heart now and forever.

I exited the bathroom feeling a little more like myself, especially now that I was wearing full undergarments and not just a pair of knickers and a loose gown. To my astonishment, Rhys was standing next to our mum, and they were giggling. I couldn't believe he was here and of all things giggling. I was overjoyed at just the sight of him and, from the look on his face when he turned to see me up and dressed, he was also. He held out his arms in anticipation and I rushed towards him to give him a hug. I was relieved at the sight of him and when we hugged, I could actually feel the two of us exhale as if we had been holding our breath until we met again.

"Hello beautiful. I've missed that smile," he whispered in my ear.

"I've missed you. I'm so relieved you're alright," I whispered back.

We broke off the hug and I was finally able to see up close and personal the results of his altercation the day before. His cheek has some bruising, and his lip was in fact split, but it could have been a lot worse. I did my best to not draw too much attention to it, but I hoped he knew how much that act of bravery or quite possibly pure rage meant to me.

"So, is it true that I get to go home today?" I asked.

"That's the hope. They said there were a few more things that they wanted to address before that happens, but they seemed confident that today was a good day. Would you like me to order you some breakfast?" Mum said with a hint of excitement in there.

"No, thank you. Someone already took care of that for me."

A slight grin appeared on my face as soon as I realized I would see Tyler again. Unfortunately, another one of my physicians entered the room first. It was time for my discharge instructions and mind-numbing follow-up. I understand it is required, but it's so tedious. To be honest I wish they would just hand my mum the paperwork and send me on my way. He went over the usual items and follow-up instructions, but on the last item he mentioned a word that caught my attention.

"My apologies doctor, would it be possible for you to repeat that last part?" I blurted out.

"Ms. Walsh, as I was telling your mother, you will need to come back in for some follow-up testing. Initial testing for sexually transmitted diseases and pregnancy may not always be as conclusive as when a patient is tested weeks after their exposure or encounter. We can discuss these options more thoroughly during that follow-up appointment."

He said the words in a smooth and monotone voice, but I couldn't believe how calm he was. More importantly how calm my mum and brother were at the sound of that. Was there really a chance I could have an STD or be pregnant? I mean, I went to health class like everyone else

130

my age, but that never even crossed my mind. I felt like I was going to be sick. I got up quickly and made my way towards the bathroom once more. By the time I reached the door I knew I was going to be sick. True to themselves I could hear my mum and brother following me. I shut the door behind me, and I could hear them both thumping on the door.

"Izz, are you alright? Open the door!" Rhys shouted.

"Isolde, please open the door!" Mum added in an equally loud, but significantly more distressed tone.

"Please just give me a few moments!" I demanded.

"Please come out Isolde. We can work through this together," my mum added.

"I don't want to work through it. I just want someone to wake me up, so I can be normal again," I mumbled through the gagging.

"Alright dear. Please come out when you're ready." My mum's tone softened, and disappointment set in as she stepped away from the door. Rhys, however, didn't move. I could hear him breathing and running his fingers along the door. This was something he did since I was a child. Whenever I refused to come out of my room he would sit and patiently wait until I was ready. Almost like his way of saying he was there for me, but without saying a word. While hospital doors do not lock it is remarkable how difficult a door is to open when someone is pressing their body against it, and I had no intention of moving unless I had to. After a few moments, Rhys remained, but instead of standing he dropped and placed his back against the door.

"Mum, could you and the doc step out for a few moments to continue your discussion? I don't want to leave her, but I don't know if she is ready to hear everything that is being said," his words were soft, but direct. He's never been the type to just tell someone to get out. Well, then again no one in our family really says things like that at least not to someone outside the family. It's not in our nature to make a fuss or cause a scene.

"Rhys, are you sure? Maybe I should stay."

"Mum, please. Take care of things with the hospital, so we can take her home."

I could hear mumbling through the door like maybe that wasn't the last of the conversation, but maybe it was the last of it they wanted me to potentially hear. I could hear the room door close shortly thereafter followed by more tapping on the bathroom door.

"I apologize. You shouldn't have had to hear that," he said softly.

"You knew?"

Part of me already knew the answer, but the words came out anyway.

"Yes."

I could feel the tears welling up once again and I did my best to hold them back, but they fell anyway. I brought my knees up to my chest and rested my head on them as I watched the tears fall slowly and seep into my shirt. Just when I thought the nightmare was over, it reared its ugly head and took me under once again.

"Izz, once you were on the mend, they told us those were possibilities, but I'm sorry Izz. If I could undue all of this and take away the pain, you know I would."

"I know," I uttered through the tears, "I'm sorry I shut you out."

I heard the room door click open and Rhys began talking to someone. It was a man, but it didn't sound like my father or the physician that was just there. Rhys was being kind to him and as the voice grew louder, I knew I recognized who was approaching Rhys, but it's difficult to be certain when listening through a heavy door. I could hear Rhys trying to explain to him what happened and in the man's response I knew it was Tyler.

"Tyler?" I raised my voice to clearly be heard.

"Isolde...I mean, Ms. Walsh. I brought you some breakfast. I even have enough for your brother to join you if you'd like."

He stumbled over his words just a bit at the start, but I think he was just trying to protect me from any potential backlash a personal relationship between us would cause at the present moment. I stood up and tried to gather myself before opening the door. I wasn't sure what I would say to either of them, but I knew hiding in this bathroom wasn't the answer. As I slowly opened the door, I was relieved to see them both smiling and happy. Maybe it was a front to lighten the mood or maybe they really were just happy to see, but their joy helped regardless of the motive or meaning behind the gesture.

Rhys stepped over and hugged me tightly and, even though my arms were loosely wrapped around him, I was still able to outstretch one of my arms enough for my hand to find Tyler's. He squeezed my hand gently before letting go to step over by the bedside.

"So, I'll leave you two to it. I just needed to make sure you were alright," he said before moving towards the door.

"Please stay. I'm sure my sister wouldn't mind the company," Rhys stated.

"Not in the least. I would love it if you would stay."

I perked up quite a bit at Rhys's suggestion probably a bit more than I should have, but at least I was smiling again. Tyler nodded and sat down on the foot of the bed while Rhys set up shop in the recliner. I paused briefly and then opted to sit next to Tyler on the bed. Thought it would make more sense to sit there since the bedside table was already raised to the perfect height and began passing out different items, so I wasn't the only one eating. Probably a good thing too since this meal was clearly designed for two.

"So, your brother tells me they are planning to discharge you today. You must be excited to finally go home," Tyler spoke trying to be casual.

"Well, I'm not sure about excited, but it would be nice to sleep in my own bed once again," I said in a melancholy tone.

"I know you will be missed around here. You brought this place to life, even if it wasn't on such joyful terms," he added.

I laid my hand down on the bed in hopes that he would find the courage to take it in his. Without missing a beat, he laid his hand down upon mine and placed his fingers in between mine. That was what I needed. That reassurance and that comfort.

"I can't thank you enough for all you have done for my sister during this difficult time. It's my understanding the two of you have grown quite close," Rhys piped up in a rather cheerful manner, but it was not without suspicion.

"Yes, I believe we all need someone at one point or another in our lives and I'm just glad I could be there for her at this particular moment," Tyler bounced back.

Rhys was generally not suspicious of many but, in light of recent events, this may have flipped his personality causing him to be suspicious of nearly everyone. I didn't think it was possible for such an instance to occur, but it just might have. While Rhys couldn't possibly have spotted our hands, he looked upon us with curiosity as we continued to eat our breakfast. Something wasn't sitting well with him and, while I now have a better understanding of what withholding the truth does to people, this is something that will just need to play out a little more before I announce anything to him or the world.

Rhys continued to pry but, as his attempts failed to get a rise out of Tyler, forced him to give up his fishing expedition. They were able to bond over several different points and it was good to see them both laughing and carrying on about something other than me for a change. Not to mention it was rare to see my brother around someone closer to his own age. I did my best to chime in where I could, but in truth I was getting more enjoyment out of watching the two get along than anything I was able to contribute.

12

We were able to finish our breakfast before another interruption presented itself. Clearly, there would be no rest or peace for any patient in this hospital. Unfortunately, this time it was one of my least favorite people, Officer Chaney, back and with an attitude as expected.

"Good morning, Officer Chaney, how can we helpyou?" I asked.

"Good morning Ms. Walsh, I'm glad to see you are in a better mood. I need to go over everything with you now that you are alert, and your mother is present."

She followed him into the room with some paperwork in her hands and an ill-fated expression upon her face. This particular look caused some discontent within my brother, and it was written all over his face.

"Gentlemen please excuse yourselves," he added.

"Wait!" I shouted. "Would it be possible to have my brother, Rhys, sit in on our conversation as opposed to my mum?"

My mum looked utterly appalled at my request as did Officer Chaney.

"Please, my mum's heart has already been broken. Please don't shatter it further," I pleaded.

"This is a bit unethical, but with your mother's permission I will allow it," he glanced in her direction seeking a response.

She didn't say anything for a few moments but walked over and whispered something in Rhys's ear.

"I will allow it, but I will be right outside if either of you need me," she pointed to Rhys and me before excusing herself from the room as if threatening us that she'd be watching or something.

Tyler gave my hand a quick squeeze before standing and attempting to exit the room.

"Tyler don't wander far. I may have your statement, but I have a few more questions for you once I'm finished here."

He nodded before picking up my breakfast tray and stepping out.

"How are you feeling Ms. Walsh?" Officer Chaney asked.

"Much better, thank you."

"Good. I have several questions and depending on your answers to those questions I may have others. Please be aware that all responses you provide to me today will be included as part of your official statement. Do you understand?"

"I understand," I said anxious to begin.

"Mr. Walsh, do you understand?"

"Yes, I understand."

"Please explain to me the events that lead you to take a walk in the woods last Thursday."

"I needed to clear my head as I told you before," I said agitated.

"Ms. Walsh, being vague will not help your case, so the more you tell me now the better I will be able to do my job," he insisted.

"Fine. I was home from school when I heard a commotion at the front door. Apparently, my other brother, Liam, had brought a lady home for lunch and I decided to give them some time alone. Hence my need for fresh air."

"So, they came home for lunch. Why would you feel the need to leave if they were just there for lunch?"

"Well, they were home during lunch period, but they weren't having lunch exactly."

I could feel myself start to sweat as I watched him purse his lips and raise an eyebrow. He can't seem to let anything go and while I discourage anyone from tattling on sibling this was not the time to lie or avoid the question unless I absolutely had to.

"Based on their behavior I believe they came home to have sex."

I winced at just the sound of it and when I saw Rhys's reaction, I knew that he was nowhere near prepared enough for that revelation.

"Did this happen often?"

I shook my head.

"Did you recognize the girl?"

I shook my head again.

"What did you do after that?" he pressed.

"I took the bottle of whiskey I confiscated from Liam's room, and I quietly headed downstairs before rushing out the back door. My hope was of making the memories of the past week fade away and allow me to sleep without dreaming for at least one afternoon."

"But why leave the house?" he questioned.

"I didn't want to be present when my brother decided to bed a lady in the next room over from mine." It felt strange just to say it out loud, so hopefully this would end that discussion and we could move on.

"So, you went to the woods and proceeded to get drunk. What happened after that?"

"In my inebriated state I believed that a wonderful man had come and swept me off my feet and began to romance me."

"And in turn you did what?"

"Well, considering I thought this was a dream I began kissing this man just for the sheer pleasure of enjoying the fantasy. After all, I'm not the only one who can attest to having those types of dreams or fantasies."

Officer Chaney did not appear to be pleased with my response, but he took a few notes and then looked back up at me.

"Please continue."

"When I realized it wasn't a dream and it was Derek whose arms had been wrapped around me, I resisted."

"Did you specifically tell Derek to stop?" Officer Chaney inquired.

"I pleaded with him to let me go and when he didn't, I refused to cooperate causing this to happen," I lifted my shirt a little to emphasize my point by showing him my bruised torso.

"So initially you resisted, but then gave him your permission?" he looked perplexed.

"No, I didn't."

"But we have a statement from Mr. Strom stating you gave yourself to him. Did you or did you not tell him just before the alleged assault that you were his?" he demanded.

"Alleged? I didn't have a choice," I spat back. "I did what I had to do to survive and while I'm not proud of it, I'm alive."

"Officer Chaney, who's side are you exactly on here?!" Rhys piped up appearing very agitated at the sudden twist.

"I'm on the side of the truth," he bit back.

"Then try to remember that she is the victim here," Rhys added.

I proceeded to explain the situation in vivid detail hoping this would appease the officer and this nightmare would be over. As I struggled to recall the broken memory of that afternoon, I did my best to keep my eyes closed and focused. Periodically, Officer Chaney would interject with another question but overall, he remained quiet which I'm sure was not an easy feat for him. I wanted to give him information, but not too much. After all Rhys, one of the closest people to me and he had to hear the tragic tale in great detail for the first time while unable to react for fear of making the situation worse.

"Officer Chaney, I didn't submit to him out of desire. I did it out of fear. This wasn't the first time he…assaulted me. And I wasn't ready to die."

I concluded that chapter of the story in hopes that it would end his questioning. Unfortunately, what I failed to realize was that he didn't know that in the forest that afternoon wasn't the first time Derek brutalized me or tormented my mind nor did Rhys and Officer Chaney was quick to capitalize on my oversight.

"How long has this been going on Ms. Walsh?" he genuinely sounded concerned.

"What day is it?" I looked up at him only to meet a look of surprise on his face.

"You don't know what day it is?"

I shook my head and watched the two of them shoot a concerned look over at the other.

"It's Friday Izz," Rhys added.

"Then two weeks I believe. It's started at a football game one Friday night and has plagued my mind and body ever since."

Rhys staggered to his feet and stumbled back towards one of the walls. The blood drained from his face, adhe began to look frantic.

"Mr. Walsh, do we have a problem?" Officer Chaney placed his notepad down on the vacant chair and directed his attention towards him.

"Oh Lord, forgive me," Rhys proclaimed.

His eyes were focused on me as if he'd fallen into a trace. His mind was rapidly flipping through memories trying to bring all the pieces together.

"I remember now. Izz was dirty and covered in scrapes. She claimed they were from a fall, but my sister has never been clumsy. She became troubled. She couldn't sleep and when she did, she would cry out in pain just as she did when…"

He abruptly stopped and clasped a hand over his mouth trying to suppress his shock. Officer Chaney seemed baffled at Rhys's sudden corroboration to my story.

Even though I knew he would have more questions for Rhys he let that urge slide for now and pressed onward.

"Please tell me what you remember of that Friday night and be as specific as possible."

Officer Chaney's tone soften. He was getting somewhere. He picked his notepad back up and sat down next to me. I did my best to describe the events of that terrible night in vivid detail as I watched my brother's face turn from anger to sickness.

"Do you remember refusing his advances or saying no?" Officer Chaney interjected.

"Of course, I did! I didn't want this to happen!"

"Then why go with him?" he added.

"Officer Chaney, up until two weeks ago I trusted a person until they gave me a reason not to. Derek was a desirable man, well-liked at school and comes from a prestigious family. No one could have prepared me for the monster I discovered."

"What do you mean by *was* desirable?" he inquired.

"Meaning I once thought he was, but have since learned my lesson," I snapped at him.

"Ahhh, I understand. Well, I believe that is all I need for now, but I will be in touch if I have any further questions."

He stood and placed his notepad inside his suit jacket while pulling out what appeared to be a business card. He extended it towards me in hopes that I would accept.

"Please take this and if you think of anything else, don't hesitate to call." He turned towards Rhys and gestured towards the door. "I have a few more questions for you if you could please step outside."

Rhys nodded and pushed himself away from the wall in one swift motion. Clearly, ready to take on the world or at least appeared to be. He leaned over and kissed my forehead. It wasn't long before they both left, and I was alone once more. My mind was drained, but still reeling over the ordeal. Was that really all I could remember? Was that going to be enough? What's going to happen when I return to class? The more I thought about everything the more overwhelmed and nauseated I became. Before I had a moment to plan my escape, my mum came back into the room with what most likely was two cups of hot tea. She may be predictable, but she is always trying to put others needs before hers.

"Officer Chaney seemed pleased. Hopefully, his visits will be minimal once we've taken you home," she gave a slight smile and we both understood.

"We can only hope. Thank you for letting Rhys stay with me," I said softly.

"I have never understood the two of you. Thick as thieves and always have been," she sipped her tea before continuing. "When we first brought you home, he was instantly drawn to you. Liam never enthralled him much. He was cranky with deafening cries, but you would just smile at him."

A smile appeared on her face, and I could tell part ofher was reliving those moments in her mind. She was happy again however brief it may have been. During this whole ordeal I never stopped to really think how she felt or how my father felt or how anyone else felt for that matter.

I was so focused on trying to forget the nightmare I forgot to build again. Maybe that is part of the problem. I was trying to be who I was before this all happened, and that lady doesn't exist anymore. She fell down the rabbit hole and someone else emerged.

"Forgive me, they do not teach parents how to deal with misfortune such as this," she said softly.

I shrugged and gave a little smile.

"That makes two of us," I said.

She smiled in return and for no reason at all we started laughing. It reminded me of when I was a kid, and Iwould just burst out laughing for no reason at all. Liberating, but it has the potential of making one look completely mental. Guess that's one good thing about being a kid, you just don't care what other people think. For a moment, we looked like two crazy kids without a care in the world. This catastrophe has strained our relationship a bit, but from the sight of us right now you wouldn't know it. I wanted to hang onto that moment, but I knew it wasn't meant to last. I wasn't sure how I was going to move forward, but I knew I couldn't stay here.

The telephone rang moments later and broke up our laughter. We both appeared to be frozen in space as the phone continued to ring. To my knowledge this was the first time the phone has rang since I arrived or at the very least since I became lucid. Who could it be? My mum seemed slightly irritated at the call, but even with reasonable effort I could not discern as to the reason.

"Oh, for goodness sake," she blurted out as she jumped up to answer the call.

"Hello?" she answered.

I'm not sure who or what she heard on the other end of the line, but I could see her body relaxing.

"It's for you."

She turned and held the phone out towards me.

"Who is it?" I asked.

She shook her head and shrugged her shoulders. I took hold of the phone and held it to my ear.

"Hello?" I said softly.

I could feel my mum's eyes upon me and then I heard his voice which brought a smile to my face.

"Hey, we don't have much time. Do you think you can get away and meet me at our place in five?"

It was Tyler and from the sound of his voice he was smiling and now I was too.

"Yes, of course. Thank you."

I hung up the phone softly and did what I could to hide my delight.

"Mum, I'm going to take a brief stroll, just to clear my head a bit would that be alright?"

"Alright dear. Don't be gone long."

She gave a quick smile and started pulling things out of the closest and bedside table. A bit preemptive in my opinion, but she is being hopeful, and that kind of spiritshouldn't be spoiled. I quickly fluffed my hair before heading out the door. I didn't want my excitement to be blatantly obvious, but it was hard to contain. I felt like my immaturity was starting to show when I couldn't stand being away from Tyler. The trauma may have been what brought the two of us together, but he was becoming my own personal brand of heroin. With each smile and each touch, I became more and more addicted to him.

I did my best to stay quiet and unseen as I made my way around the nurse's station and down the abandoned hall. My heart was beginning to race as each step brought me closer to him and before I knew it, I was nearly there. The morning light was drifting across the tile floor warming its surface. I was reminded of the first time I stepped down this hall. The sunlight was shining in a slightly different direction, but the warmth of its light could be felt through my slippers. It was one of the first moments where I felt alive again. Granted, I cannot recall physically dying in the last week or so, but emotionally I've never been more certain of anything in my life.

While attempting to keep my pace steady, I did what I could to work on my breathing. If I wasn't careful, I was going to arrive sounding like a panting pooch and that look isn't good on anyone. I could feel a wave of butterflies begin to swarm in my stomach and I was beginning to feel light-headed. I seriously need to get a grip and just focus on what really matters. He makes me happy.

I stopped just shy of the corner and took one final deep breath, anything to make me appear more relaxed than I truly was. Then I exhaled and took the plunge. I leaned around the corner hoping to catch a surprise glimpse of him without his knowledge and I did. He appeared to be pacing and lost deep in thought.

"A penny for your thoughts," I said softly.

"Oh, hey, you weren't supposed to see that," he snickered.

"Debating anything worth sharing?" I smirked.

"Maybe," he smirked back as we walked towards each other. "I know the timing for what I'm about to say couldn't be more inappropriate, but I'm afraid if I don't, I will regret it."

"Alright," I said with a fair amount of skepticism in my voice.

"I like you, probably more than I should, but I do."

He closed the distance between us, and I could feelmy hands start to clam up. My eyes didn't leave his and the lack of blinking was forcing them to start watering.

"Please just say whatever you need to say before..."

I couldn't finish the sentence. The tone of this whole conversation was making me extremely nervous, and I was afraid if he didn't spill it soon, either my heart was going to explode, or I was going to melt into a puddle on thefloor. My body must have been tensing up because I noticed his posture changed.

"I'm sorry, I'm all inside my head and this isn't how I wanted this to happen," he muttered.

I breathed a sigh of relief and smiled. I realized I wasn't the only one who was awkward in situations like this and that made me relax.

"Ty, I like you too."

He took me in his arms and kissed me softly in the warmth of the morning light. At first, I could feel myself tense up bracing for something that I was confident would appear, but when nothing terrible happened my body relaxed and turned into that of a rag doll, mellow and malleable. I placed my hands upon his waist and pulled him closer to me. His lips were soft and pressed gently against mine. It wasn't perfect but was what I needed. He knew what he was doing and broke the kiss off when we both still wanted more. I couldn't pull myself away, but I noticed he wasn't trying to move away from me either.

I felt his eyes upon mine, waiting for me to open my eyes or say something. When I finally found the courage to open my eyes, I found myself staring at his chest afraid to look in his eyes. It wasn't my first kiss by any means, but this was the first time I felt apprehension over what it could have possibly meant. What were his intentions? What were mine? Why was I so comfortable with him touching me, kissing me, but jittery when almost anyone else does? Was this a farewell kiss or one inviting me to see him again?

"Please forgive me, I just need a moment," I whispered.

"Are you alright?" he whispered back.

"Yes, of course. I just need to catch my breath."

He snickered just a little and it made me look up at him. Laughter is contagious and before I knew it, we were both giggling like children in a school yard.

"Any chance you give me, I will do what I can to take your breath away." He smiled and it was mirrored on my face.

"Please don't let today be the last time I see your face...or the last time we kiss," I said softly trying to hide my hunger for more of his sweet kisses.

I could feel myself blush and I had to turn away for fear of embarrassment. When I did, he leaned in and kissed my ruby red cheeks causing the redness to spread like wildfire. His kisses were tender and sweet, not anxious, or desperate, and he behaved like someone out of an old movie. He wanted to be there for me, but not so much that

I would be frightened or shy away. I gathered my courage and turned to face him. His eyes were beautiful in the morning light reminded me of water found at Slieve League Cliffs of Donegal back home. They were nearly the opposite of mine not only in color, but brightness. The way he gazed upon me was pure and foreign to me. Other than family I can't say that I experienced a man looking upon me the way Tyler did and without another thought on the matter I raised myself upon the tips of my toes and kissed him. He embraced the kiss and encompassed my body in his arms. It only lasted a few moments and if these were the last moments I had with him, then I would have been given the perfect ending, or perhaps the perfect beginning.

"If you ever need me," he took my hand and put a piece of paper in it, "you will find me there."

"What happens if you need me?" I inquired with hope in my heart.

"I will find you. I will always find you," he smiled.

To my surprise, my name was called over the loudspeaker and I knew our time was up. I could feel disappointment set in, but I had to do what I could to keep my spirits up. We would find each other. Five simple words that at one time would have meant very little but have now become my source of hope and happiness.

"Time's up Isolde. Remember what I said," he said reassuringly.

I nodded and let him kiss my cheek once more. As I started to walk away, I paused momentarily to take in everything once more as I was overflowing with emotion. I didn't turn around, but I knew he was watching me. I attempted to gather my thoughts and while I was trying to do so, I could feel the tips of his fingers gliding over mine. I was tempted to turn and stay with him, but I knew if I did, it would only make leaving that much more difficult. It was the reassurance I needed and his way of letting me know that he was there even though I had to move forward for a while without him. I wiggled my fingers against his as my way of acknowledging his gesture and then I stepped off towards the unknown.

13

I arrived back at my room to be greeted by several familiar faces and one unfamiliar face.

"Welcome back Ms. Walsh. I'm here to take out your IVs and take your vitals one last time," the nurse said.

"Fantastic, please do," I said followed by a sigh of relief.

I followed her lead and laid down on the bed where she proceeded to remove both of my IVs and run the usual vitals. Everything seemed to be in order and, as I panned around the room, I could see that my belongings were carefully packed up and waiting for my departure. Whether I was ready or not they had determined it was time. I heard the staff going over everything with me and my mum once more before they brought in a wheelchair encouraging me to take a ride.

"I'd rather walk myself out if you don't mind," I stated.

"Ms. Walsh, this is hospital policy. Please take a seat," the nurse responded with a disapproving tone.

I raised one of my eyebrows and glared at her as a way of responding to her disapproval with my own.

"Alright then, I will need to walk with you," she added.

I nodded and grabbed my coat before making my way towards the door. I'm not sure who she thought she was but telling me what to do right now was not going to go over well. There was some chatter as we made our way down the long corridors to the main entrance. More than likely from a few meddling nosy nellies, but nothing more than I expected. All the whispering was making me feel a bit more self-conscious than usual, however. This is one of the prices you pay for living in a small town. There will always be whispers and a person's secrets are never really secret for long. A scandal like this one may take months or even years to blow over.

We stepped through the sliding glass doors where Rhys was waiting with the car. Unfortunately, nothing could have prepared me for the reporters that surrounded us shortly after we cleared the threshold. I didn't realize how uncomfortable the attention made me until I noticed everyone starting at me and jutting out questions. I felt like I was being verbally assaulted, and I became increasingly nerve racked. The thought of what everyone must be thinking about me was starting to make me panic. Don't say a word, just keep moving.

Despite my best efforts they continued to nudge themselves in front of me and it was really starting to make my blood boil. They pushed and pulled each other as if they were fighting their way to the front row of a Beatles concert. Ambitious, but in the end still pathetic. The sound of the crowd and their continual questions began to sound like that annoying hum that comes from your refrigerator when it kicks on. I could hear it, but it didn't sound like anything distinct anymore. Maybe my mind was going numb to protect what was left of my sanity.

Only a few steps more and I was in the car with the door closed quickly behind me. Lunging into the car must have caused me to twist a bit more than I was prepared for and I was reminded that while I appear to be in good health my ribs weren't exactly healed. Thank goodness for decent pain killers or I'm sure I'd be in more pain than I could stand. I could feel the pressure once again with every breath and I was already beginning to count down the hours until I could have my next dose.

The reporters were persistent and continued to shout questions at us and tap on the windows. Rhys did his best not to hurt anyone while trying to get in the car or as we drove off. I think my head was starting to hurt more than my side and I held my head in my hands. It felt good to shield my eyes from the light. It was unusual how unaccustomed someone can become to the light after only a matter of days with very little. The darkness of the den began to appeal to me and was looking forward to relaxing there hidden from the world. Thankfully, we only lived a short drive from the hospital, so I wouldn't have to endure for long.

We arrived at the house where I was greeted by Liam and our father. It feels like it's been ages since I saw them. Liam must have been ill since he actually hugged me. The last time we hugged was over a year ago and I remember it perfectly. It was the last time we confided in each other about anything, and we sealed the moment with a hg We ventured to America the next day and have rarely spoken since then let alone hugged each other. He seemed a bit uncomfortable at the idea but offered it to me freely. My father seemed equally uncomfortable, but clearly relieved to see me home.

"I've missed you," he said with a smile, but tears in his eyes.

"I've missed you too," I gave a brief smile and hugged him as tight as my strength would allow.

We headed inside and my mum, true to form, started her usual pampering routine. She had Rhys escort me into the den where they clearly planned on me staying for a bit. There was a large stack of books on top of my favorite blanket, and I could hardly wait to settle in. Unfortunately, our house was starting to feel like the hospital with everyone constantly checking up on me. I knew there would be an adjustment period, but my goodness, I've walked thirty feet and been asked if I'm alright at least ten times. I did my best to cooperate, but I was starting to become annoyed.

Rhys wasn't very talkative which was out of character for him, but I could hear my folks whispering in the kitchen as Mum began prepping lunch and some sweet treats from the sound of things. Soon would come the tea and biscuits to tide me over until I was either ready for some more rest or a light lunch, neither of which was particularly appealing to me at this point, but now that everything is out in the open, there would be no refusing her attention. I mean, I was relieved to be home, but I'm more the suffer in silence type. Based on everything that happened over the last couple of weeks, suffering in silence didn't really help much, but I've never been one to hurt someone else even if it would have helped me.

Mum came in the room with some tea as expected and sat down on the edge of the couch cushions next to me. She sat there for a moment staring at me as if she were trying to find words befitting of the moment, but they were never found. An uncomfortable smile graced her face before nodding and heading back towards the kitchen. Rhys tried to pretend he wasn't witnessing the whole awkward moment, but very few things evade him. He had picked up a book and was attempting to read, but with his eyes darting between me and the book I'm not sure how he'd have even finished a page.

"You can stop pretending to read now," I said while raising one eyebrow.

"I'm doing my best," he snickered.

"I just want to be normal again and maybe even a little boring," I scoffed.

"You could never be boring. It's not in your nature," he smiled. "Besides, you deserve a lot of credit for what you were trying to do."

"Trying was the key word and everyone still got hurt," I mumbled.

"You were trying to do what you thought was right. Just because it didn't pan out the way you hoped doesn't mean your heart wasn't in the right place."

"I just can't handle the way everyone looks at me now."

"There is a lot of emotion surrounding you right now and people don't know how to react," he lowered his book. "Izz, it will take time."

I nodded and sipped my tea. I was hoping by the time I arrived home my life would have started to make sense again, but I was still plagued by questions. There will be time I'm sure when the vast majority of questions would cease to flood my mind, but I have to wonder when would that be? I've never been one for instant gratification. Well, unless chocolate is involved, but in this case, I feel an exception should be made. While I continuedto sip my tea and nibble at the biscuits that were just brought in, I could feel the tension in the room mounting.

It was becoming so thick you would need a knife just to cut through it.

"I think I'm going to head up to my room," I said.

"Don't even think about it Izz." Rhys added still pretending to read.

"Well then, can everyone stop acting like I'm on suicide watch. They wouldn't have discharged me if I wasn't alright," I blurted out annoyed at the whole situation then I noticed my father stepped into the den and was only a few feet away from us.

"You're not alright and may never be again, but until you're over the worst of it, we are going to keep a watch on you," he said sternly.

Unfortunately, I didn't realize that somewhere along the line I started rolling my eyes out loud and when I did, he went from looking concerned to extremely irritated. If he'd have been a Saturn V rocket, this would have been the moment when the engines would have been ignited and he was getting ready for take-off.

"I understand," I said softly hoping to dodge a bullet.

He left the room and headed back towards the kitchen to continue the discussion that he and Mum must have started earlier. Upon his return the whispering commenced once more. I never understood why folks whisper. If you need to have a private conversation, go to your bedroom or discuss the matter at a later date. Rhys was sitting quietly, but no longer pretending to read. He was casually looking around the room almost like a patient would when waiting for a doctor to arrive. He looked bored, but clearly it was his turn for guard duty. I wanted to say something to him, but I didn't want to upset the balance either. I turned slightly towards him and with the book lowered I could see what was left of his encounter with Derek in the hall that day. His face has had better days that's for sure, but there was something about seeing it that made me proud. I really do have an amazing older brother.

"Hasn't anyone ever told you it's rude to stare?" he glanced at me and gave a quick smirk.

"Apologies," I smirked back at him. "Do you maybe want to do something together?"

"Feel an escape coming on?" he grinned.

"You've read my mind. What did you have in mind?" I perked up at the thought.

"Here, take my hand. I'll help you up."

He extended his hand, and I accepted it with a smile.It took me a moment to stand up and get moving, but once Iwas up, he tugged me into the living room where we both flopped down on the sofa after he put a movie in. We spentthe whole time giggling over the witty repartee and the zany wardrobe the actors were wearing. While our folks and Liam had come and gone, it was nice for it to really be just us two. It was so much fun and just what I needed to lighten the mood. To those that don't have an older brother it's hard to explain the relationship. Older brothers are like a combination of a father, a best friend, and a boyfriend. They say you look nice even when you don't, defend you when you're being bullied at school, and help take care of you when you are sick. I couldn't imagine life without one.

We remained there all afternoon and into the early evening. We watched movies, read books, and giggled over silly jokes we found in a few random magazines located at the bottom of one of the end tables. I couldn't remember the last time I had this much fun. I missed the days when we could just hangout like this, but then I remembered that as we continue to get older, the time spent together become shorter and further apart, and we have to work twice as hard to hold onto each other. Then the thought crossed my mind, why am I seeing so much of Rhys? I feel like nearly every time I opened my eyes at the hospital he was there and now he is here.

"Rhys, not to annihilate the mood here, but—"

"Why have I been around so much lately?" he interjected.

"Yes actually. I can't remember the last time I saw you so much. Not that I'm complaining," I smirked.

"I felt like I was needed more here," he smiled briefly, "but don't get used to it."

"I'll do my best not to," I giggled. "Thanks for being there for me. I'm sure it hasn't been easy."

"You're welcome. Just doing what any big brother would do," he smiled.

"Well, not all big brothers, Liam would never—"

"Now, now, you should give him more credit. He is taking this really hard especially since he feels partially responsible," he interjected once more.

"What are you talking about?" I blurted out.

"Feel like taking a walk?" he raised an eyebrow.

I nodded and leaned down to don my sneakers before taking his hand to stand once more. I'm not sure how Liam could possibly feel any responsibility for what happened to me, but for reasons unknown to me, Rhys insisted that this couldn't be discussed in the confines of our home. The whole idea just railroaded me and was beginning to make my head swirl once more with questions. We grabbed our jackets and headed out the back door. We made it several feet from the house before he finally spoke.

"Do you remember the last time you spoke with Liam?" he whispered.

"Yes, of course," I whispered back, "he mentioned he heard a rumor."

"That you were with Derek, yes, but that's not all he heard."

"I'm not sure what you mean."

"Apparently, in the locker room one afternoon Derek was discussing you in explicit detail. From your body to how you responded to his touch while being intimate," he looked away from me as we kept walking. "Liam knew that what he was saying could have only been known if he had carnal knowledge."

That was the nicest way he could have worded that for my benefit. I'm sure the conversation wasn't as polite or flattering to me. I bit my lip and realized that while I was extremely uncomfortable, I could only imagine how much harder this was for him.

"And he believed him?" I added.

"What choice did he really have? It's an unfortunate fact that men tend to flaunt their conquests and with such irrefutable evidence he had no choice but to believe it. He confronted him about it in the locker room and it didn't end well, but I think it would have gone even worse if he knew what he knows now."

"Why not tell me about this back at our home?" I asked confused

"Our folks don't know about all of this, and Liam hate it if you knew he was a nice guy deep down inside," he said.

"Heaven forbid that would happen," I said with a fair amount of sarcasm.

"It's one thing when a man gives himself away so freely, but when a woman does, it's quite another. I know, sounds like a cliché, but it's true," he shook his head in disappointment. "I've never understood that double standard or why people have devalued themselves in such a way."

"Rhys, that's because you're classy and a good guy."

He smiled taking my hand in his and giving it a squeeze.

"So, what happened between the two of them?" I asked.

"When he confronted Derek, it was in front of several other classmates and unfortunately, only validated his story. Liam's fury got the best of him, and they got into a scuffle. Nothing terribly damaging and apparently didn'tlast long, but it was enough to get some unwanted attention."

"Why not just tell this to the folks?"

"It proves he knew something was going on *before* the incident in the forest happened and your reaction to his response that day in the house was not that of a terrified woman, but defensive...like you were hiding something," he stopped and looked towards me. "Why didn't you just tell someone, anyone?"

He looked terribly saddened just thinking about everything and his eyes were pleading with me for an answer. I met his gaze for a few moments and then my eyes fell towards the ground as I continued to step forward.

"Rhys, nothing I say will make this any easier. We have struggled to fit in here and while we are a good family, we will always be treated like we are not from here. I made the decision to protect our family from the shame this would cause," I squeezed his hand a bit tighter. "Little did I know I was only prolonging the inevitable."

"You let your pride get in the way, Izz," he scoffed. "I know why you hid this from the world, but you shouldn't have hidden it from us," he sighed. "When the time comes that you are ready to give yourself to a man he won'tbe thinking about this terrible tragedy, he will be thinking about you."

I nodded, "I know that now."

He nodded in return as his way of accepting my apology without one truly being given. I know I hurt him, and he knew I regretted what I did. No number of apologies from either party would have changed the outcome, so we considered the matter closed.

"So, how are you holding up?" he inquired in a quiet voice.

"I'm terrified. I've found very little peace in the last two weeks and, while there have been moments, those seem to be short lived. At least I know I have you."

"Always," he gave my hand a little squeeze, "and that will never change."

We continued on for a few more blocks before we reached the edge of the forest that I used to call my sanctuary. I don't believe it was his intention for us to wander this far, but we did. I felt like I had seen a ghost or something and couldn't catch my breath.

"Do you want to turn back?" he asked.

I stood frozen like a statue placed on the concrete walkway. My eyes were open, but I cannot recall blinking. There was something in the forest looking at me, or possibly someone. This was an ambush and we needed to go. It's not safe here. I tore my hand away from Rhys's and began to run as fast as I could away from the forest. It only took a moment for him to bounce back from the shock and then he was nipping at my heels. I felt my shoulders being pulled backwards and my feet were entering my field of vision. I was falling backwards towards the ground in slow motion. Part of me continued to resist his grasp, but as our bodies slammed down against the pavement, I could feel the wind get knocked out of me.

"Izz! Izz! Stop! You're safe!" Rhys shouted.

"He's in there! I know he is!" I began to sob uncontrollably. "We need to get out of here!"

I continued to try and pull away, but with each tug I could feel Rhys's grip tighten almost to the point of cutting off circulation.

"Izz! No one can get to you as long as I'm here!"

He began to shake me hoping it would jolt me back to his reality. Unfortunately, for him he may not have believed someone was there, but I could feel it in my gut that we were being watched. I was beginning to feel light-headed and my vision turned blurry. My heart was beating at such a rapid rate any moment it was going to explode, and my lifeless body would collapse onto the pavement. In addition, in my panicked state, my hearing was beginning to fail. I could hear Rhys's voice, he seemed very far away. My body was growing weak, tired from the struggle and I collapsed.

As my eyes began to flutter open again, I could see the dark night sky overhead and it appeared to be moving. Then I realized it wasn't moving, I was, but I wasn't walking. I tilted my head into more of an upright position and then I realized Rhys was carrying me. He was the one that was walking. I'm not sure for how long I was unconscious, but by the looks of our surroundings we were nearly home.

"I can walk you know," I piped up.

"I know, but right now you need to just let me take you home."

He kept walking and didn't look at me when he spoke. His pace was steady but quick. I could tell he was worried.

"Just try to relax, I got this," he said.

He glanced down in my direction and winked at me before shifting his gaze towards our home. He pressed onward without another word out of me and then we were home again. As he lowered my legs towards the ground, I had a thought.

"Please don't tell anyone about this. I already feel like I'm on suicide watch and this would only make it worse," I said quietly.

"Izz, it's alright to admit you're having a tough time," he gave me a hug while we stood in the darkness of the back porch. "We are all here for you, but what I saw back there looked all too familiar, and well...I'm worried about you."

"I'm worried about me too," I whispered.

He broke off the hug and proceeded to open the back door as we headed in single file. I could hear the sound of our mum's voice shout in delight at our return. Apparently, Rhys wasn't the only one who was worried, and our prolonged absence gave our mum's concern a foothold. She ran over and hugged us both before prompting me to sit down. I shook my head refusing her request.

"I need to lie down," I insisted.

She did not look pleased, but my head was throbbing to the point that standing on my own was becoming difficult. She didn't say anything in response to my statement, and after a few moments I headed into the den and collapsed once more on the sofa. I wasn't fully alert, but I clearly had not fallen into a deep sleep when I heard them arguing in the kitchen.

"Where have you been? I've been worried sick." Mum insisted.

"We went for a walk and stopped short of the forest" Rhys spoke calmly. "Something happened."

"Wait, why would you take her there?! You know she is not ready to fully grasp all of this just yet!" Mum shouted.

"We are worried about her emotional stability. Something could have happened," our father added sounding much calmer and more collected than our mum.

"Something did happen," Rhys stated. "She panicked and then collapsed in my arms. I carried her home as quickly as I could."

I could hear footsteps of someone walking, heavy on the floor. I couldn't tell the direction they were headed, but before they reached their destination, I fell asleep once more.

14

The next time my eyes, opened I found night was still upon us and the house was blanketed in darkness. I was unsure of the time, but I was awake. Not well rested by any means, but awake. I felt this urge to suddenly peel myself off the sofa, like I was being pulled towards something, but what? I slowly made my way through the first floor of the house going from room to room not finding anything unusual. Against my better judgment and restricted breathing, I began my ascent up the staircase stopping every few steps to catch my breath. It took some effort, but I was able to make it to the top with no other assistance than from the banister. My bedroom was within my sight, and I did my best to scurry there without making asound.

I rounded the frame of the door and quietly closed the door behind me. I started looking for anything out of the ordinary, but nothing obvious appeared. I flicked on the bedside lamp before grasping my side and sitting down on my bed, bewildered at the sensation I felt when I woke. Was my mind playing tricks on me or were my animal instincts taking over? I continued to scan the room for anything different, keeping in mind that in the last week my mum was surely in here to keep up appearances. Then I saw, sitting next to my armchair, my book bag. There wasn't much to see, but I couldn't mistake its color for anything else. It was a crimson red bag that was given to me as a gift my first year of high school. At first, I wasn't fond of the color, but over the years it has grown to be one of my favorite possessions.

I sat there for a moment and pondered how it came to be here. I dropped it a week or so ago in the forest and it was taken from me. By whom I still do not know, but I desperately needed to know. I stood quicker than expected and I could feel myself sway from the rush. Once I regained my balance, I tip toed toward the bag. Something about it made me uneasy as if I were reaching towards a bomb about to detonate. The bag was within my grasp, and I took one last step before grabbing it and pulling it towards me. I lowered myself to the floor and pulled the bag onto my lap. It did not appear to be changed in any way causing my shoulders to relax slightly. With the outside unchanged I pressed onward and opened the bag.

I pulled a few folders out along with some books. As I continued to crawl towards the bottom of the bag a few folded pieces of paper fell out. Since I'm generally a tidy individual jamming paperwork into my bag casually doesn't suit me, so I decided to earmark this for further investigation as I kept searching. There was something soft like cotton located there, but I was certain whatever it could have been it wasn't mine. To carry extra clothing implies I was planning on changing at some point during the day and I cannot recall having a need to do something like that since I was a small child. The object laid there in the bottom of my bag taunting me. I couldn't take it anymore. I grabbed the soft bundle, removed it from the bag and began to unfold it. It appeared to be a shirt of some kind, but it didn't appear to be one of mine. It was fragrant like that of a spring meadow and instantly made me long for warmer days. However, despite its allure I didn't recognize it.

I quickly tossed it towards the ground as if I had just been handed a hot coal and pushed myself across the floor towards my bed. The smell had engulfed my senses and I could feel it quickly settling in my lungs. How did this come to be? Why would someone take my bag and then return it with something of theirs in it? Why take the bag at all? Better still if someone took it how did they return it and when? My mind was swimming once more in questions and then one question stood out in my mind. If this shirt was left for me to find, then what else was I supposed to find?

I scooted myself back towards the bag and upended it. A few other random items fell out, but other than the shirt and folded papers nothing else was out of sorts. I decided against my better judgment that I couldn't wait to unveil the contents inside and I began to unfold the last one that fell out of the bag. I quickly skimmed the first note and realized that I didn't recognize the handwriting, so I drew my attention towards the signature at the bottom. This note was from Derek? Why would I have a note from Derek? This must have been meant for someone else. In a frenzy I grabbed the others and began opening them as fast as I could. They all were from him. I opened the first one again and then the next and then the next. I read them line by line in no discernible order.

Isolde, I can't stop thinking about you. I think about you all day and every night. Please call me.
-Derek

Baby, I don't want to hide anymore. I'm yours.
-D

Beautiful, why do you tease me so? This morning in the hall took all my restraint not to maul you. I want you.
-Derek

Izzy, you were amazing on Friday. Just thinking about it makes me hot. Meet me in the woods tomorrow?
-D

Baby, please stop being mad at me. I can't take youavoiding me. I'm so sorry about the other night. Please meet me at our place?
-D

I read the notes repeatedly to the point I was nearly ill. I didn't understand. I don't recall ever seeing these notes before, but if I didn't receive them how did they come to be in my bag? I could feel myself spiraling, but I had no idea where to go or what to do. I dropped the notes I was holding and got to my feet. Home is supposed to be safe,but when your home is filled with emotional landmines it becomes your own personal war zone. I had just stepped back into the line of fire.

I reached to turn off the light and then headed toward the door. The house and hall were still quiet. The words Derek wrote had leapt onto my skin and refused to let go. I didn't want to be alone for fear of Derek finding me. I wasn't sure how he could, but something told me he would. So, I went to the only person who could understand, Rhys. I crept down the hall, doing my best not to make a sound, until I reached his door. I lightly tapped on the door and when he didn't make a sound, I turned the knob and stepped inside.

"Rhys?" I whispered.

When there was no answer, I walked over to his bedside and laid my hand upon his exposed shoulder. His body gave a sudden jerk and he quickly sat up.

"Izz, are you alright? What are you doing up here?" he muttered in surprise.

"I just don't want to be alone. May I stay with you tonight?" I replied.

"Yea, of course. Come here."

He sat up and held out his arms for me. I fell into them and leaned my back against part of his chest. He wrapped his one arm across my chest holding me in place and gave me a gentle squeeze.

"Anything you want to talk about?" he whispered.

I shook my head in response and I could feel him nod in return. I closed my eyes and did what I could to focus on one thing at a time starting with my breathing. He pulled the covers up over me and just sat there with me as the worrying subsided and my breathing returned to normal. He didn't say anything else, nor did he move. He just kept me safe as the monsters of my mind were settling in. I fell asleep there leaning against him like we did as children.

The hours flew by like minutes this time and then I was awake once more. Rhys was sitting quietlyby the window just staring out, surveying the land so to speak. Without Tyler, I didn't realize how much I was leaning on him and how difficult this must be for him. I continued to watch him without making a sound. He slowly sipped warm coffee from a cup while his unwavering gaze remained fixed on something outside.

"How long have you been awake?" I said softly.

"Awhile," his focus remained unchanged. "Had a bit of trouble sleeping."

"Sorry about waking you last night."

"Izz, I cannot protect you from your mind, but I can help you with anything out here," he waved his hand in a panning motion as if to emphasize his point of the physical world.

"I'm having some trouble separating the two and I'm starting to lose track of what is real." I could feel the tears welling up and before the day had even begun and I already felt defeated.

"I noticed you were trying to refresh your memory last night," he picked up a few papers that were sitting on the floor to his left. "Are you sure that's such a wise idea?" his tone changed and now he was being quite serious.

"How did my book bag get in my room?" I sat up and spoke with a tone to match his own.

"He brought it by a couple of days after you were admitted into the hospital. He claimed you forgot it in the forest earlier that week and he knew it meant something to you."

I wasn't sure what to say. I'm not sure what bothered me more, the fact that Derek had been to our house or the fact that Rhys knew about the notes.

"Please don't misunderstand. I wasn't going through your things. I noticed them on the floor of your room, and I didn't know what they were until I read them,"he looked at me disapprovingly.

"It's not what you think. Don't you see what he's trying to do?" I spoke up. "He planted those to make his side of the story seem like the truth."

I climbed out of bed and headed over towards him where I knelt beside him. When he wouldn'tlook at me, I grabbed his chin and pulled his face in my direction.

"Rhys, you know me. I wouldn't compromise everything I believe in over a pretty face. Please help me."

He paused for a moment before jerking my hand off of his chin.

"What do you expect me to do that the police aren't already doing?" he said with a scowl.

"Help me prove he's not who he seems."

"So, you want me to help you declare war on Derek Strom?"

I nodded.

"Alright, I'll do what I can to help you, but you have to stop keeping secrets from me."

I nodded again and the deal was struck. I struggled to power through the sleepiness my legs were feeling from kneeling for so long and stood up. Slowly I dragged my legs until the pins and needles had subsided and headed back towards the door.

"Thank you, Rhys."

"For what?" he replied.

"For always being on my side."

I rounded the door frame and headed to my room to collect a few items before heading to the bath. Felt like days since I had bathed, but in truth it was probably more like hours. The days and hours were blurred, and I needed to do what I could to create a fresh start. I reached the bath and locked the door behind me. Before I finished undressing, I closed my eyes and stepped in front of the mirror. I tried to remember my before but struggled to find the image in my mind. I let the moment pass and opened my eyes once more. While I failed to remember the lady that I once saw in the mirror I now saw a woman standing before me. Wounded and scarred, but alive. My body was nearly healed, but I was unsure how to mend a broken mind.

I stepped into the shower and did what I could to let the worries of last night wash off in order to fully be present today. Soon I would be expected to return to classes and that would be a struggle all its own. The pressures I'm going to face will be the equivalent of being lodged in a vice grip that is slowly tightening for extended periods of time. We need to get to the bottom of this and prevent my already fragile walls from collapsing down upon me.

15

I finished in the shower faster than expected and hurried back to my room. I did what I could to get dressed quickly and decided to head downstairs for some breakfast, anything to try and get myself back into the routine of things. Rounding the banister at the bottom of the steps I heard a knock at the door. I nearly leapt out of my skin by the sheer shock of it and for a moment I was frozen in place. Unsure whether to answer the door, Liam sprung up from the sofa and opened the door. I was surprised to even see him awake at this hour, but I was glad that he was there at this very moment. As the door opened, I saw a man holding a large box with a ribbon on it. The two exchanged greetings and small talk while Liam signed for the package. Soon they said their goodbyes and the door was closed once more. I turned and began walking towards the kitchen when I felt a hand touch my arm.

"It's for you," Liam said.

"Are you sure?" I was stunned.

He nodded.

I reached out to grab the box and walked slowly into the kitchen. This was no ordinary box. It was large and black with matte finish wrapped in a dark red silk ribbon. I arrived at the kitchen's island where I slid the box down onto the surface. There was no card to be found on the exterior of the box and I was at a loss at who would be sending me such a flamboyant gift. I placed my hands on the face of the box, slowly untied the ribbon, and let it fall back towards the counter. I caught a glimpse of Liam slightly off to my left. He must have followed me in, and I didn't realize it due to my focus on the box.

"You know it's just a box. It won't bite," he said sarcastically.

I frowned, "Thanks for the revelation."

I lifted the cover of the box and flipped it over on the counter. The inside was filled with tissue paper covering something that appeared to be the identical shade of the ribbon that previously encompassed the box. There was a letter folded and laid upon the tissue paper. I picked it up and began to unfold it. It wasn't a bill, thankfully, but it was a note for me. The handwriting appeared to be familiar, but rather than stand there debating who this gift might have been from I decided to read on.

My dearest Isolde, please honor me by joining me for the homecoming dance next Saturday. My heart is broken without you.

Forever yours, Derek

I gasped and dropped the letter. Liam took no time picking up the letter and helping himself to reading its content. It wasn't long before we both grabbed at the tissue paper to see what remained in the box. It was lovely and a deep crimson red. I grabbed what I could and lifted it up and out of the box. It was a full length, off the shoulder, long sleeve, floral lace evening gown. It was breath-taking.

Part of me was touched by the gesture and the other part repulsed by it. Why would he send this to me? Why pursue me after I've accused him of such vile acts? Not sure how long we were standing there, but my silence prompted further assistance. Liam called for back-up.

"Hey Ma, can you come here for a minute?! I think Izz is having a stroke or something!" he bellowed.

I'm not sure what she was in the middle of, but I heard a loud thud followed by fast moving footsteps. I felt I blinked, and she was there.

"Isolde, are you alright? You look like you've seen a ghost," she said startled by the sight of me.

Liam didn't say a word, just stared at the gown I was holding. In turn, she began staring at that gown. All of us locked in place at the sight of this beautiful gown. My mind couldn't fathom its cost, nor did I want to dwell on that. I was so intently focused on that thought I nearly missed seeing Liam hand our mum the letter out of my peripheral vision. She quickly skimmed the note and after a quick re-read she raised her head, but not in shock like we did. More like she was trying to put things together in her mind. Probably the equivalent of what Liam would look like if forced to solve a chemistry equation on the spot.

I dropped the gown on the counter suddenly. "Send it back. I can't stand to look at it anymore."

"Are you sure my dear?" Our mum said softly.

I nodded. "I want to speak with Officer Chaney. He can't keep doing this to me."

Mum nodded and walked towards the phone where she began to dial. Liam didn't say anything only placed a hand on my shoulder briefly and nodded as if in confirmation. I think he too was getting tired of all the drama that has infected our home. I felt like this was all some deliberate and cruel joke played upon me in hopes of ruining my family's good name. I couldn't let that happen. I waited for Mum to hang up the phone before I spoke again.

"Is there anything he can do?" I inquired.

"He will be over shortly. We can all discuss it then," she replied.

I retreated to the den where I sat and waited for the infamous Officer Chaney to arrive. I was growing impatientas the minutes passed, but just as I was feeling the wait time was going to be too much there was a knock at the door. My mum answered the door and showed him into theden. I did my best to stand and greet him as he was introduced to me once more.

"Thank you for coming, Officer Chaney. Please have a seat."

My mum smiled and gestured towards one of the armchairs near the sofa where I was sitting. He accepted and sat down with his hands folded in his lap. As Mum gave him a brief synopsis of the reason for his presence he inquired about the gift and the note that was found within. She ventured into the kitchen and retrieved the items requested and he glanced them over.

"Mrs. Walsh, as you remember from our previous conversations, I cannot arrest Mr. Strom at this time." She nodded in understanding. "Is there anything we can do? I mean, to help ensure he keeps his distance."

"I will make your concerns noted, but I feel that attempting any further action at this time would be ill advised," he turned and looked in my direction. "Isolde let me be clear. We have your statement and I have statements from your classmates, family, numerous onlookers, and Mr. Strom. We have nothing that corroborates your account of what happened."

"Wait, what about what Rhys said or the blood in the locker room?!" I blurted out.

"Yes, I'm aware of what you are referring to. Please understand, both of your stories place you at the same places at the same times. When you were brought to the hospital while you were injured and significantly malnourished you did not present with defensive wounds which suggests either you knew your attacker, or you weren't really attacked."

"But the physician said he believed there was enough to suggest I was sexually assaulted. Was he mistaken?" I became very defensive.

"Ms. Walsh, that conversation occurred before Mr. Strom's statement was taken. Yes, he was questioned when you were brought in, but not to the full extent until days later."

I could feel my face fall deep into concentration mode trying to think of a way out of this.

"So, you're saying he is just going to get away with it?"

"Ms. Walsh, his testimony is nearly identical to yours with the one exception being the accusations of sexual assault."

"So, essentially, it is my word against his?"

"That's correct."

"I still don't understand how he can just get away with it," I stood up frustrated and began pacing.

"We have eyewitnesses siting the two of you together in the hall and at the football game. He admits to cutting class to secretly meet you in the woods as the two of you had planned."

"But that's not true!" I interjected.

"Then why keep the notes?" he fired back, and Icould tell he was growing impatient with me.

"I can't explain how they came to be in my book bag, but I can assure you this is not what you think."

He turned towards my mum, "Mrs. Walsh, unfortunately there isn't evidence to support your daughter's claim."

"Are you able to provide some sort of protection for her?" she said softly.

"At this time, no. He is not harming her nor threatening to do so. Most girls would be flattered to receive such a gift."

"Officer Chaney, can I ask you something?" I spoke up drawing his attention back to me.

"Of course," his eyes became fixed on me.

"If I'm making this up then what is his excuse for keeping everything a secret?"

My tone had gone from the usual polite and courteous to just straight up rude and the change had sparked a look of anger from my mum.

"You're a practicing Catholic, are you not?"

"Yes I am."

"According to Mr. Strom, he was protecting *you* and *your* reputation. Your relationship with God may have just taken a hit, but he didn't want everyone else to know how intimate the two of you had gotten."

"Then why discuss it in the boy's locker room?"

"He was protecting *his* reputation."

"How so? He can't protect himself and protect me since we believe in different things."

"If he didn't talk about it everyone would know something really was going on, so he gave them what he could. Unfortunately, Liam heard more than Mr. Strom originally intended ending in an altercation."

I nodded and finally got it. This was a situation I now know I wasn't going to win. While I could sway Rhys to provide a helping hand the look on our mum's face said she no longer believed me and that truly hurt. I felt a few silent tears stream down my face, and he turned back towards my mum.

"Mrs. Walsh, I appreciate you giving me a call. Please let me know if you have any further questions, but as you can see there isn't much I can do at this point."

"Wait, Officer Chaney...there's been something I've been meaning to ask. Something that has confused me since I awoke in the hospital."

"Alright, how can I help?" he asked with a sound of exhaustion in his voice.

"I was told in the hospital that I was found in the forest by a classmate which now I know they referring to was Derek. How could he claim to find me like this if he was already with me?"

"Well, he may have been with you that afternoon, but he returned to class shortly after lunch and was accounted for by classmates and faculty until the final bell.

He even attended practice, and this was confirmed by his coach," he took a deep breath before continuing. "If someone was with you during that time it wasn't Derek."

"So, you're saying there was someone else that attacked me?" I could hear the skepticism in my voice.

"I'm saying there is a possibility, but since we onlyhave your memory to go on, we can't assume that is the case."

"I apologize, I still don't understand. Why did he return to the forest that late afternoon then?" I said perplexed.

"In your statement you mentioned being laid down on a blanket just shortly before the two of you were intimate," he waited for a sign of recollection from me which I gave before proceeding. "He ventured back to the site to retrieve it and that's when he found you."

"In what state did he find me exactly?"

"They didn't tell you when you woke up in the hospital?"

I shook my head.

"It was chilly out that day and while the dirt and scrapes we were able to explain, we couldn't explain some of the additional bruising found or the damages to your face. Derek couldn't recall seeing them on you either."

"Say again, what damages to my face?" I insisted.

"Your lower lip and one eyebrow were both split and you had a bloody nose. Do you recall how you might have gotten those?"

I reached up and quickly started scanning my face with my fingertips over every freckle and pore trying to find what he was referring to. When I couldn't feel what he had referred to I wasted no time rushing out of the room towards the mudroom near the back door to our home. I knew there would be a mirror there. I didn't even bother flicking on a light just ran straight over to the mirror next to the closet. The sunlight shining through the windowpane was just enough for me to see some redness around my lip and left eyebrow. I felt like my mind was spiraling down the drain as the questions began flooding my mind. Where did these come from? How could I have missed these? Why don't I remember any of this?

It was starting to make sense why no one was believing me. After the conversation with Rhys this morning, I knew doubt was beginning to consume everyone with an outcome that was becoming more and more grim every day. I turned and left the room in what could only have been the equivalent stroll of the walking dead. My feet were sliding across the floor with my lifeless arms and face to match completing my freakish walk. I was at a complete loss for words and my situation went from complicated to dire in a matter of minutes. If knowledge is power, then I needed to find a way to make my new-found power work for me. I arrived back at the den several minutes later. As I opened my mouth ever so slightly in hopes words would come to me, but they never did. I just continued to stare blankly at them.

"My dear, are you feeling alright?" my mum's voice echoed slightly throughout the quiet room.

I cleared my throat, "No, I don't."

Officer Chaney stood and faced me, "Ms. Walsh, I'm terribly sorry for what has happened to you.

I have given your mother the name of someone who may be ableto help."

I nodded. I knew I should have been more polite and thanked him for his time, but I just couldn't. He was merely the vessel that delivered the message and not the cause. My anger towards him had grown even though I knew none of this was his fault. I was hopeful this visit would have had a better outcome, but it only ended in disappointment.

"Can I have a minute, Officer Chaney? Alone if possible?" he nodded and the room slowly cleared out, but I knew my mum wouldn't be far.

"Alright, what can I do for you?" his voice said with a touch of disdain. He was clearly becoming irritated with me.

"Is there any chance you'll be able to find who did this?"

"Ms. Walsh, to be completely honest we tried to build a case against Mr. Strom, but nothing would hold up. Yes, something happened to you, but without any evidence or an eye witness you don't have a case."

"So, what am I supposed to do?"

"Go back to the beginning and start again. Even the smallest detail may help."

"Thank you," I said softly.

He nodded and we walked towards the front door. He was finished here and had no intention of entertaining anymore questions from me. I turned to open the front door for him. Just that brief opening allowed a cool breeze to rush through the opening and send a chill across my skin, but it didn't last for long. It made me long for the forest I once loved, but it would never be my sanctuary again. It was tainted and torn much like my mind. I needed a clear head to process everything, but my mind only taunts me now with anxiety and uncertainty. I needed to go back, back to the beginning and replay everything for there musthave been something I missed. Based on Officer Chaney's assessment, I must have either gone completely mental or I was attacked by an invisible man. I refused to believe either.

16

I must have been standing there an awfully long time because my mum came over to me and nudged me. Shewas smiling and I noticed she was carrying the long red gown.

"My dear, it's been a long and trying morning. I think you should lie down for a bit."

I pursed my lips, "I think so too, but why are you holding that?" I pointed to the gown and raised one of my eyebrows.

"I think you should think about it. It's a beautiful gown and a wonderful gift."

"Mum, I just can't see it that way and I can't even believe you would suggest being..." I couldn't finish the sentence.

"Listen Isolde, no one really seems to know what happened to you and while we want to believe you, it's hard to trust a broken mind."

"That's absurd! I've never given you a reason not to believe me!" I shouted at her.

"Isolde, if you can look at me now and say in full confidence Derek is the man that did this to you, I will believe you, but if you can't," she glanced towards the gown, "you'll at least think about apologizing to him."

"I don't know what happened. I mean, I know what happened or at least I thought I did, but something isn't right now," I muttered as I could feel my mind start to unravel once more.

She sighed and handed the gown towards me, "Then do what you need to do to make it right and let yourself heal. We love you."

I felt my face begin to droop and the tears were welling up once more. "I'm not sure that I know how," I sniffled. "I'm lost."

"We can figure it out together."

She wrapped her arms around me and squeezed me tightly. I held on as long as my tears would allow and when I pulled away my hands found hers. I gave a little squeeze as a way of saying thank you and began to turn and pull away. I needed to get away and really think about things. Well, probably not really. The last thing I need to do is think about things. I needed to plan my escape. I was about to make a break for it when she pulled slightly on my one arm and leaned forward extending the gown towards me. I reluctantly accepted the gown and draped it over my shoulder while I walked up the stairs.

I made it to the top of the stairs and took a brief pause, the room below was silent. If I held my breath, I could hear a pin drop and that was too quiet for me. I lightly tapped the banister with my hand before pushing myself onward until I reached my bedroom where I firmly closed the door behind me. I didn't feel the need to lock it this time which meant progress regardless of how minuscule it was. While I was leaning against my bedroom door, I tightly held the gown against my body and felt the softness and smoothness of the fabric. I wanted to toss the gown into the bottom of my closet where it could be lost forever, but my hands just wouldn't let it go. The gown had captivated my thoughts and my senses.

I raised the gown up to my nose and inhaled its fragrance. It smelled of rose and hibiscus and I instantly became intoxicated with it. My eyes fluttered closed as I continued to take it all in. I could just picture myself wearing it and I was drawn to the idea, but if I did how could I live with myself? I needed to believe in myself and trust my gut, but the gown, this gown, was unbelievable. The gown was becoming forbidden fruit and I just needed a taste. It deserved to be worn at least once, right? My eyes opened and I rushed over to the bedside where I began undressing. Once I was down to my knickers, I picked up the dress and stepped inside. Slowly pulling the dress up onto my arms I did what I could to button the back of the dress, but there were just a few too high for me to reach comfortably. No need to worry, I wasn't planning on leaving my room with it on, so no one would know I wasn't fully buttoned up.

I stepped in front of the window just steps away from the full-length mirror. With each escaping breath I felt as ifthistle was being pulled through my throat and dragged across my tongue. I began gasping for air and quickly began my search for something to alleviate my discomfort. I didn't have to hunt for long when a butterscotch candy caught my eye. I quickly unwrapped it and launched it intomy mouth. Within seconds I started to feel the dryness andirritation to calm down. Rather than wait another moment I stepped in front of the mirror and exhaled. It was as if Istepped out of a fairy tale.

I reached up and let my hair fall onto my shoulders. The rich color of the gown was a perfect match for my dark hair, and it couldn't have been more perfectly fitted to me. It was as if someone had custom made this piece just for me. I placed my hands over my stomach and began touching the fabric once more. I couldn't believe how soft it felt and again how perfect the fit was. I turned slightly to see the backside of the dress. It was even more beautiful than the front. The petals were long and stretched out onto the sheer fabric that provided the illusion of being naked while still allowing a woman to keep some of her modesty. The neckline in the back fell far below anything I had worn before and while there was an illusion of modesty, I still felt very exposed. While the gown was full length there was an extension towards the rear giving it a slight train. Very elegant and formal. If the gown would have been made in white, I don't believe there would be a wedding dress as beautiful as this one.

Just wearing the gown brightened my dreary mood and brought life back into my face. I continued to scan myself in the mirror allowing me to take what little joy I could from this rare and unwelcome gift. I wasn't ready to take it off just yet, but I knew the time was coming. Just a few more minutes I told myself, just a few more minutes. In the midst of my delight, I heard my window slide open and a gust of air rushed in blowing my hair over to one side. The gust quickly drew my attention towards the window where a figure was stepping inside. It took a moment to take in the figure, but once I did, I felt as if the wind had been knocked from my body. I did not gasp for air or move from my position as I already knew there was nowhere for me to go.

"Derek, you need to leave...right now or I'll scream." My voice was quivering.

"Izzy, baby, I just had to see you and I couldn't resist seeing your reaction to the dress. He advanced towards me. "You look so beautiful right now."

I scanned his face and noticed while he was smiling, his once stunning face was terribly beaten, stemming from a blackened eye flowing into a bruised cheek with a broken nose and split lip to match. This was clearly from the altercation with Rhys and after seeing him I would have to agree with Tyler. Rhys had been kind. I'm surprised more damage wasn't done, but he may have been stopped before it could be taken any further. I began to step backwards towards my dresser as he continued to advance in my direction. Clearly, I took one too many steps and slammed into it causing a sharp pain in my lower back. I winced from it, but I didn't take my eyes off of him. Was this another threat or had he finally come to finish the job?

"Easy baby, I wouldn't want you to hurt yourself."

He stepped into my personal space as I opened my mouth to scream, but I was quickly silenced by him placing his hand over my mouth.

"Please don't, I just needed to see you," he added softly.

"Don't you think you've done enough? This is all your fault after all," I hissed.

"Isolde, stop. I've done nothing to you that you didn't welcome."

"Are you saying I asked for you to break my bones and rape me?" I spat.

"Izzy, don't you think if I'd have done those things someone would have been able to prove it by now?"

I raised my hand and slapped his cheek, hard. The sound of his teeth smashing together brought me a taste of satisfaction, however small it was. He brushed his hand slightly over his cheek feeling the warmth from the impact.

"Please don't do that again. I'm not here to hurt you. I just need you to remember."

"Remember what?" I said defiantly.

"This," he leaned in and kissed my cheek softly.

I opened my mouth to scream but was quickly met with his hand over it muffling the sound. I jerked away and turned my face away from him like so many times before. He looked towards me with disappointment, but he was not surprised this time.

"Izzy, baby, I'm so sorry for everything that happened, but this wasn't my doing."

He didn't wait for a response before kissing me hard forcing my back against the dresser once more. I tried to pull away from him, but it only spurred him on. He wrapped his arms around me pulling me swiftly towards him. I barely noticed my struggle for breath since the pain from extending my body in such a way was consuming mc. I needed to break myself away from his grasp and fast. During my struggle I knocked some things off my dresser causing them to crash onto the wooden floor beneath our feet. Thesound didn't break his concentration and, in an effort, to calm me, his hands found mine. His fingers became interlocked in mine, and he squeezed them tightly.

Was he trying to breakmy fingers or simply control me?

It reminded me of that afternoon in the forest. Fora few moments, I was torn between two sides. The side that desperately wanted the man of my dreams and the sidethat was greeted by the monster. For him, however, it wasa complete role reversal. Was he a monster or hopeless romantic? Was this really part of some elaborate ruse or was he just delusional? He was acting like nothing ever happened. I could feel myself becoming sickened over the entire ordeal and I just wished I could remember everything. There must be proof somewhere. It would be the only way I could move forward. Unfortunately, the sound of the picture frames and jewelry box hitting the floor was clearly heard by someone else and there was a knock at the door.

"Isolde, I heard a noise. Are you alright?" my mum's soft voice came through the door.

My eyes darted between the door and Derek's eyes. I could feel my heart pounding in my chest. I only had about fifteen seconds or less to decide what to do before she would come through the door. He leaned towards me and quietly shushed me.

He whispered, "I have nothing to hide, but you need to decide if you do."

I hesitated. I didn't have anything to hide, so why was I hesitating. My mum always believed me in the past, but after everything that was said earlier, and me now wearing the gown, I don't think me saying he's a monster and I'm afraid of him would be so plausible. I had no choice, but to lie to her.

"I'm alright Mum, just slipped and knocked a few things over. That's all," I did my best to shout without raising any alarms.

"Alright dear. Get some rest," she shouted in return.

I waited until I heard footsteps walking away before exhaling. What did I just do? I had the perfect opportunity to prove I hadn't gone completely mental, and I didn't take it. Why did I protect him or was I really just protecting myself? I was trying to perceive everything from all possible angles, and it was making me dizzy.

"Now, where were we?" he smirked just before leaning in and kissing me once more.

"Derek, I'm confused and I'm not sure what is going on." My voice was shaky.

"Are you afraid someone will see us together?" he asked.

"Yes...I mean, no, I don't know anymore." My voice was still shaky and now I could feel it spreading to the rest of my body. I began to shiver like I had been left out in the cold too long without a jacket. He began stroking my arms in an attempt to warm me up enough to stop the shiver that had taken over.

"You need to leave," I forced the words out of my mouth in hopes that he would listen this time.

"Please let me stay. I've been forced to stay away from you for so long already."

He looked saddened by the thought of leaving, but I couldn't tell if he was just acting or that if there was something there.

"Besides, there is something I need to tell you."

"Alright, what is it?" I asked softly.

"Here let me help get you out of this dress first." A grin appeared on his face, and he was almost playful in the way he said it.

"But I'm only wearing my knickers under this," I raised an eyebrow.

"Baby, why do you tease me so? I wouldn't dream of breaking your bedroom rule, but at least let me warm you up."

Wait, did he just say bedroom rule? What is a bedroom rule and better yet, what was *my* bedroom rule? He didn't wait for a reply before leaning in and kissing my neck softly. I turned sharply forcing his kisses to land in my dark curls. I wrapped my arms tightly around myself hoping to keep him at bay for a little while longer. I felt him step away for a moment and that's when I heard a click near my door. I turned my face quickly and saw him standing near the entry door to my bedroom. He was locking it, but why? Was this another act of protecting my honor or was he afraid that he might be caught?

"What are you doing?" I asked sharply.

He snickered, "Just trying to get you to relax. That's all."

"The bedroom rule, what is it?"

He grinned.

"What is it?" I insisted.

He sighed, "I've been in your room before, but you're adamant you won't have sex with me here."

"Forgive me, how many times have you been here before?" I said sounding puzzled at just the thought of it.

"I'm not quite sure how many times, but several," he walked towards me forcing me once again to step backwards only this time towards the bed.

"Prove it," I hissed.

"Alright, in your closet over there," he looked towards the closet then back at me, "your shirts are organized by color."

"I'm sure lots of people do that. Tell me something else."

"The picture we knocked over earlier was of you and your gran back in Dublin just before your family immigrated here. From what you've said she still lives there. In your nightstand, you keep your favorite book, some new and old photographs, and a few handheld puzzlegames for when you feel restless."

He walked over towards my full-length mirror before continuing.

"And behind here is where you've been hiding us," he flipped the mirror around revealing several Polaroids of us together.

I shuffled over towards the mirror with my mouth gaping open nearly the whole way. What just happened here? I'm not sure how someone could know the things he knew just like that, but in turn I can't believe if we were together that I could have forgotten something like that. I stared at the Polaroids for several moments trying to piece everything together. These are photos of us laughing and kissing. We look happy.

"We can be happy again, Izzy," he looked towardsme trying to get me to smile.

"But after all that I said, I..I..I..." I couldn't finish the sentence. I felt terrible and my mind began swimming in guilt. I reached for the dresser to help support me as I was feeling a bit faint. I closed my eyes and tried to grasp the new information that was laid before me without completely losing my grip on reality. Derek had come up behind me and began brushing my hair off my back. I could feel his luscious, soft lips start kissing my shoulders and his hands were beginning to fumble over the buttons on the back of my dress. I think he was nervous. I didn't realize that a situation like this could make him nervous.

"Derek, I don't think this is such a good idea," I whispered as I turned towards him.

He didn't say a word. Just cupped my face in his hands and kissed me softly. I brought my hands up and rested them on his forearms. They were warm and taunt much like the rest of his body. I pushed back on his forearms hoping he would stop as I don't think I could continue to resist him for too much longer. At this very moment, I wasn't sure whether slapping him or kissing him would give me more satisfaction I just knew he needed to leave. As he pulled away, I could feel my breathing increase. I bit my lower lip as I contemplated letting him kiss me again, but I was lost at whether that is what I really wanted or was I just trying to please his inner beast. I still wasn't sure if I believed everything that I'd been told recently, but it was hard to deny.

"I think I need to lie down for a bit. This has all been a lot to take in. I hope you understand."

He nodded in agreement, "Alright, I understand," he kissed my lips once more before turning and walking towards the window. I stepped over towards my bed as I heard the window slide open once more. A chill burst through the opening, waking up my senses.

"Derek," he turned back towards me, "I apologize. I'm not sure what or who to believe anymore."

"All is forgiven. I just look forward to the day we can be together again."

"We are together now, are we not?"

"We are, but I long for the day when you are no longer afraid of me. I miss you," he stood briefly in front of the window just looking at me before he spoke again. "You're so beautiful Izzy."

Between the dress and the way he was looking at me I felt empowered and in the spirit of healing I stepped towards him and kissed him. I needed to know if I felt something, anything for him. If we were together there should be a spark or something there, right? Seconds after our lips connected, I knew it was the wrong thing to do, but I did my best to power through. I embraced the moment, and he did too. He wrapped his arms around me and continued to kiss me until that simply wasn't enough anymore. He pulled away to strip off his jacket and my hands could not help themselves. I slid them under his shirt to feel the warm body that hid beneath its surface. I waited for a sign of what to do, but nothing happened. Not a memory or shock to my senses had awakened in me. I was on my own at least for the moment and that was truly frightening.

He noticed my hesitation and peeled his shirt off revealing his chiseled arms and torso. I pulled myself towards him hoping he would stop if I showed him any sort of affection. When I felt him fumbling over the buttons on my dress once more the sensation jolted me back to reality. I jerked away from him. Well, I attempted to, but his grip was not easy to shake. He didn't appear to be as bothered as he waspreviously and that was new.

"Baby, we don't have to do anything you don't want to do," he whispered as his breathing remained heavy and deep much like my own.

I was afraid to be alone but knowing I couldn't fully trust myself yet meant that I should be careful who I share my life and my bed with. With everything that happened that day and all the evidence now laid before me; I was beginning to wonder if I was the one that was delusional. I don't think he would have forced himself upon me at that very moment, but I didn't think it through inviting him back in by kissing him the way I did. What was I thinking? Oh wait, I wasn't thinking or maybe I was thinking too much.

"I need some time, to remember everything," I whispered.

"Well, don't take too long. I really would like to show you off in that dress," he grinned.

"But wouldn't that ruin your reputation...I mean, being seen with me," I could feel my body bracing for his reaction.

"Izzy, I care about you, and I just want you," he kissed me again bringing our bodies together however brief the moment was before peeling his body off of mine. He stepped back and reached for his jacket. He donned it in one swift motion, but when he reached for his shirt, there was something different about it. I could see that he was smiling almost like he was remembering something pleasant. He stood there quietly for a moment or two as if he was trying to hold onto it for a little while longer.

"Everything alright?" I said softly.

"Yea," he turned towards me and held the shirt out for me to grab. "I think you should keep this. At least for now."

"Why should I keep your shirt?" I said puzzled.

"It was the first one you ever took off of me," he grinned, "it should bring back great memories."

I took it willingly and brought it up to my face where I briefly inhaled his scent. I was surprised to find that it smelled exactly like the shirt I found in my bag, but why roses? Was this simply a cologne he wore to draw women in or just a simple laundry detergent his mum uses. As he was turning to leave, I grasped the back of his jacket and pulled him back slightly. The leather smelled as expected and when I didn't find what I was looking for I stepped in front of him and led him towards me by the collar. As I buried my face in his chest, I could smell roses once more. Very much like the gown I was wearing. It was as if this the scent just radiates from his pores. It was everywhere and intoxicating. I couldn't tell what he was thinking or even what the expression was on his face, but I felt his arms wrap around me and hug me softly.

"I'm sorry, I was just remembering something," I mumbled while pressed against his chest.

"I'm not complaining. I can stand here with you all night," he responded as he leaned down and began nuzzling my cheek. "Please kiss me," he whispered in my ear as his fingers began stroking my cheeks.

"I don't think I can," I whispered back.

"But you just did a moment ago."

"That was a mistake, and I shouldn't have."

He continued to nuzzle me and touch my face with his hand. There was no sense of urgently or pressure to his touch, but I could tell he was bothered, and I was torn.

"Please Izzy, look at me," he threw his head back out of what I can only assume was sheer frustration. I remained buried in his chest. I couldn't bring myself to look at him. When I didn't respond he dropped to his knees suddenly and placed his face against my stomach while grabbing my waist with both hands. He didn't say anything, but his grip was desperate and unsteady. He wasn't nervous like when he was fumbling over the buttons to my dress, but he was struggling with something. He was vulnerable. Everything I thought I knew about Derek was rapidly dissolving.

"I'm so sorry Derek. I know this is hard for you, but I need time."

I felt the words catch in my throat as I struggled to push them out and I closed my eyes. I could feel him tugging at my waist, pulling me closer to him, but I wasn't pulling away from him at least not physically. He wasn't verbally pleading with me anymore, but his actions were his way of screaming at me.

"Derek," my eyes fell upon his face pressed tightly to my stomach.

He looked up at me and then kissed my stomach softly. I've seen him like this before, but where. Was it in a dream or was this an actual memory? I didn't know for sure, but in his current state I didn't figure I had long to debate the matter. I felt like the room was spinning and my heart was beating so fast I could barely keep up. Come on brain, remember. Remember something, anything!

"Izzy," he grabbed my hands and encompassed them in his own. "You accused me of beating you and raping you." The sound of those words caused me to flinch as if the words had somehow managed to manifest themselves physically and strike me which only caused his grip to tighten.

"And I'm still here. We haven't just been together for weeks, it's been months."

There was a sense of urgency in his voice now that hadn't been there previously. He wasn't trying to get me to remember anymore he was trying to force me to acknowledge his pain, his struggles. Really step outside of myself and see this catastrophe from his perspective. My whole body was shaking, and I felt like I was going into shock. I couldn't catch my breath and my heart was racing. How could it have been months? The memories I do have are so vivid and I can't remember him even speaking to me before that night at the football game. I had to say something or do something before one of us exploded or worse before my family heard us and began beating down the door.

I knelt bringing my cool cheek next to the warmth of his and whispered in his ear.

"Please calm down...someone will hear you."

"Come with me, please," he turned his face slightly and pressed his lips against my cheek.

"Where do you want to take me?" I replied softly.

"Anywhere."

"I can't do that right now, please forgive me."

I hoped he would let the matter rest, but true to form he was going to take advantage of what little time he was able to steal away with me. His forehead creased ever so slightly while clearly pondering his next move. He had nothing left in him tonight and I could feel his drive failing him. Who was this man before me? He was not boastful or cocksure, but vulnerable. Nothing like the monster I'd seen in weeks or even months prior. Was this the type of moment he was protecting from the world? His vulnerability and his affections for a woman born without privilege or prominent origin. I couldn't be sure and while the evidence was compelling me to believe there was more to his story, no, our story than I previously was led to believe I couldn't allow myself to be oblivious anymore.

He began to rise to his feet lifting me up alongside him. I was at a loss for words and even though there was so much left that needed to be said the both of us remained silent. I turned and walked towards my bed where my clothes from earlier were still laying. I suddenly became aware of the fact the gown I was wearing nearly completely unbuttoned and I was freezing. I crossed my arms in an effort to warm myself just a bit, but unfortunately it did little to comfort me. While the bitter air continuing to rush through my window wasn't helping the chill, in a way I was glad he came through my window that afternoon. I turned around just in time to see him stepping through the opening and onto the branch. I couldn't let him leave like this.

"Derek," I said suddenly, and he turned towards melooking hopeful. "Thank you for the gown. It's lovely."

"Just seeing you in it was thanks enough. Please think about joining me for the dance."

"I will."

I smiled and this was a smile I truly meant. Something about the way he was looking at me brought a sense of joy that had been only found sparingly over the last few weeks. He smiled in return and once again turned to make his way down the tree. I quickly stepped towards the window where I found his shirt laying. I picked it up and brought it to my face once more and took in the scent. It was beautiful and once again reminded me how kind he has been to me recently, a bit creepy depending on how you look at it, but kind. I glanced out the window and saw he had already made it down safely and was running out the back to avoid any potential beatings Rhys might have dealt out if he would have seen him leaving my room like that. I closed my window and decided it was time to take off the gown. However, instead of donning my old jeans and sweater I decided to just lie down for a bit with nothing, but my knickers on and his shirt. Maybe it really would bring back some fond memories.

I stared out the window for some time trying to picture him sitting out there, waiting, and watching me. Thethought made me uneasy and forced me to focus intently onthe idea that what if this wasn't the first time, he'd been sitting out there watching me? While I thought about asking him that during his brief visit, too many other questions were at the forefront of my mind during that time that seemed far more important than that one. However, based on his reaction I couldn't assume he was spying on me for malicious intentions, but the idea of him seeing me in the ways that he did sent a chill down my spine.

17

Hours later there was a knock at my door with no particular urgency in the taps, but they continued for several minutes. As my eyes fluttered open my window came into view, and it was open. I could have sworn I closed it earlier today, but it was clearly unlatched and swung open turning my room into that of a northern igloo. I sprung myself out of bed and quickly headed to the window where I quickly and quietly closed it. The knocks continued as I rushed towards the door.

"Just a minute," I called out.

In a panic I quickly unlocked the door and swung it open. Unfortunately, there was one thing I forgot to check and when I saw the look in Liam's eyes it reminded me that I was nearly naked and wearing a man's shirt. Not exactly something I should be wearing considering everything that has happened recently.

"Uh ok, not what I expected," he cleared his throat, "there's a guy on the phone for you, from the hospital. It sounded important," he cleared his throat again.

"Sure, just let me grab something to put on." I stepped over to my closet and grabbed the first shirt that was big enough to cover Derek's and then slid on a pair of jeans before pushing my way past Liam. I rushed down the steps trying to do my best not to keep whoever was calling waiting. Unfortunately, I wasn't the only one who was curious since Liam nearly ran into the back of me when I stopped to pick up the phone.

"Will you get out of here! I doubt this is something YOU need to be involved in," I snapped at him.

I picked up the receiver and tried to appear calm and collected even though I was a bit disheveled.

"Hello, this is Isolde."

"Hey Isolde, how are you feeling?"

It took me a moment to place where I heard the voice before, but when I thought about it for a moment I knew, and my heart leapt with excitement. It was Tyler. I did my best to try and hide my enthusiasm, but I couldn't stop the grin that began consuming my face.

"I'm doing well considering everything. Thank you for calling to check on me," I tried to be as nonchalant as possible considering there were prying ears and eyes on me nearly the time now.

"I just had to check on you and I didn't want to alert the media of my feelings for you. I hope that's alright."

"I completely understand, and I appreciate you reminding me," I replied trying to sound aloof. I didn't want to alert anyone here either, or things could become dramatically more complicated.

"I know you are coming back in for a follow-up in a few days, but I really would like to see you before then if I may."

I began pacing back and forth between the den and the kitchen pretending to be bored, but really it was more to muffle the sound from my side of the conversation than anything else.

"I will have to check with my folks, but I think that should work. Any particular time?"

I could hear him smile in his voice and it reminded me just how much I loved his smile. "I'll wait for you outside the hospital tomorrow morning when my shift is over at nine. Talk soon."

"Thank you again for calling," I nodded and hung up the phone hoping that my performance was believable enough to avoid any potential follow-up questions.

"Who was that dear?" My mum appeared out of nowhere and I jumped at the sound of her voice. "Are you alright my dear?"

"Yes Mum, of course," I sounded startled. "Just a routine follow-up call from the hospital."

I was rushing and needed to slow down, giving enough to be believable, but not so much that it sounds suspicious.

"They were checking to see how I was and make sure I was aware of my follow-up appointment," I said, sounding much better.

"Alright dear. Are you hungry? You missed lunch."

"I hadn't realized, but yes I am. Thank you."

"Did you think about what I said? It may be a good idea to bury the dead."

"I did, a little. I'm still just really confused about all of it."

She looked at me a little puzzled.

"I just mean that if everything that was said is true then I feel like I lost more than just my dignity."

"Isolde, there are some details of your case that the doctors and Officer Chaney wouldn't share with us since you're of a certain age, but that might be another place to start."

I gave her a worried look.

"It's just a suggestion. We just want you to get better."

I nodded, "I'm just struggling to believe that I could have been with someone, but not have any recollection of it. Is that even possible?"

"Anything is possible really. The staff at the hospital made no mention of a severe head injury, but that doesn't mean one didn't occur," she sighed.

"Before all of this happened, did I act any different than usual?"

"Yes of course, but to be honest I just figured you were finally outgrowing being my little girl."

"Oh, any idea about how long? Since you noticed a change, I mean." I was biting my lip anxiously awaiting her answer.

"Well, perhaps it's been several weeks now."

She responded rather quickly at first, but then took a few moments before adding the specifics.

"Maybe a month or two at best."

While it wasn't what I was hoping to hear it did help a little. "Thanks Mum." I turned and began venturing back towards the stairs when she hollered in my direction.

"Isolde, you forgot to eat lunch!"

"Oh, right, I'm not hungry," I continued forward when I heard her footsteps rapidly approaching me.

"Doctor's orders. Take this and enjoy."

She held out a plate for me to grab but I did not.

"I will be up to check on you shortly to make sure you've eaten," she insisted.

"Mum, it's alright. I'm alright. I don't need to be monitored every second of every day."

She raised her one eyebrow and didn't seem the least bit amused.

"I'd say the evidence points to the contrary."

She didn't move a muscle only continued to stare at me until I caved in, took the plate in my grasp, and trotted up the stairs to my bedroom. Upon my arrival I promptly shut the door and locked it. There's something about leaving my door open now that really makes me uncomfortable. Mum may insist that I need to be checked on constantly, but I wasn't going to make it effortless for anyone. Nowhere in my home felt safe now and I would soon need to find another sanctuary where I could think uninterrupted and unsupervised. Don't misunderstand, I appreciate everyone's concern over my well-being, but the restrictions are handicapping my recovery. Granted if they knew Derek had been in my room earlier today, then they really would be watching me and my room a bit closer.

I began eating my lunch as Mum insisted and once again my attention was drawn to the gown slung over the end of my bed. I ran my fingers gently over the fabric and brought back the memories from early today. Then I remembered the photos on the back of my mirror. I stepped over to the mirror and carefully scanned the photos for anything that looked familiar. Most of the photos were just of Derek and I, but then I noticed it. While most of the photos were taken up close there were a few that had to

have been taken by someone else. I was able to see the full
length of myself and Derek, but I have no idea who would
have taken these. There were photos from in the forest, at
the football game and here in my bedroom. In none of the
photos do I appear to be distressed or worrisome and that
surprised me more than there being photographic evidence
of our "relationship".

I continued to scan the photos and most appeared to
be the same as any other couple would possess. We either
appeared to be smiling at one another or kissing in the
majority, but it wasn't what we were doing in the photos
that drew my attention as much as where the photos were
taken. They were all taken on the days I was attacked
except for two. Those ones were taken in my bedroom and
placed at opposite sides of the mirror to make it seem like
we were actually looking at each other. The photos were
clearly capturing private moments between Derek and I.
Wearing his arms in the photo as opposed to a shirt leaves
little to the imagination as to what we had just done or what
we were about to do. For someone, who doesn't like to be
tied publicly to any one woman I have an awful lot of
evidence that would suggest otherwise.

I didn't seem to be alarmed by anything I saw, nor
did they appear to be tampered with. These were all
polaroids and those are hard to fake since there is no
negative. I pulled one of photos out from behind the frame
that was holding it and tried to focus on it. Derek was
lying on top of me and kissing me. Our eyes were both
closed, and I could tell he snapped the photo since his one
arm was outstretched towards where the camera would
have been. I can only assume this was a post coital kiss

since all we both seem to be wearing was each other, but again only an assumption. I glanced around the photo for a clue as to when this might have been taken. I found nothing noteworthy.

I placed the photo back where I found and looked again at the remaining photos. They weren't hung in any particular order, and nothing was off limits. To let yourself be photographed in such a compromising position either leads me to believe we wanted to be photographed or this was proof he really didn't assault me. However, if he knew they were there why wouldn't he have told the police to further prove his innocence? Maybe he really was telling the truth and the photos were kept a secret for not only my benefit, but to prove his innocence to me. Post coital photos are scandalous, so I know now why they were hidden. However, someone else had to have been there and that was the witness I needed. I stood there pondering that thought for a moment when I got the idea of where to start.

I headed over to my bookshelf where I quickly began fingering through the titles until I found the yearbook from my sophomore year. I remember pleading with my folks to purchase it since it was supposed to be the beginning of a beautiful thing, but now looking at it all dusty and faded it just seemed bittersweet. I slid back into my armchair and began combing through the pages looking for anyone appeared near or next to Derek in the photos. If Derek asked someone to photograph us together then it would have been someone close to him or a paid professional. Paid professional would have been out since there would be too many lose ends that would have arisen when the incident hit newsstands, but a friend may have done this for him. I continued to flip through the pages, but while there were photos of him with others, they didn't appear to be the same people twice other than the team photos.

Unfortunately, time had gotten away from me once more and there was a knock at the door. I got up and unlocked the door before cracking it just enough to see who was on the other side. I wasn't given any time to react before there was a push and the door swung open allowing my mum to step inside. I don't believe she meant to shove the door open with the force she did, but I think she was growing impatient with my erratic behavior.

"Hello dear, finish your lunch?"

"I haven't had a moment to just yet."

I completely forgot my mirror was still flipped revealing the photographs I had at one time carefully hidden. She was moving towards them and the closer she got the more her mouth began to gape open.

"Mum, I was just about to take a bath and relax...could you come back later?"

I stood up and scurried over towards her trying to usher her out of my room before she saw any more than she already did. Unfortunately, she wasn't interested in being distracted as her eyes were fixed on the photos like a dog fixated on a bone. She placed her hands on me and slowly began pushing me out of her way. She wasn't trying to hurt me; it was more like someone moving canned goods in a cupboard trying to get to the one they wanted. She was standing very close to photos now and her eyes were darting between as if she was watching a tennis match. I felt myself inhale deeply and hold my breath as her hand reached up and covered her mouth. She appeared to be going into shock. I don't think I've ever seen her in shock.

There was no doubt she was alive, but I can't recall ever seeing her this lifeless. I couldn't hold my breath anymore and when I exhaled it was like I had just thrown gasoline on hot coals. Her voice projected from her in such a tone that was only audible by man's best friend. When she turned towards me her voice became amplified and hurt my ears.

"Isolde how dare you! You shame yourself and our family! Why would you lie to us, about this of all things?!" she began pacing across my room, but her eyes never left mine. I held her gaze as long as I could before I was forced to blink and when I did, I couldn't bear to look at her anymore.

"Mum, it's not what you think...I promise!" I felt the words catch in my throat and knew already that a part of me was lying to her.

She pulled the photo of Derek laying on top of my naked body and thrust it inches away from my face. I could feel the anger radiating out from her body like a shock wave.

"Then explain this!"

"I can't," I mumbled.

"Explain this!" she screamed again.

My mum has never screamed at me like this before. Come to think of it I've never seen her this livid before.

"I can't!" I cried out.

"You lied to me, you lied to everyone and for what? Lust in your heart! We taught you better than this...you should be ashamed of yourself!"

I heard footsteps rapidly approaching and realized that the shock wave of fury from my mum had traveled to other parts of the house and drew some extra unwanted attention. My brothers and father were standing inside the doorway and their eyes were the size of cue balls.

"What in God's name is going on here?" our father bellowed and just the shear sound of his voice made me cower in fear.

"Have you seen these?!"

My mum stepped over and pointed towards the back of my mirror.

"And this one of that man defiling our daughter, our little girl!"

My father went to my mum and began hugging her. Anything I'm sure in an attempt to calm her. She was very upset. The only time I've seen her worse than this was when my grandfather died, and she wasn't so much livid as she was inconsolable. I stood, reached for my sneakers, and ran towards the door. Rhys was blocking my exit with his body and when I attempted to push past him, he gave a verbal and physical rebuttal.

"Don't leave like this. It will only make matters worse if you do," he whispered.

"I can't stay," I whispered back.

I pushed my way between my two brothers and just as I was about to step down onto the first step I was pulled backwards. Rhys grabbed my upper arm with enough force that I was not only stopped dead in my tracks I nearly fell backwards.

"Let me go," my voice gave no room for misinterpretation.

"Where are you going?"

"Just let me go," I demanded once more as I struggled to free my arm from his grip.

"You're going to him, aren't you?"

That struck a nerve. I didn't even know how to respond as the shock of his question gut-wrenched me and I felt my heart sink in my chest. He really believed I would go to Derek after everything that I said. It broke my heart. I tore my arm from his grip and rushed down the remaining steps.

"Izz come back!" he shouted.

I didn't even acknowledge his request. I grabbed my coat before reaching the back door, swung it open and made a break for it. I wasn't sure where I was going or what I was doing, but I knew I couldn't stay there. Nothing felt right anymore, almost like I was dreaming all the time now. Is that even possible? I know people with certain conditions can experience hallucinations for short periods of time, but for one to last for days even weeks seems impossible somehow.

I thought about what Officer Chaney said earlier, go back to the beginning. I needed to take myself back to that Friday night and try to retrace my steps. I turned sharply and began running towards the school. I didn't make it far before I was reminded that I was still healing and should probably take it a bit slower. I walked the remainder of the way while clutching my side in hopes relief would soon find me.

I arrived at the school a few minutes later and casually walked around to the rear parking lot. There were sleeping buses hidden there like they were the night I was attacked, but everything looked different in the afternoon light. I didn't believe I could get into any trouble for being here, but I did my best to maintain a low profile just to be on the safe side. I reached the backside of the first one and then the second one carefully scanning each area for anything that looked familiar, but I found nothing. I leaned against the side of the sleeping bus and tried to think of that night. Nothing particular seemed familiar, but that could have been since it was so dark by that time of night. I slammed my eyes shut and tried to replay everything from the time Derek walked up to me until my friends and I reached the car to leave.

He walked towards me, and we began chatting. We were making small talk as we veered towards the buses when he said something else. As I now think of it, he wasn't saying how attracted he was to me he was saying something else entirely. We were still walking, but I attempted to slow the moment down in my mind like pressing pause and fast forward on a VCR at the same time. He was saying he was sorry, but sorry for what? I pushed the play button in my mind and began moving the memory forward again. As we rounded the first bus, he took my hand in his and he was smiling. While we were walking, I tried to count the buses in my mind, so I could have some idea whereabouts were we actually stopped. The further we walked the closer in my mind we became. I did not remember us kissing until we stopped, but in my memory, he was kissing my hand and my neck as we walked.

I stopped the memory dead in its tracks focusing on our behavior towards each other. This wasn't the first time we had held hands; it couldn't have been. He took my hand in his without so much as an awkward glance. The memory continued to play in my mind and soon we arrived at our destination. It played out in my mind almost exactly like it did previously, but this time I cannot recall ever saying no to his advances. In fact, when I think of it now, I wasn't saying no I was saying we shouldn't. My response caused us to begin arguing in such a way that was foreign to me. Arguing didn't occur often in our house, but when it did it would end with whiskey and slamming doors. Ours was filled with bickering and passionate kisses, but what were we bickering about?

My eyes opened suddenly. Was this a false memory or an actual one? Two weeks ago, I would have bet my life on my account of what happened here that night, but now I'm not so sure. I just can't believe how my life has been flipped upside down in a matter of days. Before this I was alone and led a relatively uneventful life, but now it was nearly unrecognizable. Now each day is filled with surprise and mystery. I desperately wanted to know what we were arguing about that night, but the thought of dwelling on it any longer seemed unbearable. Unfortunately, like most women, and teenagers for that matter, letting go wasn't something in our vocabulary.

I peeled myself away from the buses and began walking. Generally, when I needed to gather my thoughts, I would head to the forest and just breathe in the fresh air and all would seem right with the world again, but after everything that happened there, I just don't think I can. I couldn't take the risk of remembering something different than what I believe really happened there. While it would make sense to want to know the truth, finding out it could be the complete and total opposite could be devastatingly dangerous to my mind.

18

As I was walking out from behind the school, I noticed Rhys's truck rush by. Rhys has always been a very law-abiding citizen or at least that was what I was led to believe, but at this present moment his driving was quite erratic. Where was he going in such a hurry? I have been known to be particularly swift on foot and it wasn't long before I got the idea that I needed to follow him. I tried to maintain a low profile, but I had a lot of ground to make up if I was going to even attempt to keep up with him. I began sprinting and after only a few moments I felt incapacitated by the sharp pain in my side. I had to stop and do what I could to catch my breath. Stupid broken ribs. I wish they would just heal already, so I could be done with that mess.

For several minutes, I stood there nearly doubled over attempting to catch my breath. I was dizzy once more and I began seeing spots everywhere I looked. I knew on some level that I needed to stop and rest, but I forced myself to work through what pain I could and continue. The truck had long been out of my sight, but I was able to catch the general direction it was headed before I had to stop. I decided taking a few shortcuts was the only way I had even a remote chance of catching up to him.

My breathing became more and more labored as I pressed onward, but I just had to know where he was going.

I wasn't egotistical enough to believe he was out looking forme, but this wasn't the first time in the last week he had ventured outside of his norm in pursuit of something that involved me. That I think distressed me more than anything. The collateral damage from this debacle is rippling out to ever corner of my life with no end in sight. I wanted to know the truth, but I was beginning to wonder if the cost of it all was worth it.

After cutting through some side streets and a few backyards I was able to at least hear his truck nearby. As I began walking towards the sound I realized, while the sound of his music may have been how I found him, it was being drowned out by an argument. A very heated argument between two alpha males by the sound of it. I rounded the street corner to find I had stumbled upon a very ritzy cul-de-sac of homes. I wasn't familiar with this street or any of the homes on it, but something told me that I didn't belong there. These were vast, elegant, and custom-built homes. The kind you would expect to see a successful physician or barrister residing in not someone like me. Someone of my social standing could only dream of living on a street like this one.

As I continued to wander towards the sound. I realized how peculiar I must look. I was clearly trying to spy on two people arguing, but I was doing it in plain sight. I scurried over towards a nearby tree line and did my best to blend in. I continued moving towards them and, as I got closer, I could clearly hear two men arguing outside of the large mansion at the end of the lane. Clearly, one was Rhys, but it wasn't until I was nearly on top of them before I finally placed the other voice. It was Derek's. I couldn't tell if Rhys drove there to find me or to hurt him...again. I was feeling terribly divided as to who's side I should be on since I now know I have connections to both of them. Rhys was my blood and my family, but if Derek and I had what we appeared to have then he must have meant something to me. I was oddly protective of that.

"I won't ask you again, where is she?!" Rhys demanded.

"I already told you she's not here!" Derek shouted back, "I asked her to leave with me and she refused!"

"What do you mean you asked her to leave with you? And when was this?" his voice was raised, but he wasn't shouting anymore.

"I care for her, and I know I can help her remember what really happened that night."

"When did you see her?" Rhys shoved him back a step.

"Earlier today, after Officer Chaney left."

He was defiantly staring Rhys down at this point, almost as if he was challenging him.

"What were you doing in our home?" Rhys demanded.

"I needed to see her," he paused. "I've been kept away for far too long and I needed to tell her something."

"I think you need to leave my sister alone. She deserves better than being another notch in your bedpost."

Derek put his hand on Rhys's chest and attempted to push him back towards his truck. Rhys wasn't having it and pushed back.

"She's not a notch on my bedpost!" Derek exploded, punching Rhys in the face. "It may have started out that way, but she means more to me than that now."

Rhys retaliated and soon they were in more than just a pissing contest, they were at war over something I couldn't bring myself to remember. I watched in horror as Derek and Rhys continued to hit each other and throw each other down on the ground. They were equally matched in size and anger that normally would have made for an interesting fight, but I only saw disaster if this continued.

"SSSSSTTTTOOOOPPPP!" I screamed with every fiber of my lungs. "You're going to kill each other! Please stop!" When they turned and looked in my direction, I hadn't realized how close I actually got to them while I was listening until I felt the pavement beneath my feet. They both quickly rushed to their feet and began heading in my direction. Derek was moving a bit quicker, but Rhys didn't hesitate to grab him and pull him back.

"Get away from her!" Rhys shouted as he rushed over to me where he found me clutching my side once more. "Izz, are you alright? Where have you been?"

"Rhys I'm alright, really, but please stop. You're better than this."

I touched my brother's face and tried to wipe away some of the blood. I saw Derek approaching us, his face was bleeding as well, and he was grasping his shoulder.

"Listen Rhys, I know you don't trust me, but I need to tell your sister something before you decide that knocking all of my teeth out is in your best interest."

"Absolutely not! Izz, get in the truck. I'm taking you home," Rhys insisted.

"No!" I shouted in protest. "I need to know; I want to know what..." I couldn't finish the sentence.

Derek stepped forward only to meet Rhys's hand in his chest once more. "That's as close as you're getting to her right now."

"Take your hand off of me," Derek growled. "Trust me if you're this upset about a photo you won't want to hear what I have to say to her."

Rhys looked disturbed and suddenly very concerned about the path this was going down. He turned his back on Derek and whispered to me. "Are you sure you want to talk to him?"

I nodded and watched him walk just a few feet away towards his truck where he propped himself against it carefully watching Derek's every move. Derek stepped towards me and reached for my hand, and I withdrew it before he could touch it.

"Please let me hold your hand. I—"

I cut him off surprising even myself. "Two weeks ago, we were together at the football game. Do you remember?"

He was taken back by the question, "Of course."

"We were arguing about something," I watched his face change from hopeful to saddened as he was beginning to see where this was going. "What were we arguing about?"

"Umm, this isn't something I think you'd want your brother to hear."

"Well, I'm not leaving, so you better tell her." Rhys interjected still leaning against his truck.

"Well, we've been having sex for months now and the last several times we've been together...well...we didn't use anything."

Rhys's postured straightened and he was now glaring at Derek. I felt the wind get knocked out of me.

"You lie," I spat, "I would never."

"Well, you would, and you did," his defianceastounded me.

"Wait, so if I was upset with you for forgetting to use protection, why would you have attacked me?"

"Well, I did, but I didn't attack you."

"Izz, he just told you everything you need to know," Rhys interjected, "he admits to having attacked you, now let's go!" he growled.

"No, it wasn't like that," he turned and glared at Rhys before returning his attention to me. "You were upset and were trying to leave. I didn't want you to leave upset."

"So, you restrained her and raped her?!?" he demanded. In a matter of seconds Rhys had moved from being by the truck side to being right on top of us and his blood was boiling. Derek reached for my hand once again and briefly connected with it before Rhys casually slapped it away as if it was a small fly or something. Derek was growing irritated at Rhys's very presence and his continual interjections were not helping matters. Well, maybe not helping Derek's cause.

"I grabbed you to stop you from leaving, but you fell and hit your head," Derek added.

"So, you left me there...alone and hurt." I could hear the irritation in my voice. How could someone who supposedly cares for you leave you alone and hurt in a dark parking lot of all places.

"Izz, I left because you asked me to. You wanted to keep our secret and leaving there together could have blown our cover."

"So, you're saying someone else raped me? You had nothing to do with it?"

"I'm not saying that at all," he sounded surprised at my response.

"Then what?!"

"You weren't attacked in the sense you are thinking."

"Then tell me what sense I should be thinking!" I could hear the words catch like thistle in my throat. He was toying with me, but why?

"You weren't raped, but you were definitely mauled."

"I still don't understand. What happened to me and my clothes?" I was starting to cry. I couldn't take the pressure much longer.

"I tore them in the heat of the moment," he grinned.

I gasped at the sheer audacity of his response. It's one thing to say such a thing to me privately, but in front of my eldest brother was going too far.

"While I'm sure you enjoy reliving the fact you defiled my baby sister behind the high school, you didn't answer her question," he stepped even closer to us, and this time Derek flinched and stepped back from me. "So, get to the point and soon," his tone was gruff and insistent.

"Relax, I will tell her, but you need to step back." Derek tried to match Rhys's tone and dominance, but it ultimately failed.

"I'm not moving from this spot until you tell her," his eyes were fixed on Derek's and suddenly I understood. While Derek's true and intimate connection is with me, my brother was judge and jury. Derek couldn't stall any longer.

"You told me you were late," Derek said softly.

"Late for what?" I think I already knew the answer but needed to hear it from Derek's lips.

"You told me you might be pregnant and how frightened you were. We argued about how to handle it if you, I mean, if we were."

I didn't realize I was falling until I noticed Rhys lunging towards me with hands outstretched in an attempt to catch me. They caught me just in time and for a moment they weren't arguing anymore. I could hear them shouting at me trying to get my attention and bring me back to them, but I was lost in the fog and my head was spinning. This would explain the secrecy, well some of it at least. Growing up in a Catholic household, premarital sex and having a child out of wedlock are more than just mortal sins. They are things that would cause a family to disown a child regardless of whether or not the child confessed and did penance or not. I knew this is why my mum was so upsetby the photographs. In her eyes, I not only sinned against myself, but against the family and against God. I could pray for forgiveness, but there was no way to know if she would forgive me. I needed this to be a dream for I know longer knew what was real.

I looked up at them both as my mind began to clear and Rhys's words became clear. "We need to take you to the hospital, now."

Derek appeared to be in agreement, but if his testimony was true then who attacked me in the forest that afternoon?

"No, it's alright, I'm alright," I slowly sat up. "I just felt a little weak."

"Izz, we need to know if you're alright," Rhys said.

Derek placed his arms under my arms and helped me up to my feet. He held me close while I regained my footing. I desperately wanted to know the truth and I believe Derek was letting his guard down just enough I may finally hear his side of the story. Something Officer Chaney would never dream of telling me. I heard the truck door open and my brother beckoning me to go. When I didn't respond I felt a tug at my arm attempting to pull me away from Derek.

"Izz, we need to go. You need to go back to the hospital. If there is a baby, they will be able to confirm that and help you both," Rhys said softly.

Hearing that word jolted me back to reality. "I'm sorry come again."

"Izz, your brother is right. With everything you've been through we need to know you both are alright."

Derek sounded concerned and it was extremely perplexing to hear them both in agreement on something. However, I don't believe I was pregnant with the amount of blood I lost in the hours following our encounter at the football game. It would be hard to imagine anything could have survived that. Part of me was insistent he was lying, but there was something tugging at my heart strings. It would explain so much if there was any kind of validity to his sideof the story, but if there was, I would have to wonder how delusional I was for not remembering any of this. For now,I needed them to both believe that I believed Derek's side of the story. I reached up and tried to wipe the blood from his face.

"Derek, what if there isn't a baby anymore?"

"What do you mean? Why would you say that?" he jerked his face back and sounded so hurt.

"I was in the hospital for nearly a week, and no one mentioned that I was. So, if I was, I may not be anymore," I did my best to appear upset about the thought of losing a child and by the look on his face he was too.

"Please let me go with you. I love you and you shouldn't be alone when you find out for sure."

"What did you say?" My eyes widened and I held my breath.

"Please let me go with you," he repeated.

"No, not that part. The other thing you said."

"I love you."

This was the part when he takes me in his arms, kisses me passionately and then carries me to bed where we make passionate love for hours. Well, that's how it would be in a typical love story. Unfortunately, while I wanted that to be my response I was frozen in place. Completely in shock once again over a few small words uttered in my present, but luckily, I didn't faint, nearly faint or become ill this time.

"Izz, are you alright?" Derek whispered.

"Yes, I think so," I turned toward Rhys. "I can't go with you. I'm sorry."

He slammed the door to his truck and walked towards us. "Please come with me. We don't have to tell anyone, but the physician why you're there."

"I know, but I think there is some business Derek and I need to attend to here."

Derek let go of me and watched me hug my brothertightly. I whispered to Rhys, "He's lying, I can feel it. Please don't go far. I may need you."

19

Derek reached for my hand and led me toward the back entrance of his family's home. He seemed pleased with my sudden interest in joining him, but I don't believe I had any other choice. This may be the only chance I get for him to open up to me. In addition, knowing the nature of the conversation we were about to have, I know it would only have hurt Rhys to hear it. A few steps later we were at the door, and I could feel my heart racing. As Derek turned the knob and opened the door, I could see Rhys staring at us from the street. He was worried and afraid for me and with good reason, I was walking into the lion's den. I felt like the truth was finally in sight and some battles cannot be fought with fists.

I took quick mental notes as we walked through different hallways and rooms until we arrived at what I can only assume was his bedroom, where we were still hand in hand. I glanced around the room and noticed nothing there appeared to be familiar. He removed my coat and tossed it on a nearby chair before leading me towards the bathroom. I left him standing in the doorway near the vanity while I searched for a washcloth. I don't believe this was his intention, but it would be a nice distraction for both of us. I turned the faucet on and waited for the water to warm. I began soaking the cloth until it was completely saturated and warm to the touch. I reached for him and pulled him fully into the light. I looked upon his face with sadness that brought tears to my eyes. His face which was once so perfect and smooth was badly beaten and broken. This is where the path of hatred and mistrust has brought us, and no one was leaving unscathed.

I rung the washcloth out and began wiping the blood from his face. While the warmth of the cloth was perfect for removing dried blood, it caused a stinging sensation when brushed over his open wounds. He would periodically wince as the cloth passed over those particular spots, and I would do my best to reassure him it was for the best. He didn't say anything to me, but his eyes watched me carefully. There was something he wasn't saying, but the fact that I chose to go with him over Rhys gave him a false sense of security and dominance. On some level, he believed that I trusted him.

I was nearly done with washing off his face when I noticed that there was blood on his shirt and hands. I took his hands one by one and placed them in warm water while my fingers brushed over his battered knuckles. His face was in far worse shape than his hands, but I wanted to help him get cleaned up. I felt at fault for everything that had happened and while I wanted him to believe I was truly sorry; I didn't exactly know how to show that without it coming across as false. I needed him to believe we were on the same side. I didn't trust him, and the feelings were not mutual, but sometimes we all need to wear masks when seeking the truth. I needed to create the illusion of a connection in hopes he would slip up.

I dried his hands and then my attention was drawn to his shirt. The blood on it didn't feel damp anymore, but just the sight of it made me uneasy. I reached out with one hand and touched the blood patches on his shirt and began tracing them with my fingertips. I wasn't sure if these stains were only from his face or if there was an injury I couldn't see because he was still clothed. I looked up at him hoping he understood what I was asking without even saying a word and he did. He reached back with one arm and pulled the shirt over his head groaning as he pushed through his discomfort. I helped pull it the remainder of the way off and dropped it on the floor.

Upon scanning his bare torso, I could see that his one shoulder was badly bruised, but other than a few scrapes iappeared his face took the worst of the beating yet again. I continued to wipe up what I could and when that was done, I moved on to adding butterfly bandages to help closethe tears in his cheek and upper arm. As I placed the last strip, I noticed he was checking me out as well. He began carefully tracing my features and every curve with his eyes and then his fingertips. There was blood on me as well. I just hadn't realized it until he picked up the washcloth and began running it across my cheeks. I wasn't injured but getting so close to Rhys and Derek in their wounded states forced some to transfer onto me. I reached down and begantugging my two shirts apart.

"Here let me help you," he said softly trying not to startle me.

It didn't startle me, but I could feel my gut telling me to run and run fast. The idea of him undressing me physically was almost more than I could bare, but I needed to allow him to or he'd never believe I came with him with good intentions. I nodded and before I knew it my shirt was off and thrown onto the floor. Even on days I was running behind I couldn't have removed a shirt that quickly. I brushed my hair back and realized I was still wearing his shirt from earlier today. It was the icing on the cake and even though I just happened to be wearing it this was exactly what he needed to see. I bit my lower lip out of sheer embarrassment, but when I did it only made him smile.

"I'm terribly sorry about my brother. He's very," I paused, "protective of me."

He leaned in and kissed my cheek, "As am I," he reached under my shirt with one hand and gracefully let his fingertips dance across the rim of my jeans touching my stomach ever so slightly. At first it surprised me. His hand was warm and caused excitement to rush over me much like it did the night of the football game. How could I possibly enjoy his touch? In this moment, I felt like a monster. I closed my eyes and just tried to focus on my breathing. I was nervous and while I still can't remember everything I had to remember, there are two sides to every story. Who's to say his truth wasn't partly true if not entirely? Today was the first time a man has ever told me he loved me, and I didn't know how to react. So, I did what I could to show him I appreciated him even if I wasn't confident that the sentiment was genuine. When opening my eyes again I noticed his were closed and his breathing was calm and shallow. He needed to rest. I leaned in and kissed his cheek before stepping out of the bathroom.

I exited the bathroom quickly to hide the look of disgust and confusion that was rushing over my face. While I enjoyed the sensation of being kissed, kissing him was making my stomach turn. I needed to imagine him as someone else, anyone else, just to get through. I kept walking trying to take in my surroundings and look for anything familiar. There were posters on the walls, trophies on the shelves of his bookcases, and photos of him and the guys. When I glanced towards the windows, I could see something reflecting on the ceiling above his bed. As I walked towards them, I could see they were photographs, but of who? I attempted to lean over to see who they were, but I couldn't bend that way with my side still bothering me.

"Every chance I got I snapped a photo of you and added it to the ceiling."

I didn't even notice he had stepped out of the bathroom and his sudden presence caused me to jump.

"But there are so many?" I said with a fair amount of surprise in my voice.

"I had help," he nodded, and a very large grin appeared on his face.

"Help from whom?" I inquired.

"Friends, classmates, it's not important really."

I scanned the photographs again. Something wasn't right about them. Several were of us together, but several of them seemed random. Like a shot taken from behind as someone was walking or a casual photo from across the room. These could have been staged but being polaroids I'm not sure how. I needed more time.

"Derek, I'm sorry, I still cannot remember everything."

"Baby please, none of this is your fault." He stepped towards me closing the gap between us to only a matter of inches. "Someone attacked you and possibly took something from both of us."

He placed his hand on my belly and our eyes met. This is why he wanted me to remember or possibly why he planted a false memory. He wanted to appear angry, hurt and alone in his suffering. More importantly he didn't want me to believe that there was even a remote chance that my suffering could have been caused by him. I placed my hand on his and while I was confident, I wasn't pregnant, I wasn't ready to take that away from him just yet. At least not until I knew for sure what really happened. I took my other hand, brushed his hair back from his face, and rested it on his neck. There was something about the way he was looking at me. He wasn't hungry for me like that afternoon in the forest, but he clearly yearned for me.

I got up on my tippy toes and kissed those luscious lips of his softly. I could taste the blood from his busted lip but having that moment with him was more important. At first, I don't think he knew how to react. He just was waiting to see what I would do. After everything we've been through and all the times I resisted him, I can understand why he would be a little reluctant. I needed to show him that I understood, and it was alright to tell me everything. I needed him to tell me everything. He was watching every move I made with increasing interest. I placed my hands on his chest gently began pushing him backwards towards his bed. He fell back on the bed letting out a slight giggle when he landed.

He raised one of his eyebrows, "I never thought I'd see that girl again."

"I don't know what you mean."

He grinned. "That afternoon you were so willing. I was relieved you had finally forgiven me." He leaned forward and began kissing my neck. "You had to have known it was me the whole time."

"I really didn't."

"So, you expect me to believe you'd have just given yourself to some random guy?" he scoffed. "Nothing you say would make me believe that. I had to seriously work for it."

"What are you talking about?"

"Come on Izz, do you really think it was easy covering all of this up? I had to call in some serious favors."

He grabbed me and pulled me onto the bed. I knew he was strong, but even injured he still posed quite a threat to me. I knew I was getting closer, but the stakes were getting higher. If he didn't slip up soon, I may already be in too deep to get out.

"What do you mean you covered all of this up?"

"Izz, I had to protect us both and that type of protection doesn't come cheap. The bribes alone cost more than your brother probably earns in a year."

"Why me Derek?" I leaned in close enough to kiss him but didn't just to see what he would do. "I mean, you could have had any lady you wanted."

He rolled over forcing his body on top of mine, restricting my movements. "It's no secret I've been with several women, but you were a challenge. That's how it all started, a bet really. You had morals...principles, if you will, and are exotic," he started taking his hands and running them along my curves and through my hair.

"Wait, what you do mean had?" shock came across in my tone of voice. "I still do."

"If you did, you wouldn't be here," he began kissing me. "Being here only validates your desire for me and your desire to continue breaking the rules."

That stung a bit, but I couldn't let it distract me. His kisses were becoming a bit more forceful now just like at the football game. He was hungry and devouring me was back on the menu. I knew biting him wouldn't end well, but so far, he'd given me nothing to really go off. I wanted to press him for more information, but I couldn't shake this feeling of fear that was once again consuming me.

"Derek, please. I don't think we should."

"Izzy, there's no need to be coy. I've had you before and I will have you again," he started pulling at my jeans trying to get them off. "Now let's get these off of you," he grinned.

I attempted to pull myself away, but when the attempt failed it only drew me closer to him. I could feel my heart begin to race and my eyes started scanning the room for anything that could help me. Coming here was a mistake and I needed to get away. If I gave him another inch, he would have me once more. That couldn't be allowed to happen. I needed to find a way to appease him so he would drop his guard and I could make a break for it.

I began tracing the muscles in his chest with my fingertips in hopes that it would calm us both. His skin was soft like suede and only made me want to touch him more. Aside from his battered shoulder and scrapes, his skin was unspoiled. There were so many things that I wanted to say to him, but I didn't want to spoil the moment. I kissed his chest and drew in a deep breath. I felt his hand slide down my side and began gently massaging my thigh. This moment had the potential to draw me in, but I did what I could to focus. I pulled my one leg up towards him and wrapped it around his hip pulling his lower body towards mine. His guard had fallen and there was my chance.

I brought my knee up hard and fast taking his breath away. He fell to one side of me, opening up my chance to head for the exit. Since I didn't know the layout of the house my best chance would be to locate the back door where we came in earlier. In a fury I rushed to my feet and grabbed my coat before bolting down the hall. I could hear him groaning as he was beginning to recover. Soon he would be mobile, so there wasn't a moment to spare. I made my way through the labyrinth of rooms and halls when finally, the door to my freedom was in sight. A few more steps and I would be there. Help isn't far. I just need to reach the door.

In my panicked state I couldn't slow myself down causing me to crash into it with a loud clanging sound that echoed into the emptiness of the space around me. I gathered myself and reached down to pull the door open, but it wouldn't budge. I tried both handles and nothing happened. I started banging on the glass hoping to be heard. This was the way out I was sure of it. I made my way back to the door with little to no difficulty, but I remember nothing of him locking the door behind us when we entered previously. My adrenaline was rapidly flowing now causing further panic and confusion. When I realized Rhys wasn't coming, I turned to notice that everything around me was silent, but it shouldn't have been. His family home was vast, but I refused to believe he could move about without making any sound. As I continued to scan the room for any sign of him there it was. The keypad on the wall I failed to notice when we entered the home earlier. My heart sunk in my chest. I may not be able to get out without the code. This system was clearly designed not only to keep people out, but to keep them in as well.

While there were several windows in sight there was no way to know if they would have been locked or not also, but I had to try. I leapt myself into action and began checking the ones I could. Unfortunately, I was so focused on the windows I failed to notice he was lurking in a dark nook just shy of the window I was banging on. As he began to speak, I nearly came out of my skin.

"Izzy, baby, what's come over you? I thought we were past all of this," he started walking towards me forcing to step backwards in a panic. "I wouldn't have hurt you."

"You lie," I hissed.

"I have no reason to. You're the one fighting me. I'm solely here defending myself," he held his hands up as if to show he was surrendering.

"Then let me go," I hissed again.

"Now see that's something I can't do until you come to your senses," he stepped in closer. "I can't have you going out and undoing all of my hard work," he pointed to a chair nearby, "Please sit before you hurt yourself."

"No!" I shouted. "You can't have me!"

"I already have, and I will again until I'm satisfied."

"Never again," I spat.

I swerved wide in hopes of avoiding his grasp, but he was too quick for me and before I knew it, I was grappled and slung over his shoulder flailing like a small child throwing a temper tantrum.

"Put me down! Someone please help me!" I cried out.

He squeezed me tighter as a suggestion, but I couldn't stop myself. Someone would hear me. They had to, they just had to. He may have me restrained, but I wasn't going to go quietly. I continued to scream and flail about doing any damage I could along the way. When my attempt to injure him failed I began my work on his family home. If there was a photo framed on the wall, I was knocking it down. If there was a window within reach, I was going to try and break it. I may have given in before, but I'd rather die than let him win again.

I felt my body growing tired and I knew I wouldn't be able to hold out much longer, but I had to keep trying. Every fiber of my being was pushed into being heard, but no one came to my call. I was beyond terrified and as we reached his bedroom once more, I knew my chance of escaping was rapidly dissolving. He dropped me onto his bed suddenly and in my exhausted state crawling seemed to be my only option. He quickly saw through my plan and restrained me once more. This time, however, he made sure to keep me face down, so there would be no more cheap shots to his manhood. Unfortunately, this took away my ability to see what he was really planning to do and that only heightened my fear and anxiety.

"Derek, please. Please, don't do this. This isn't you," I pleaded with him. "I could be carrying your child," I wanted to gag as the words crossed over my lips.

He quickly grabbed me and flipped me onto my back before crawling on top of me once more.

"Izzy, there is no baby at least not that I know of, but I must admit it helped convince you to come inside with me," he flashed a diabolical grin, "The look on your brother's face when he not only knew I defiled you over and over again, but knocked you up as well was worth it."

I couldn't hide the surprise I felt as the truth came out. He seemed pleased at my reaction. There was a part of him that knew I was starting to believe it all. This was all part of his plan to get me inside once more. As long as I went willingly, he was covered just like that afternoon in the forest. Coercion is difficult to prove and even with Rhys witnessing the conversation that occurred outside that wouldn't be enough to prove malicious intent and Derek knew it. He has done his homework and was continually working two steps ahead of me. His body was pressed against mine once more as a form of restraint, but he had no intention of just letting me lie with him. He was beyond that now.

I didn't know what was left to do or say at this very moment. I knew I was trapped and despite my efforts to attract attention to the matter all had fallen on deaf ears. Out ofsheer exhaustion I could feel myself fading from the light, but my mind wasn't ready to give up just yet. I needed to keep him talking as a distraction.

"Have there been others?" I whispered.

"What does it matter?" he uttered.

"I would hate to think all of this attention and time spent plotting was all for my benefit."

"No, most can't wait for the moment when I take them to bed, but not you," he began kissing me once more. "You would rather watch the city burn to the ground before giving yourself to me."

Keep him busy I thought. Keep him interested.

"So, you seek fire?"

He grinned, "Yes."

"Then fire you shall have."

My eyes narrowed and a diabolical grin to match his own appeared on my face. I refused to go quietly into the night as a vessel for his depraved intentions. I brought my face towards him and without so much as an awkward glance I turned and bit his neck as hard as I could. If I would have been able to rip his flesh, I would have. In a panicked response he let go of one of my arms and I repeatedly began smashing my fist against the other side of his neck and shoulder. He tore himself away briefly in what I can only assume was shock before returning to kiss me. I rejected his advances and bit his lip as my counteroffer.

When I finally released his lower lip from my teeth, I felt something cold and hard against the side of my face. It happened so quickly that I hadn't even noticed he had drawn his hand back and was bringing it towards me. The momentum from the impact caused my face to turn quickly forcing a sharp pain to run down the side of my neck. The blood that had pooled in my mouth from his lip and neck shot out of me spraying the bedding and headboard. I refused to go quietly and began to scream again. He struck me again and this time with enough force my ear began to ring. I was becoming disoriented, and, in his rage, he tore the shirt from my body. I tried to push him away from me but was unsuccessful. It only ended in more pain.

I attempted to holler for help once more but was met with resistance when I tried. I once again found myself at his mercy and after struggling for several minutes I knew I couldn't best him. He knew it too. He dealt one final blow to my ribs causing me to gasp for air. I needed to breathe to stay alive, and he knew that pain would be more than enough to hold my attention. He began removing my sneakers and soon my jeans would be next. There was nothing more that I could do.

"Izzy, I do love you, but you should have just given yourself to me," he paused, "I'm a man that has and always will have what he wants. I've decided I want you."

I began kicking my legs about as my arms clung to my sides. Anything to protect what I could. He grew tired of the struggle and grabbed my ankles one by one restraining them until the pressure became too great and I conceded in defeat. My legs fell lifeless on the bed and I had become his personal rag doll. It wasn't long before he had my jeans undone and nearly off when he leaned in and began whispering to me.

"Now, try to behave yourself. I plan on having you as much as I want tonight with no interruptions."

I wanted to say something to him in return, but by the time the words came into focus in my mind I heard a thud and Derek fell lifeless on top of me. Unfortunately, collapsing on top of me like that forced me to stay frozen in place and I wasn't sure whether friend or foe had found me. Then I heard Rhys's voice.

"Izz, I'm sorry it took me so long, but I'm here now."

I couldn't particularly focus on his image, but I could hear him. Derek's weight began to shift, and I started to panic once more. Thankfully, Derek wasn't shifting his weight, Rhys was in an attempt to get him off of me.

"Let's get you out of here."

As I attempted to sit up, but we both became very aware that I was naked at this point. As uncomfortable as it was, I knew Rhys wasn't even remotely looking at me in that way. To him this house was on fire and getting me out was the only thing that mattered.

"Oh Izz. I'm sorry. Umm, here let me cover you with this."

He stripped off his jacket and quickly wrapped me in it. It was warm and soft taking the edge off my chilled skin. I attempted to stand, but quickly collapsed. Rhys wasted no time picking me up and carrying me to the nearest exit. Where we ran into the same problem as I did earlier. They were all locked. I'm not sure how he got in, but clearly it must not have been an option to get us back out or he would have used it. I wasn't sure what we were going to do, but Rhys true to form took initiative. He gently set me down in a nearby armchair and went to work on finding a way out. Seconds felt like hours as time pressed on and even though I wasn't myself I knew we were on borrowed time. We need to get out of here.

20

I'm not sure how we escaped, but I awoke to the sensation of Rhys running. He was breathing hard and moving quickly. I couldn't tell if we were being chased or if he was just fighting against time. The truck couldn't be far, and I longed to be protected inside its walls. A few quick steps later we were there, and I was placed inside before Rhys climbed in and started the engine. He placed his hand upon my shoulder as I lay beside him and quickly pulled away. Neither one of us said a word, but I could hear him struggle to hold back the tears. I don't know what he saw or how much he heard that day, but something in that house changed him.

He continued to drive on, but the destination eluded me. I took a chance in the hopes of discovering the truth and I may have just broken what good was left in me. I did my best to just close my eyes and rest, but every bump or shift in the road caused me to flinch. I may never be able to rest again, but somehow knowing Rhys was with me gave me hope. He was the good I needed to see in the world, and he may never be able to make this go away, but he would do what he could to make it right.

It was as if I blinked again, and the truck came to a screeching halt. Wherever he was headed, we had arrived. He didn't say a word before opening the truck door and pulling me out towards him. After being in a warm truck the cool crisp air outside of it raked across my bare skin like I was being drug through rose bushes. I grasped him as hard as I could. He crossed the threshold, and the bright lights nearly blinded me. We were back at the hospital.

We cleared the double doors and he shouted for help. He didn't have to try for long before several people came and took me away. Rhys followed quickly behind as they began to flood him with questions. He started to answer them, but something stopped him. As they were attempting to uncover me, he just turned and looked away saying nothing more. Part of me believed he was respecting my privacy as best as he could, and the other partbelieved he couldn't handle seeing what was left of me. I could see him vaguely in the distance and his eyes were covered shielding him from the light with the other outstretched. I couldn't make out what he was saying, but he appeared to be pointing towards something or someone as a random person appeared before my field of vision.

"You're safe now."

I remember trying to respond, but whether or not the words were audible I cannot remember. Over the next several minutes and maybe even hours I only saw bits and pieces of the world around me. I was moved to an interior room where the curtains were drawn, and the lights dimmed. At times there was someone sitting in the darkness near me, but who they were I do not know. There was no sound other than that of a monitor or two. No one spoke and I did not speak either. At least not until sometime later.

Waking up once again in a hospital should never become anyone's norm, but I'm finding it comforting. I'm protected here. Even my own home didn't give me a feeling of protection anymore. I began scanning the room for anything that would have been familiar to me, but there wasn't anything other than a chill in the air. This one wasn't from an ajar window or door more from the room in general, but I could be particularly sensitive to temperature since I was only wearing a gown. I pushed the call button not sure what to expect from the other side. There was no answer. Something's wrong. Someone always answers.

There was an all too familiar knock at the door before it swung open revealing my visitor. It took a moment to focus on the figure before me, but when they spoke, I knew the voice all too well. It was Jean.

"Hello darling, how are you feeling?"

She smiled as she walked closer to me. I didn't move nor did I say anything to her which wasn't like me. As she reached my bedside, she reached out towards me, and I flinched. I'm not even sure why. I don't believe she was there to harm me, but I couldn't help my reaction.

"I'm cold," I croaked.

What was that? My voice sounded weak and raspy. Almost like what you would expect a smoker of thirty years to sound like. Not at all like what I used to sound like. I cleared my throat and tried again.

"I'm cold."

"I'll bring you a warm blanket." She turned to walk towards the door and then stopped. "You're safe here. He won't be allowed in as long as I'm here."

Then she stepped out before I could respond. I wanted to thank her for not only remembering me, but for being kind to me. I know she isn't in an easy position and my reaction probably didn't help her. It was only a few moments before she returned with a large blanket in tow. I noticed this time she didn't close the door behind her however and I wasn't sure what to make of it. I could see a man in uniform standing just outside the door and I presumed he was either a security guard or one of Officer Chaney's henchmen. I was indifferent to his presence, but the door ajar concerned me. Anyone could be lurking around the corner, and I wouldn't see them coming.

"The door," I whispered.

Her attention was drawn to my face, but not towards the door. As she looked intently upon me my eyes never faltered from the door finally forcing her to look upon the door. She turned briefly towards the door and then back to me while she covered me with the warm blanket.

"What about the door?" she said softly.

"It's open," I mumbled.

"You're alright now."

I quickly turned my attention towards her and grasped her wrist by chance.

"Please don't leave me alone in here."

She carefully placed her hand upon mine, "You're never alone here. We have a good team of people here to help you," she smiled, "Maybe even a few familiar faces as well."

I knew she was being coy, but the second the thought crossed my mind a smile was brought to my face. Tyler. The surprise I never saw coming. When I hear his voice and see his face it makes my heart leap with excitement. Then I remembered, we were supposed to meet in the morning. That is if morning hadn't already passed me by. I was afraid to ask for him directly, so all I did was give a brief smile. Thoughts of our last encounter warmed my cold heart and left me distracted if only for a few moments.

By the time I snapped out my trace I noticed Jean had vanished and I was alone once more. I lay there cowering in the bed trying to shield myself from the outside world when I heard a noise in the hall. The sudden noise startled me and caused me to jerk under the mass of blankets that now covered me. The noise didn't appear to be from someone attempted to enter or cause trouble, but more than likely a general sound from the looming worker bees. Every sound caused me to nearly climb out of my very own skin. I felt crippled by my inability to cope with the basic sounds around me and I knew I needed some help. I pushed the call button once more.

"May I help you?" A voice called out through the intercom.

I didn't know what to say. I knew I needed help, but I didn't know what exactly I should or shouldn't be asking for either. I couldn't possibly expect them to cease all noise in the facility, could I? I must have stayed silent too long as I heard the intercom click off. I hovered my finger over the button once more but was unsure whether or not to press it again. I attempted to click the button once more, but once again all was silent. The door opened without warning and there stood a male figure in the dim light. In my skittish state, I could feel fear beginning to crawl all over me and soon I would need to run. I told myself to remain calm, but my body refused to heed my advice as I began to spider climb up the bed. The figure stepped forward and I could not hide my fear anymore.

"Someone help me please!!" I cried out as I braced myself against the side rail.

The figure was moving quickly now. I closed my eyes as tears began to rush down my face. I wanted to cry out again, but I couldn't. Frozen in fear I clung to the railing and began to pray for someone to please come and save me. The man sat down on the bed beside me, and I gripped the railing tightly. His warm hand grazed my cheek brushing the tears back. My eyes were clenched shut tighter than a drum and I refused to open them. He was moving in closer and closer when I heard it. Ever so faintly the first time, but louder and distinct the second time. He wasn't shouting at me, but more trying to break through the wall that was there to get to me.

"Izz, it's me." I could feel his arms trying to wrap around me pulling me towards him. "I'm not here to hurt you."

At first, I thought my mind was playing tricks on me, but as my eyelids began to part and my vision focusing, I could see his face. Tyler had found me just like he said he would and, although, I was skittish moments before seeing his face relaxed me considerably. I didn't know what to say, but I realized it didn't matter. We didn't need words to be exchanged in order to grasp what the other one was feeling. I wrapped my arms around him and rested my head on his shoulder. Tears were falling from my eyes, but they were not out of fear anymore. We sat there for several moments locked in an embrace like two long lost friends being reunited after years of separation. I missed him terribly.

"Izz, are you alright?" he whispered. "I've been so worried about you." He paused briefly and kissed my cheek. "When I found out you were brought in, I was beside myself."

"I've missed you," I whispered.

"I've missed you also. I didn't realize how much until just now."

He relaxed his grip as did I and I laid myself back down slowly. What happened may have only taken a minute or two, but my reaction took every bit of the energy I had restored. Feeling depleted I lay there just looking upon his face wondering how I ever survived without him. He was the support I never saw coming and a kind-hearted soul to help bring me back to the light. Our hands found each other's and as we sat there, hand in hand, I saw his face fade from the light. He was deeply saddened by something, and it troubled me to see him like that.

"What's wrong?" I whispered.

He cleared his throat and turned away from me. He was breathing deeply, but he did not appear to be in distress. I gave his hand a gentle squeeze to let him know I was still there.

"What is it?" I insisted.

"I was told about what happened when they brought you back to this unit, but no words could have described what I'm seeing now," he turned towards me, "Why would you risk your life like that?"

"I just wanted answers. I never meant for it to go that far," I hung my head, "I was baited into a trap and both Rhys and I fell for it."

"What trap?" he said looking quite perplexed.

"There were photos of us together and Derek said I was pregnant in front of Rhys. The whole thing was just a mess. I thought if there was any validity to his side of the story maybe I really am mental and fabricated it all, but if it was all fictitious then I had to know. I felt I needed to do something since the police have nothing, but I made a mistake."

I could feel my face grimace and my body tighten in anticipation of his response. I was embarrassed by my actions, and I was terrified he would turn away from me justwhen I needed him the most. As much as it pained me, I had to look at him. I looked upon his face not knowing what I would find, but there was compassion in his eyes.

"Do you think I'm a fool?" I whispered.

"No," he responded. "I think you want to see the good in humanity, but it has let you down." He bit his lip once more and I remembered how much I adored that. "Just know that I never will."

Without missing a beat our bodies were pulled together like magnets and his lips found mine. His kiss gave me butterflies and I longed for more of his touch. He was incredibly gentle with me partially I'm sure since we both knew I was in fact breakable, but partially because I believe that was his nature. He was a man of simple pleasures and the act of kissing me softly or running his fingers through my long hair seemed to be enough. I've never experienced anything like him, and something told me there may never be another one like him to cross my path. I had to walk through fire to get here and while I can't say I would do it all again I can say he was worth it. I knew we couldn't remain as we were, but we tried to hold onto it if we could. Unfortunately, we were brought back to reality too soon when there was a knock at the door. We parted quickly as a means of protecting each other, but Tyler didn't venture far. We were both on edge and while I knew I was more protected here than anywhere that didn't mean that everyone was on my side. Thankfully, it was Jean who opened the door. She smiled as she entered the room and politely closed the door behind her.

"I see you two found one another."

"Yes, we did. Thank you, Jean," Tyler said politely.

Jean leaned around the bed rail to turn on some additional lighting. "I need to run through a few items with Ms. Walsh. Care to assist?"

Tyler glanced down at me as if seeking my approval to do so. We crossed a line and now our relationship wasn't just professional. He was a student and a member of my care team, but I could feel myself falling for him. I nodded. I wasn't overly comfortable with him examining me, but I wasn't uncomfortable either. I think I was more beside myself at the fact he was seeing me at my most vulnerable state than anything else.

Since I had not been awake long, I hadn't fully taken in how I was feeling or what state I was found in. The pain was minimal, but as they began changing dressings, I realized there was more to this ordeal than I initially thought. I continued to listen intently trying to pick up anything that sounded familiar. Contusion and tear seem to be the favored terms, but there were others. I hadn't noticed the tenderness in my cheek and jawline until they were attempting to remove the dressing.

"Darling, are you alright?"

I grimaced, "I think so. I just hadn't noticed the pain much before now."

"It's about time for another dose of pain meds. When we are finished, I will go and fetch those for you."

I nodded, "I'd appreciate that. Is there anything I can have to help me sleep?" I smiled awkwardly. "Every little noise in here just…bothers me I guess."

"I understand."

She turned back to Tyler and was about to continue with the examination when I interjected once more.

"I'd like to see my brother, Rhys, if that's possible. There's something I need to tell him."

"Unfortunately, we been instructed to not let you have any visitors until the doctor and Officer Chaney have spoken to you."

There was something about the way she said it like there was another shoe that hadn't dropped yet. I may have been out of sorts and exhausted, but something told me something was rotten in Denmark. I just needed to find out what that something was.

"What's going on?" I asked.

I turned towards Jean and focused heavily on her face. She wouldn't look at me. She didn't seem like the type to follow orders without question, and I could tell she knew something. I know there are rules against the nursing staff telling a patient too much about their condition or about someone else's, but I deserved to know something.

"Where's Rhys?" My tone was becoming more insistent.

Jean looked up at me and then to Tyler when I heard her whisper, "She doesn't know."

"What don't I know?" My eyes began to dart back and forth between them. "Please someone tell me what is going on?"

Jean quickly pushed the call button, and a voicecame over the intercom.

"May I help you?"

"Karen, it's Jean. Can you page Dr. Jordan and Officer Chaney? Ms. Walsh is alert and awake."

"I will do that now," the voice responded.

"Will someone please tell me what is going on? I want to see my brother. Now!" I demanded.

"Darling, I need you to take a breath." Jean tried to sound calm and reassuring, but all it was doing was irritating me.

I needed to get out of here and fast. Something was terribly wrong, and I could feel it. My pulse was beginning to race, and my breathing quickened. Panic would soon set in. Making a break for it seemed like my only option. If he was here, I would find him. I just had to. I pulled the blankets back exposing my bare legs. In seconds I felt a chill come over me and a desire to stay hidden came over me. I needed to push through that feeling and force myself up. I swung my legs quickly to one side and white knuckled the railing. I was going to stand with or without their help. As the adrenaline raced through my body, I took one quick breath and pulled myself up. However, I didn't account for Jean or Tyler's reaction to my defiant behavior.

Just as I stood, I felt Jean's arm grasp the back of my gown, "Darling, you're not well enough. Please lie back down."

Not knowing Tyler that well I figured his actions would mirror hers, but I couldn't have been more wrong. He wrapped his arms around me and pulled me in close.

"Ty, please tell me he's alright."

I placed my hands upon his waist and tugged at his shirt. I wasn't trying to remove his shirt I just needed to grab something without hurting myself or someone else. I could feel myself start to cry. I don't even know what I was crying about. I was so overcome with emotion it has nowhere to go, but out my eyes. He leaned down and brushed my hair back away from my forehead.

"I need you to breathe with me," he whispered.

"Tyler, please help Ms. Walsh back to bed," Jean insisted.

"I don't think I can," he uttered.

"Tyler, look at me," her tone hardened, "if you cannot separate your personal feelings for Ms. Walsh from the requirements of your position you will need to remove yourself from her care team."

I couldn't see what she was doing, but I could feel her reach out and touch him.

"I say this for your protection and hers. It's not safe," she uttered just above a whisper.

He inhaled and exhaled slowly trying to sync our breathing. As I felt his chest rise and fall, I felt my own start to mimic his. He was warm to the touch and his arms being tightly wrapped around me took the chill from my skin. My once panicked heart was beginning to slow itself down and I could feel myself growing weaker. The adrenaline was leaving my body and taking with it most of my worries. Replacing the adrenaline was its ugly cousin exhaustion and I was a slave to its will. I felt my body relax in Tyler's arms where he continued to hold me close.

21

I must have passed out briefly for when I opened my eyes, I found Officer Chaney concentrating all of his energy on Tyler and I. I could feel Tyler tense up slightly and I knew how suspicious this must look. I'm not sure whether it bothered him because of how it looked or what it really was. Regardless, Officer Chaney seemed very interested in how he found us. Jean must have, also, noticed this and quickly tried to divert attention from us.

"Officer Chaney, it's good to see you. Ms. Walsh has been having a difficult night-"

He cut her off, "Oh, I'm not so sure about that. She appears to be quite comfortable to me."

He took a few steps closer to us and his energy was already suffocating me. I relaxed my arms and slowly reached behind me to feel for the bed. I needed to sit down and let Tyler and Jean take their leave. There was no way for me to know what Officer Chaney would have to say, but something told me they weren't to be a part of it. I watched him watch me as Tyler and Jean helped me back into bed. When they were finished, they both turned to vacate the room but were met with resistance. I was not sure why at the time, but unfortunately Officer Chaney's methods are not always apparent.

"I suggest the two of you remain here," he glanced at Jean briefly then focused hard on Tyler. "I've noticed the two of you have grown quite close."

He turned and stepped even closer to me stopping within inches of my bedside. While he entered the room arrogant as usual something is different this time. He looked upon Jean and Tyler with suspicion, but when he arrived at my side exhaustion is what I saw.

"Ms. Walsh, do you remember what happened yesterday?"

"I think so."

"Can you please tell me about it?"

"Alright, where would you like me to start?"

"From the time I left your house until when you woke up here."

He pulled up a chair and sat next to me as I walked him through the tragic events that led to my readmission. By the time I was through Jean couldn't even look at me, but her tear-stained face will resonate throughout my mind forever. Tyler was pacing in the room with his face hidden from my sight. I do not believe weeping was in his nature, but the tale I told would be hard for anyone to shake off. I may never be able to separate myself from it and this would always be what brought the two of us together. When there was nothing more to say I just stopped and stared at Officer Chaney. I was hoping to see a sign of recognition, but there was nothing. He had made some notes during the tale, but for the most part just observed me. I couldn't presume to know what he did or didn't know, but up until now he has always been at least one step ahead of me.

"Officer Chaney, where's my brother?" I sat up and leaned towards him. "I've given you what you've asked for, now please let me see my brother."

He leaned forward in the chair resting his elbows on his knees. "Ms. Walsh, shortly after you were brought in, your brother was asked to remove his vehicle from the ambulance bay. He was happy to do so of course, but unfortunately during that time there was an incident."

I looked back at Tyler and found his hands were folded just in front of his mouth. Whatever Officer Chaney was struggling to say Tyler already knew it wasn't good news.

"Officer Chaney, where is my brother?" I pressed him.

"Ms. Walsh, the information I'm about to tell you will be difficult to comprehend and accept in your current state, but against the advice of your healthcare team I've decided to divulge that information to you now while you are in a controlled environment rather than withhold it."

I felt a knot form in my throat, and I could barely breathe. My eyes were beginning to well up with tears and I felt like my heart had just stopped.

"When Rhys exited the building, he was gone for several minutes prompting a member of security to check on him. Unfortunately, it appears he was ambushed in the parking lot causing the delay."

"No, that can't be, by whom?" my voice was barely above a whisper.

"We can only assume that Derek was trying to get to you when he encountered Rhys in the parking lot." He leaned towards me and touched my hand. "Rhys was stabbed multiple times and left for dead."

I couldn't believe what I was hearing, and I was afraid to ask about the elephant in the room. Not because I couldn't, but because I don't think I could handle the answer, but I needed to try.

"Is he—" I started to say it.

"He's still with us, but the surgeons are working tirelessly to repair the damage. I don't know much more than that."

"And Derek?" I mumbled.

"We haven't been able to locate him, but we have footage proving it was him. We will have an officer stationed outside of your door at all times until he is found," he gave my hand a gentle squeeze. "I'm sorry it had to come to this."

I physically felt like I couldn't breathe. Like the air was there, but I was no longer able to take it in. The news hit me like a brick, and I was crippled from the blow. At that moment, I would have given anything to trade places with him. It should have been me, Derek wanted me, and Rhys was just the collateral damage, the splinter that became lodged under his fingernail. He knew this would draw me out. The initial pain that found its way to the pit of my stomach was turning into rage.

"You don't get to say you're sorry to me," I growled, "you knew he was dangerous! Now Rhys may die, and you still don't have the man responsible!" I shouted.

I forced myself to stand quicker than expected causing Officer Chaney to jerk back suddenly.

He stood quickly and placed his hands on my shoulders. "Ms. Walsh, we are and have been doingall we could. We will find him," he said firmly trying to sound confident.

I pulled my arms up causing his arms to fall off me.

"Just get away from me," I started to cry. "Get away from me now!" I shouted with every fiber of my being. "This is all your fault!"

I hadn't noticed Tyler or Jean in some time, but it wasn't long before Tyler stepped between us. Jean was trying to usher Officer Chaney out of the room as I continued to scream at him. The words came at him like a barrage of missiles aimed with intent to kill. I tried to hit him with my hands, but he was just out of reach. In my frustration I hadn't realized Tyler was now behind me attempting to restrain me from hurting myself or Officer Chaney. On any other day I wouldn't consider myself a violent person, but I was no longer myself. The anger and fear had consumed me at least for the moment.

I heard the door slam behind them and once again I was alone with Tyler. I started to calm down and I could feel his arms relax. He slowly lowered us both towards the floor where I fell into his arms and wept uncontrollably.

"This can't be happening, Ty, I can't lose him, I just can't," I mumbled through the tears.

"Hush now," he kissed my forehead. "We have to believe he will make it through. He's strong like you and look at all you've survived." He pulled me even closer to him and took deep breaths. Anything to calm me and bring me back to him. "I'd give anything to trade places with him. I know what he means to you."

I rose to my knees and wrapped my arms around his neck hugging him as much as my body would allow.

I whispered, "But you mean something to me also and I don't want to lose you either."

I turned slightly and kissed his cheek. The tears were still falling, but not as rapidly now. I could feel the dampness already in his shirt and all along his cheek. I needed to try and pull myself together. I wasn't sure how, but I knew I needed to try. He rose to his knees almost as if he was prepping to lift me up, but he didn't move anything further. Baby steps now. My heart felt broken to match my broken body, but his kindness never faltered. I tried to slow down the tears and breathe with him. Inhale. Exhale. Inhale. Exhale. The fire that had grown inside me was dying, but my love for him was growing with every moment we were together. I didn't know when our next chance to be alone together would come, so I had to take the moments as they came. It wasn't perfect, nor would it probably ever be, but I wanted to have that moment with him. So, I did. I laid kisses across his cheek until my lips found his. He didn't care that I was battered and broken or that my face was tear stained. He cared for me, and those kisses were my candle when all other lights had gone out.

It wasn't long before I knew our moment had passed and my attention was once again drawn back to the chaos. I broke off our kiss and turned my attention back towards the door. I didn't want to leave him, but I needed to try and see Rhys. I reached up and wiped the tears from my cheeks before turning back towards him.

"Do you think I'd be able to see him?" I whispered. "Just for a moment."

"I don't know Izz. We can try, but the most they may allow would be through a viewing window."

"Can we at least try? Please, there's something I need to…I just need to see him if I can."

"Alright, let's go."

He stood quickly taking me with him. In truth, it was probably for the best as I wasn't the fastest mover these days. He helped me gently sit down as he reached behind me pushing my call button. I didn't want to face Officer Chaney again anytime soon, but I refused to stay in this hostage situation any longer than necessary. However, this time I was greeted by an unfamiliar face. Tyler seemed to recognize the intruder, but I failed to catch the name as it was spoken.

"My apologies, who did you say you were?"

"I'm Dr. Prescott, if you're ready I have a few items I'd like to go over with you."

"I actually would like to see my brother if you please. I may not get another chance."

"Ms. Walsh, your brother is still in surgery. Once he is out and in recovery that is the soonest you may be able to see him. I'm sorry."

I glanced at Tyler and then back to Dr. Prescott. "Isn't there some way I can be with him?"

"I'm sorry again. That's just not possible right now," he turned towards Tyler, "If you would excuse us Tyler, there are a few items I need to go over with Ms. Walsh."

He nodded and headed towards the door as Dr. Prescott stepped towards me.

"If either of you need anything please just give us a call," Tyler said just before exiting the room closing the door behind him.

"First of all, Ms. Walsh, how are you feeling?"

"I'm not sure how to answer that. I'm just trying to survive at this point."

"That's understandable. How's your pain?"

"Tolerable. Can I ask you something?"

"Of course."

"Does it say anywhere in my chart that I'm pregnant or that I might have been?" I couldn't bear to look at him, so I turned to face the wall towards my right.

"No, you're not pregnant," I held my breath for a few moments more. "Nor were you ever pregnant from what we can see."

I let out a huge sigh of relief. I don't know how much of me really believed it was ever true, but the fact that the truth is out there greatly comforts me.

"Are you alright, Ms. Walsh?"

"Based on everything you've seen and what you've read in my chart, do you believe this could all be a dream? Like I'm delusional or something?"

"No, I don't believe so. Everything that has happened to you is as real as I'm standing here."

"Is it normal to feel this way?"

"Everyone responds to trauma in a different way. This is just your mind's way of processing everything. It will take time for your mind to catch up with your body, but you will heal."

"I think I understand. Is there something else you wanted to discuss?" I looked back towards him.

"Yes, the results from the exam that was performed by Dr. Jordan last week have come in and I've already informed Officer Chaney. As you've already asked, you are not pregnant, nor did you contract any sexually transmitteddiseases during either of those encounters. Considering you've only had one partner there is a good chance that theevents from earlier today will not change those results."

"Forgive me but did you say only one partner?"

"Yes, that's correct. I cannot confirm if any of your other injuries were caused by multiple assailants, but sexually there was only evidence of one male. Both you and Mr. Strom have already confirmed he was that male and laboratory testing reinforces those testimonies."

I sighed in relief. This was the first bout of good news I'd heard in ages.

"In addition, I wanted to let you know that all your blood work has come back relatively normal and while you've had some new injuries, your fractured ribs from last week are healing nicely. I know it doesn't seem exciting, but thisis good news."

"I suppose so. When will I get to go home?"

"We would like to keep you for observation at least for 24 hours. However, with your brother currently in critical condition and Mr. Strom still unaccounted for, this may be the safest place for you."

"I'm not safe anywhere to be honest. At least, I haven't felt that way in weeks."

He stepped closer and placed his hand on my shoulder. "Just try and get some rest. We will do what we can to get you home as quickly as possible."

I nodded. The nod only confirmed my understanding not that I believed him. Believing anyone was difficult for me these days. Derek was the mayor's son and part of a respectable house or so I thought. He couldn't have pulled off a cover up this large without assistance and if his father knew but did nothing there wouldn't be much out of his grasp. Not to mention there was no way for me to know who was on his payroll. Another reason why I was reluctant to come forward since I would be attacking one of the wealthiest and most respectable families in Warwick as an outsider. I could wait no longer. Derek would find me, and I had no intention of sitting around waiting for that moment.

"Can someone please let me know when my brother is out of surgery? There is something I need to tell him."

"Of course," he smiled and then turned to exit the room. "Is there anything else I can do for you?"

"Not unless you can change the past," I smirked.

He smiled politely and exited the room. I felt like I should have asked more questions or been more concerned for my well-being, but I wasn't. I laid back in the bed and did what I could to get some rest, but once again every little sound seemed to set my teeth on edge. I was in a constant state of unrest and unable to heal. I couldn't shake the feeling that I was putting Rhys in danger by staying here. Granted there is security here, but Derek couldn't get to me last night and it didn't stop him from attempting to take my brother's life. It wouldn't be long before he tried again.

I struggled to get some rest and after about an hour I reached my limit. I wanted Tyler to come and lay with me as he did once before, but I didn't know how to ask for something like that. Being forward was never my strong suit unless it was winning a debate in class and this type of request was the furthest from that I could think of. I felt safe with him and in this dimly lit room I felt very cold and alone despite what might have been looming just on the other side of the door. A voice came dangerously close to the door, and I couldn't take it anymore.

I removed the leads attached to me followed by my blood pressure cuff and some other random wires before moving to the side of the bed. This time was significantly worse than the last time and I knew my pain meds must be wearing off. I couldn't let that slow me down. I stood quickly and soon felt a crippling pain in my side causing me to nearly double over. I was in agony, but I needed to keep going. I quickly began tugging at my IV trying to break myself free without tearing it from my flesh in the process, but my efforts were to no avail. So, I was left with a choice: take a seat or add to the pain in order to reach the bag. I wasn't a quitter, and I knew what I needed to do. Quickly taking a deep breath I reached for it. Unfortunately, I was not able to flip it off the hook, but the sheer weight of me pulling on it tore the loop that held it up. I was relieved.

I pulled the bag towards my chest and began to shuffle my way towards the bathroom door. I hadn't realized how warm I was under those covers until they had all fallen off me leaving the room's chill to scrape across myskin. I understand that part of why hospitals keep the temperature like they do is for the benefit of the staff and to slow the progression of germs, but for those of us recovering while only wearing a thin gown are frigid.

Thankfully, the bathroom was only a few more steps away. While lying in bed, the door never seemed that far away, but now that I'm walking hunched over and clasping my side, it seemed miles away. Each step gave me little satisfaction, but something told me in there I was safer than being out here.

I took my final step and slid into the door holding the handle for support. Seemed like any attempt at a real action caused me crippling pain and exhaustion. There were moments as I shuffled across the floor that I felt I was barely breathing. Drowning, but I still found breath within me. I hung onto the door for only a few moments when the chill provoked a response, and I pulled the door open. It didn't take me long to round the door closing it behind me. The walls were colder than I imagined, but it was much quieter inside. I leaned against the wall for support and turned the shower on. I was grasping for anything that would warm the small space up and drown out any potential noise coming from the hall.

It didn't take long to warm up and I was relieved at the peace I found from just the noise of running water. As the room began to fill with steam, I stepped towards the sink hoping to catch a glimpse of myself in the mirror. Part of me was afraid to take a glance, but I just had to know whatthe world was looking at. I placed my hands down on the sides of the sink and leaned in. Every fiber of my being knew I was looking at myself, but at the same time it wasn't me. I could see the breaks in the skin, swelling around my left eye and the bruising along my cheek and jaw. Nothing about this lady looked like me, but sometimes denial is the only comfort we have.

I climbed in the shower using the handrails for support and lowered myself onto the shower floor. The water burned my skin forcing pins and needles to dance across it. Once the pain subsided the warmth of the water actually soothed my skin, but the sensation brought back unwelcome memories of that first time. I now knew that those memories may never fade, but I would have to learn to suppress them if I was ever to move forward or forever be consumed by them. With that thought in mind, I leaned against the shower wall and quickly fell asleep in the warmth of the waterfall.

22

My eyes fluttered awake to find I was still in the shower and there was loud banging on the door that was starting to make my head hurt. Thankfully, the water temperature hadn't failed me, or I'd have been bordering onhypothermia by now.

"Ms. Walsh, it's Dr. Prescott! I'm coming in now!"

The banging stopped and the door swung open with a violent shove. At least I wasn't standing in its wake, or I'd have more than a bruised face and broken ribs to talk about.

"Quickly now, we must get the water turned off!"

I felt the water shut off cutting off my reliable heating source. In addition, by opening the door a flood of cold air rushed in and clung to my already soaked gown causing my body temperature to drop. I couldn't have been in here long, but the way the nurse and Dr. Prescott were moving about you'd think I was there for days. Unfortunately, since this was a bathroom there was no window or clock for me to tell the time. Any guess would have been more than likely incorrect.

"Ms. Walsh, what have you done?"

"I couldn't sleep, and I was cold…so I came in here," I mumbled.

"Dr. Prescott, there's blood everywhere and I'm not sure where it's coming from." The nurse uttered.

"Let's get her up and out of that gown."

I pushed the nurse away in protest. I didn't know what she was referring to, but the idea that they were just going to undress me like that appalled me. I prayed I misheard him.

"Ms. Walsh, I'm not trying to hurt you, but you're bleeding. Please let us help you." The nurse spoke in a quiet tone. I wasn't sure if she was trying to be unheard or if that was just her manner, but I appreciated her kindness.

I nodded and slid forward as they both attempted to help me up. Dr. Prescott's bedside manner had dramatically changed from before, but he was young and I'm sure he would get better over time. As I stood the water rushed down my skin as if it was falling from a waterfall, running smooth and fast across my skin, but then crashing on part of my creased gown. As the droplets struck the white shower floor, I could see the once crimson drops now a valentine red glaring back at me. I was still bleeding, but from where?

The nurse quickly grabbed some towels and a fresh gown before dismissing Dr. Prescott from the room. While he may have been my doctor, he was a young man no less and seeing my body without my consent I would not approve of. She handed me a towel for me to attempt to cover myself before she began stripping the saturated gown off of me. I wasn't comfortable with being undressed by a woman I didn't know, but I didn't appear to have much of a say in the matter. It didn't take her long to find the source

of the bleed and I was relieved it was only my IV. I must
have pulled it out while I was sleeping.

"I'm terribly sorry…. I didn't mean to," I mumbled.

"It's alright. We can fix this. The water just made
it looks much worse than it was."

She gave a slight smile and worked to cover it and
get me back into a gown. I'm not sure what drew their
attention to my room, but I was anxious to find out. We
entered the room where Dr. Prescott appeared to have set
up shop at my bedside and was rapidly entering notes into
what appeared to be my ever-expanding chart. I was
ushered back to my bedwhere thankfully pain meds
awaited me. Since the nurse was unable to inject them in
my IV, I was given a shot in the arm just before she turned
to grab another IV kit.

"Ms. Walsh, your brother is out of surgery," I grew
still waiting for the other shoe to drop. "It's touch and go,
but it's out of our hands now."

"When can I see him?" I mumbled.

"Since we are unsure when or if he will wake up
you can see him now if you like."

"What do you mean if?"

"Your brother suffered severe life-threatening
injuries to several of his vital organs. The physicians have
worked tirelessly to keep him with us, but there is nothing
more they can do at this time."

I nodded.

He glanced at the nurse in the room, "If you could
please call the orderly to take her, I'd appreciate it."

"Yes, Dr. Prescott."

She quickly finished what she was doing and rushed
out of the room. Either she was incredibly well-trained or

she was very new to her position. After being within the confines of a hospital for several days you notice things and the majority take orders well, but not like this one. This one had either been beaten into submission or recently undergone military training. Regardless of her behavior, Dr. Prescott remained with me watching me closely.

"Ms. Walsh how are you sleeping?" he asked softly.

"Unfortunately, I'm not as you can tell. I collapse from exhaustion and fear," I mumbled again.

Why do I keep mumbling?

"What are you afraid of?"

"Nearly everyone now," I tried not to mumble this time causing my voice to project slightly louder than I expected.

"If you'd like I can prescribe something to help you sleep or something to take the edge off?"

"No, thank you. While I do not enjoy being frightened of my own shadow, I enjoy being present," I tried to smile, but it just came off as awkward forcing me to quickly glance away out of embarrassment.

The door opened shortly after revealing a very patient and smiling Tyler.

"Understood. Please let me know if you change your mind." He turned towards Tyler, "Please take Miss Walsh to the ICU. They are expecting her," Dr. Prescott saidna booming voice as he stood and stepped towards the door.

Dr. Prescott leaned in and whispered something to Tyler just before leaving the room. While I was interested in what that could have been, I was overjoyed to see Tyler again. He locked the wheels to the wheelchair in place before walking towards me. Taking my ankles in his warm hands he gently swung my legs towards the bedside before pulling my arms up onto his shoulders. I could feel his arms wrap around my waist and I already knew I wanted to kiss him.

"Alright beautiful. Let's get you up and out of this bed," he winked at me and before I knew it, we were up. We didn't linger for long as the door to my room was open and while I couldn't see anyone, I was certain we had an audience. With an arm still wrapped around me he helped me not only reach the wheelchair, but carefully slide down into it. He stepped away briefly to seek a blanket and I was grateful for the gesture as I was once again chilled by being anywhere other than under the covers. He didn't say anything but did his best to get us off and down the hall before the prying eyes became speculating whispers.

A short ride later and he was pushing me into the elevator where we could be alone once more. As the doors began to close behind us, I let out a sigh of relief. It was good to be alone with him once more. I felt his hand lightly touch my shoulder and I reached up to place mine upon his. I was nervous about seeing Rhys and something told me he knew that. He stepped around me and quickly before tapping a large red button on the control panel causing the elevator to come to a complete and abrupt stop.

"Ty, why are we stopping?" I said softly.

He knelt in front of me as I began to quiver with anticipation. He reached for my hands in an effort to encompass mine in his.

"Izz, we will be there soon, and I wanted to prepareyou for what you are about to see." My eyes grew wide.

"There will be a lot of equipment nearby, several of which are working to keep him alive. He cannot breathe on his own, so there has been a tube inserted to help him." A few tears dropped from my eyes, but I couldn't take my eyes offhim. "Due to the injuries his torso more than likely will notbe covered since the dressings are being changed quite frequently. There will, also, be several lines leading to and from his body in order to help monitor him a bit more closely." I felt the hair stand up on the back of my neck causing a shiver to run down my body. "Izz, do you understand everything I've said? I just don't want you to be frightened. You may not have much time with him."

I nodded breaking my focus, "I understand," I cleared my throat. "Do they know if he will ever wake up?"

He shook his head, "It's too soon to tell," he leaned in closer placing one of his hands on my cheek to wipe the tears away. "Izz, they won't let him go without a fight."

I closed my eyes and clinched them tightly closed in a poor attempt to hold back the tears. I couldn't imagine my life without Rhys, nor did I ever want to have to. Tyler hadn't shifted from his position as I expected only patiently waited for my approval to lead us on, but I wasn't ready just yet. I needed just another moment to gather my strength and my courage for that moment. Finally, I opened my eyes once more and leaned forward to kiss his cheek softly. I was never going to be ready for this moment, but I was glad I had him there with me to help get me through it.

He stood once more and tapped that same red button once more causing the elevator to jerk back into motion startling me slightly. Neither one of us spoke, but his hands were gently rubbing my shoulders trying to smooth the tension that was building between them. It helped. I continued to take deep breaths as the elevator continued to descend floors knowing all too well, we would soon be there. The elevator came to a stop and as the doors drew apart, I could see the inside of the ICU. The walls were a light honey color and glistened in the early morning light. The air smelled fresh and cleanser-free to my surprise. In addition, this unit was much quieter than the one I was in and other than the sounds from a horde of monitors working overtime there was very little sound at all.

We arrived at what I can only assume was the nursing station where we stopped once more. The counter was lower than most, more than likely allowing the staff full viewing access to all of the patients at any given moment just by doing a 360-degree turn. I could see several men and women hard at work when I noticed Tyler was already addressing one of them in a very subtle manner. They werewhispering, but they weren't hiding anything they were saying more as if they were being respectful of the patients that had been passed into their care. Their conversation provoked little interest for me and as I waited, I began to scan the rooms looking for anything or anyone that appeared to be familiar to me. There was nothing.

I turned back towards Tyler in hopes that would be his cue for us to get a move on, but he wasn't there. I shifted my weight a little more when I noticed him coming out of a room fully gowned and masked up. I was terribly confused and beyond my raised eyebrow I'm sure my face mirrored my inner most thought on that one. It appeared he was carrying something for me as well and before I even knew what was happening my hands were being cleaned and he was sliding my arms into a surgical gown and mask not all different from his own. Feeling battle ready we began to head towards Rhys's room.

As the space between us and the room diminished, I could feel my anxiety climbing causing me to start sweating and trembling all over. I must have looked ridiculous, but I was terrified for what I was about to see. The incessant beeping of monitors grew louder as we approached the threshold where we stopped. I felt Tyler's hand once more reach down and stroke the back of my neck and shoulder. This was my last chance to turn back if we were going to, but I couldn't let that happen. We needed to press onward.

He pushed me across the threshold where Rhys came into full view and the smell of death nearly overcame me. I clasped my hands over my mouth trying to calm myself as we continued to move closer. As I looked at him there was no denying this was my brother, but it wasn't at the same time, very much how I look at myself in the mirror now. This wasn't the Rhys I knew. My brother was young, handsome, and vibrant. This man was cold and lifeless. As Tyler warned there were tubes and cables in various places hard at work, but the breathing tube was the most difficult to take in. I watched a machine forcing breath into his body causing his chest to rise briefly then it took the breath back out of him. At this very moment, he was more machine than man.

There were dressings covering the majority of his torso, but there was one particular one that caught my attention. It was large and very blood stained. I couldn't see what it might have been covering, but its placement was what concerned me. It was from only a few inches below his collarbone down through what I was assume was his bellybutton. They said he was stabbed but gutted like a fish would have been more appropriate. I felt the wheelchair stop just shy of his bedside and even though we had stopped moving I still felt myself propelling forward towards him. I reached out a trembling hand in an attempt to touch him when Tyler spoke.

"Try not to touch any of the dressings. They were very specific about this."

I think he knew what I had been focusing on and tried to pull my attention away from it.

"What happened to him?" I whispered back.

"They had to open him up further than anticipated to repair the damage," he leaned forward and placed his hand on my chest. "The bone here that protects your heart had to be broken in order to save his life."

"Can he survive this?"

"I believe he can."

I nodded. I lowered my trembling hand on top of Rhys's. It was terribly cold as if he'd been working outside in December with no gloves on. It sent a chill up my body and down my spine causing me to shiver. Tyler pulled his arm back giving me the space I needed to draw myself closer to Rhys. I know it would have never been allowed, but I wanted to climb in bed next to him as I did when we were children. I know he wasn't dead, but somehow his spirit, his essence seemed terribly far away. I lifted his lifeless arm towards me and held it close trying to use my own body heat to warm him. I desperately wanted to tell him something, but I didn't know if I had the strength to stand.

"Ty, I need to tell him something. Can you help me up? I'm afraid I won't be steady on my feet right now."

"Of course."

He stepped to the side locking the wheelchair in place and wrapping his arm around my side. I laid Rhys's hand down in order to grab Tyler's and soon I was up once more. I was quite unsteady as we stepped towards the head of the bed, but Tyler never faltered in his support. He stepped just slightly behind me to provide what privacy he could for us but kept his hands firmly on my hips. As I leaned in and placed my face slightly against Rhys's I began to whisper.

"Thank you for saving me and for always being there for me when I needed you….and even when I didn't. I couldn't have asked for a better brother. I need you to come back, I'm not ready to lose you yet," I sniffled, "This is all my fault." I kissed his cheek, "I'd gladly give my life, so that you may live. Please come back. I love you."

I leaned back and ran my fingertips across his cheek wiping away the tears that had fallen. I stood there for a moment trying to remember the sound of his voice or his laughter. Never thought I'd have to work so hard to remember something so simple. Rummaging through my mind I remembered us together in the kitchen just a couple of weeks ago and he was making me breakfast. I could see his smile once more in my mind and reliving that memory made even his scent come back to me. I couldn't comprehend the battle that must be waging within, but his body looked and felt as if he'd already passed on. I took his hand in mine once more and squeezedit gently. The thought of leaving him at this very moment pulled at my insides, but I knew if I would stay, I would beg for death before the end. God doesn't bargain nor accept trades, but in this case, I hoped he would make an exception.

As I turned back towards the wheelchair, I felt myselfstarting to breakdown. My body and mind had already been strained from the events of the last few weeks, but thisobliterated my spirit. I wanted to demand that someone let me stay, but I think staying would consume what was left of me. I struggled to focus on the moment as I carefully satback in the wheelchair. I think Tyler could tell my emotions were on borrowed time and soon I may not be able to contain them. He quickly spun me around and backacross the threshold. Where he found a quiet spot near the desk to strip off our masks and gowns.

"Hang in there with me," he said softly as he turned and rushed towards the elevator.

I could feel the pressure and anxiety mounting. While I physically didn't stab Rhys, he was still in here because of me and I would have to live with that the rest of my life. I never really knew what true pain and suffering was before all of this, but what I do know is while the lesson is being learned I would do about anything to undue it. I closed my eyes and did what I could to calm my nerves, but nothing could get that image of Rhys out of my head. We reached the elevator where Tyler quickly closed the doors and tapped the red button stopping it in its tracks.

"Izz, are you alright?"

"No, but I think that's normal, right?" my voice cracked.

"Yea, it is. Do you need a minute, or would you liketo head back?"

"Take me away from here," I looked up at him and I could see the shock on his face. "Please, he's not safe as long as I'm here."

"Izz, I can't. It's not safe for you if anyone really knew what was going on between us let alone me kidnapping you."

I reached for his arms and pulled him towards me.

"Ty, you're not kidnapping me if I go willingly. Please help me get out of here."

Izz, think of your family and of your health. How could this possibly help?" he knelt in front of me placing himself within inches of my knees.

"I trust you and we both know you wouldn't hurt me."

He let out a sigh and while I knew he was trying to

do the right thing part of him was tempted by my offer. His hands dropped onto my knees where he began to gently rub them most likely as a distraction while he was working things out. He remained there for several moments before his concentration finally broke. He placed his hand on the back of my neck pulling me towards him kissing me softly. He didn't need to say anything, but a deal had been struck.

I felt his lips travel from mine onto my cheek and then onto my neck. We couldn't linger for long or someone may become suspicious of the stagnant elevator, and we knew we had to stop. Tyler pulled himself away from me and quickly got up before tapping the button forcing the elevator back into motion. I sat there trying to wrap my head around what was happening between us, but it couldn't be easily explained. The remainder of the elevator ride was spent in silence. Most likely we were both contemplating not only what was happening between us, but the line we were about to cross. This wasn't going to be simple, but it was one of the only cards I had left to play.

The elevator soon came to another stop just before the doors slid open. Tyler wheeled me through the halls and back to my room where he quietly closed the door behind us. His silence was concerning, but I was determined not to let it deviate me from the path I had chosen. He continued to move about in silence taking time to hook my monitors back up as I rest on the side of the bed. I went to pull my legs up when I felt his hand land on my knee. When I jerked in surprise he reached up and placed his hand just shy of my lips.

"It's alright. Let me help you."

His tone was oddly formal and as he slowly pulled my legs upward, he spoke once more.

"I can't simply walk out of here with you or I'll be implicated as well. Do you think you remember how to get to the chapel that I took you to when you first woke up here?" he whispered.

I nodded.

"Go there. There is a window in the Reverend's old office that can be opened. You can climb out there. Once outside make your way to the tree line and follow it down about a block where you will find a beige Jeep. The doors will be unlocked."

"But what of the guard outside of my room?" I whispered.

"I think now would be a good time to say a few more prayers for your brother," he winked and instantly I knew.

"Thank you."

He smiled and turned towards the door. Soon I would be out of this prison and out of harm's reach at least for a little while longer. No one knows about us, and it needs to stay that way. As soon as he exited the room, I reached for my bed rail and pulled myself towards the side of the bed. My toes grazed the tile floor and sent a chill up my body. Where were my sneakers when I really needed them? Then I remembered that Rhys carried me out of Derek's with only a coat to cover me. Where was his coat? I was just about to set off to recover it when there was a knock at the door. I needed to get my legs back in bed before I got caught. Thankfully, as the door opened, I noticed it was Tyler accompanied by another nurse.

"Hello Miss Walsh, how are you feeling? Tyler tellsme you're still feeling a bit cold." The nurse walked over and began running my vitals again.

"Yes, just can't seem to get warm."

"And your pain?"

"Tolerable, I suppose."

She turned slightly and nodded then went back to her work. While I know she was doing her job the incessant beeps from tinkering with the IV were about to push me over the edge. Tyler walked over with a large warm blanket and began covering me with it. At first, I wasn't sure why, but then I noticed he had placed something next to my hip. I dare not look at it now, but I was curious as to what it could be. I made sure to keep the blanket scrunched up around me, so that attention may be drawn away from the conspicuous lump next to me. The nurse turned back towards me just as I was attempting to cover my arms.

"If you don't mind, I'd like to take a look."

"Oh, my apologies. Of course," she caught me off guard and I nearly stumbled over my words.

"Please turn your face towards me. Tyler, would you mind turning on the overhead lighting?"

She placed her hands on the sides of my face turning it towards her. As the lights came on, I was nearly blinded by them causing me to squint. She appeared to be measuring something, but with the way she mumbled it was difficult to discern. She continued her mumbling and began checking the wound on my neck and abdomen with Tyler's assistance. While I wasn't uncomfortable with the constant exams, being undressed by a woman earlier and carefully looked over by my love interest has put me in an awkward predicament. I've never been vulnerable around really anyone other than family or my best friends and in here I've never been more vulnerable.

The nurse finished quicker than I expected and before I really had time to react, they were out the door. I rummaged through the covers to see what could have possibly been hidden within. I pulled out a pair of sneakers and some blue fabric. I began to unfold the fabric and quickly realized they were scrubs. Apparently, Tyler had thought of everything and realized sneaking out of here in a hospital gown probably would attract some attention. However, I couldn't just put them on and walk out of here either. Flopping about in the bed I managed to put the sneakers and the scrubs on before rotating towards the side of the bed. I wasn't sure how much time I had, but it was better to be ahead of the game than behind. I gathered my strength and stood quickly hoping my tenacity would be enough to get me through this. To help conceal the scrubs I put my gown back on and rolled the pant legs up, so they could no longer be seen. I felt and probably looked ridiculous. As a last-minute touch, I grabbed a robe that was draped on the foot of the bed and quickly put it on. Looking down at myself I appeared to be a bit heavier due to the extra layers, but the scrubs were covered. I was ready.

Taking my IV pole in one hand I made my way to the door with little to no difficulty. I placed my hand on the handle and opened it slowly for a quick assessment of my surroundings. If I hadn't been in the hall earlier today the layout would have thrown me off since I was in a different part of the unit during my previous stay. I opened it further to find that the guard has abandoned his post. Upon further inspection I noticed the nurses were, also, absent from their post. I slid out the door and closed it quietly behind me. Trying to act as nonchalant as possible I began walking down the hall without any particular urgency to my step. As if I was any patient just out for some fresh air. I was nearly there when I heard a voice call to me. I didn't recognize it.

"Excuse me, Miss?" The male voice called.

I chose not to respond, but my hesitation before taking my next step suggested I at the very least heard him.

"Miss, stop right there!" he shouted.

I could hear footsteps walking towards me. I didn't recognize the voice shouting at me, but for once that didn't surprise me. I stopped moving forward and slowing turned in his direction using my IV pole for support.

"Where do you think you are going? You're not to leave that room without the proper authorization," the officer insisted.

"My brother is dying, and I need to consult the onlyperson that can help him. So, unless you intend to violate my rights, I suggest you let me continue on my way."

I felt myself choke up towards the end. Part of me

knew I was lying, but the other part of me knew I was right. As a patient there are certain items they can restrict, but they cannot refuse my right to practice my religion.

"Then let myself or a nurse go with you. Now is not the time for you to be alone."

"Being alone is exactly what I need now."

"I'm sorry Miss. I will have to insist."

I sighed and turned to begin walking down the hallway once more. I didn't say a word, nor did I intend to, but I could periodically hear the older officer attempting to make small talk. We rounded the corner and I found myself finally in a familiar setting. I knew it wasn't far, but each step was beginning to feel heavy as if bricks had been fixed to the bottom of my feet in an attempt to lock me in place. While I was refusing to let my exhaustion overcome me, I knew sooner or later I would have to succumb to its will.

We reached the end of the hall where I turned sharply to find the chair still there from days before. The space felt cooler than before, so I was thankful for the extra layers. I continued towards the chapel door and to my surprise it was left unlocked. As I stepped inside, I noticed how terribly dark it was inside and decided to reach for the nearest switch. The room appeared to be lit by electronic candlelight which only drew my attention to how intricate the architecture of the room really was. It was stunning. The officer attempted to follow me inside, but I stopped him just as he crossed the threshold.

"I'd like to be alone if you please."

"Miss Walsh, as we discussed earlier you are not to be left alone."

"I'm not alone and you shouldn't be here. Please wait outside and I'll come out when I'm ready."

I added a quick smile in hopes of looking less suspicious. He appeared to have bought it and quietly vacated the room closing the door behind him. I wanted to stay and truly take in this magnificent chapel, but I knew there wasn't time. I quickly scanned the room for any possible exit when I noticed a door about a third of the way up on the far side. As quiet as I could muster, I slinked my way towards the door and turned the knob. It, too, was unlocked. Glancing through the opening it appeared to be the office Tyler had referred to, so I quickly slid through the open doorway before shutting the door behind me.

The office was as ornate as the chapel much to my surprise. This must have been here for a hundred years or more and reminded me very much of our home back in Ireland. It was carefully and meticulously crafted to not only be intricate, but to last. I hope to one day come back here and admire it further. This room was not lit, but the window gave the valuable light I needed to navigate the space. I reached the window and glanced downward in an attempt to estimate the drop. It was enough that the impact would cause a jolt to my system, but not so much as to shatter my insides. In an adrenaline-fueled fury, I pulled out my IV and used the gown to stop the bleeding. Once I was certain it stopped, I peeled the gown off and dropped it to the floor.

My focus was then drawn to the window. There was a simple turn lock that rotated easily allowing the window to fall open. It was going to be tight, but I was certain I could fit through. I took a breath and accessed the drop once more. The garden space was in view for multiple parts of the hospital, but if I was quick enough, I should be able to drop relatively unnoticed. I held the frame for support and climbed up onto the window before turning and sliding my legs out. The movement already hurt, but there was no turning back now. I latched onto the frame once more and slid as far as I could go before, I was forced to let go.

The impact came quicker than I expected causing the wind to be knocked out of me. I laid there on the ground for a moment gathering my breath and my strength before rolling to one side. I needed to get up. Even if someone hadn't seen me fall, I was on borrowed time before someone would notice me laying here or missing from my unit. With my adrenaline still flowing I rose to my feet. I pulled my hair back out of my face and dropped my arms at my sides trying to appear as if I was just taking a morning walk. I did receive a few awkward glances, but nothing more than I would have expected in the now frigid morning air. I pressed onward trying to recall Tyler's instructions. Follow the tree line to the jeep. I had now reached the backside of the main building and the tree line was in sight. I wanted to bolt towards it, but that would have drawn unnecessary attention. I kept walking.

Reaching the tree line put me one step closer and

while I knew a city block wasn't far the frigid air was beginning to comb its way through my hair and across my skin leaving me with a burning sensation I couldn't shake. Once several feet past the initial tree line, I made a sharp turn and began power walking towards where I was led to believe the Jeep would be. Increasing my speed allowed me to warm up slightly, but ultimately my goal was to reach the Jeep where I could hide in the comfort of its four walls.

It wasn't long before it was in my sights and when it was, I couldn't wait any longer. I was freezing and in pain. Those two factors forced me to sprint towards the Jeep where I quickly opened the back door and leapt inside slamming the door behind me. In hindsight, I probably should have been a tad quieter, but it's a little late for that now. As I glanced around, I noticed a large hoodie hanging over the front seat and I quickly snatched it. Anything to keep me warm. I continued to glance around noticing the entire Jeep was clean. Yes, there were some books and paperwork, but overall, very clean and organized. During my search of the Jeep, I was pleased to find a blanket as well. Either he was very prepared for my escape, or he kept this handy in case of an unexpected breakdown. Either way, I was grateful and before I knew it, I had drifted off to sleep.

23

The sound of the door slamming shut brought me quickly back to consciousness. I jerked back as I could feel someone touching my shoulder only to realize it was Tyler. I gave a sigh of relief.

"Ty, I'm so glad you're here."

"I've missed you too." He turned forward and started the engine and a rush of heat washed over me. "I'm glad you made it out alright. I was worried," he sighed. "They are looking for you I hope you know...with as much ferocity as they are looking for that monster."

I swallowed and whispered, "Then we need to get out of here. It's not safe for either of us if we are seen together."

He nodded, "Where would you like to go?"

"Wherever you feel safe?"

He turned his face quickly towards me, surprised by my response.

"I don't feel safe anywhere, but I want you out of harm's way," I whispered.

"Alright, I know just the place."

As we began traveling down the road, he started telling me about his family home and how long they have lived there. It was a charming tale and brought back the warm fuzzy feeling I had while getting to know him at the hospital. Rarely did he seem taken back by a situation or uncomfortable around me, and that was a relief since my situation was far from typical. Despite the events of the last twelve hours Tyler seemed very relaxed and social. I wasn't quite sure where we were headed, but I was enjoying the journey.

We pulled up to this quiet little house hidden away on some old county road several miles outside of town. Gradually I noticed the house we arrived at was the house he described to me earlier. Granted I did say take me where he felt safe, but I never would have imagined he would have taken me home with him. He continued to chatter on as he helped me out of the backseat. Describing various things from his father to the expected weather due to be upon us later that day. He was slightly nervous I could tell, but it helped me to relax knowing I wasn't the only one. We walked inside where his father was making breakfast. He didn't seem to be startled by Tyler's arrival, but when I rounded the corner, his face lit up.

"Hello there, who might this beautiful young woman be?"

"Morning Dad, this is Isolde. We met at the hospital."

"Good morning, sir," I extended my hand towardshim and he accepted. "It's good to meet you."

He seemed a tad startled at first, but with all the damage done to my face right now I cannot blame him for taking a second glance.

"Wonderful to meet you," his face lit up with excitement. "Would you like some breakfast? I made more than enough."

I smiled. Now I know where Tyler gets it from. His father is equally matched in pleasantries and kindness.

"I'd love to and thank you for offering."

We sat down at the kitchen table to enjoy a wonderful breakfast and the pleasant company of each other. His father reminded me of my own. Very welcoming to anyone he encountered which is very different from the suspicious nature of the majority of townsfolk in this small town. It was refreshing. I offered to help clear the table and clean the dishes, but of course he declined. Tyler took me by the hand and led me towards a room near the back of the house. I wasn't sure what the destination would be, but when we arrived, I realized he had brought me to his bedroom. I walked inside without question and took a seat on the bed. He pulled the desk chair over next to the bed and looked upon me with admiration though I'm not sure why.

"Shouldn't we at least close the door," I said softly.

"I can if it would make you more comfortable, but it's really not necessary. My dad respects boundaries."

I nodded and watched as he took a seat near me leaning in and taking my hands in his.

"Izz, you're safe here and don't have to hide, more importantly, we don't have to hide from anyone here."

Part of me felt relief that I hadn't felt in a while. I wanted to believe this could be a safe zone for us because up until now our relationship has just been trauma followed by secret kisses.

"I'm not sure how to thank you for everything you've done for me and my family."

He waved a hand in front of me and pointed to his cheek.

"I'm sure you can do better than that," I said with a smirk.

I leaned forward and kissed his smirking lips taking him completely by surprise. I wrapped my hands around his shoulders and held the kiss as long as I could. He went from tense and surprised to melted butter in my grasp. I wished in that moment we could have gone back in time and found each other before all of this had ever happened, but in truth if we did the relationship may not be what it is now. He cared for me, and I cared for him more than we both should, but the heart wants what it wants. Our age difference being unfortunate, but nevertheless it clearly wasn't stopping us. He broke off the kiss and bit his lower lip as if to stop himself from saying the wrong thing. Probably a nervous tick developed in childhood, but it really was adorable.

"Are you alright?" I asked.

"More than alright, but this…I just…please just tellme if this is moving too fast for you."

I smirked, "I will, and I think my body will keep usin check a bit. Besides, I've been falling for you since the day I met you."

His eyes darted towards mine. "Falling for me?"

"Yes, I believe I am. I've never felt this way about anyone else."

He grinned, "I was afraid to say anything out loud for fear of jinxing it, but what we have the world doesn't need to know about."

He kissed me again and again until my lips were starting to go numb forcing me to break away.

"Do you mind if I stay with you, at least for a bit? I'm afraid to leave and you were the last person who made me feel safe."

I watched his jaw drop followed by several moments of silence before he closed his mouth and swallowed.

He cleared his throat, "Of course, you're welcome to stay as long as you like."

He gave an awkward smile, and I nodded giving an equally awkward smile. I slid back to the far side of his bed and laid down hoping he would accept my invitation as he once did before. He stood and fetched a blanket from his closet and brought it back over to the bed where he covered me up. He climbed into bed moments later facing me. We didn't say anything, and we didn't do anything. He just held me until we fell asleep and that is where I woke hours later.

The morning light has changed into an afternoon of sunshine and Ty's breathing was slow and deep. I hope he was dreaming of something wonderful. Being in his company really made me happy and I wish I could stay there with him forever. Well, maybe not forever, but you get the idea. I slowly climbed out of bed and made my way to the living room where I saw his father sitting silently, staring out the window. In that moment, he seemed rather delighted by what I cannot presume to know. I stood there for a few moments trying not to disturb him, but unfortunately a young woman poised at one of the entrances to the room has a way of drawing someone's attention. He didn't move or turn towards me. Only spoke softly as to not frighten me away.

"You're awake. The two of you have been sleeping for some time and I didn't want to wake you. Is there anything I can get for you?"

"Yes actually. I was wondering if I might have a cup of tea. I'm rather parched."

"Of course. Please give me just a moment."

As Mr. Hale vacated the room, I sat down in the armchair just opposite the one he was sitting in when I entered the room. The view through the large bay window was beautiful which helped me understand part of his apparent fascination with staring out it. Yes, there was a road in view, but the sun coming up and cresting over the top of the hills was stunning. I, too, was fascinated to the point I hadn't heard Mr. Hale stepping up behind me. He outstretched a cup of tea towards me with a smile and I gladly accepted. We made small talk in regard to the weather, my background and a bit about families. Nothing out of ordinary really and it was refreshing to speak to someone about something other than the disaster that had become my life recently which he mentioned nothing of. I finished my tea and politely excused myself before retreating towards Tyler's bedroom.

When I arrived, I was hopeful to find him still in his bed, but it was now empty. I rushed over to the bedside and laid a hand where his body once was. It was still warm, so he couldn't have wandered far. Considering I just walked down the hall I'm not sure how I would have missed him passing.

"Penny for your thoughts?"

I heard his voice suddenly behind me and it made me jump at the sound. Thankfully, he had crept close enough to me when I was distracted that when I jumped, he was able to quickly steady me as opposed to letting me fall back on the bed or worse the floor.

"Sorry, didn't mean to startle you," he bit his lip once more.

"No apology necessary. That seems to happen a lot lately." I noticed his hand had fallen onto my waist, but with no apparent intention of drawing me near or pushing me away. "Did you sleep well?"

He nodded, "When I woke and you were gone, I was afraid you had left," he hugged me. "Then I heard you talking with my dad."

"He was very kind to me, and I enjoyed hiscompany."

He smiled. "I expected nothing less," he glanced towards his desk. "I have some notes to review before my exam tomorrow. My dad usually helps me, but if you wouldn't mind…," his voice trailed off.

"I'd love to," I grinned. "How can I help?"

"Great, basically skim down through the notes and quiz me. Everything on these pages I need to know, so don't hold back."

His voice was so buoyant that he was bordering on sounding giddy. He sounded the way small children do on Christmas morning. Deliriously happy and not afraid to hide their own excitement. I wished more people were like that. He sat down in his swivel chair at the foot of the bed, and I climbed further back onto the bed in hopes of steadying myself. I began questioning as I would anyone else, I was prepping for exam, but as time pressed onward, I started to have some fun by offering up trick questions and turning a phrase to see if I could throw him off the scent. Surprisingly, he was rarely misled, and I admired that. The vast majority of pre-med students are intelligent, but I wondered if they all worked as diligently as he did.

When I finished quizzing him, we turned to other topics of conversation. With him hours flew by like minutes and our laughter filled the once quiet hall. Everything felt natural with him, effortless really. If I didn't know any better, I would have guessed we had met as children and were now being reunited after a long absence. The laughter even drew in the attention of Mr. Hale as he periodically passed by Tyler's room on his way to attend to some other business. His father didn't seem the type to spy seeing how Tyler was no longer a child, but more like he wanted to witness a piece of the happiness he was hearing. I'm sure the dynamic was slightly different than what it would have been in my home.

When it was time to break for dinner, I almost hadn't noticed how close Tyler and I had become until I could feel his hand resting just slightly above my knee. We started off at quite a distance, but now we were sitting next to each other on his bed. He was leaning back against the wall allowing his legs to dangle down the side of the bed while I sat facing his left side. As I gazed upon his face, I watched his eyes slowly close. Almost like when a person is sleepy. Their eyelids flutter for a moment and then slowly close one final time before their mind drifts off to dreamland. He looked peaceful.

As a slight smile appeared on his face, I knew he was thinking of something pleasant, and I didn't want to disturb that thought or that memory. I sat there in awe of his peacefulness and longed to find that peace in my own mind. Without a second thought I leaned forward and gently pressed my lips to his and kissed him softly. The kiss didn't take him by surprise this time. I wasn't sure whether he was expecting it or if it was like a breath of fresh air and he was just trying to take it all in. I could feel his right-hand brushing across my cheek and down onto my neck while he returned my affection. While leaning towards him seemed easy enough for an impromptu kiss or two it was a starting to feel a bit awkward and straining on my body.

I placed my hands on his shoulders for support and brought my left leg across his body allowing me to shift my weight onto both legs taking a significant amount of pressure off my side. I lowered my body gently onto his lap. While the shift was a little tense at first, I could feel myself start to relax. His hands had moved down my neck and onto my shoulders moving my hair to one side. They continued to fall down my body pulling himself away from the wall and towards me. His movement was magnetic and only kept him closer to me. I heard a creak by the door, and it quickly reminded me that we were not alone in the house. More importantly, his bedroom door was wide open as I could last recall. I broke off the kiss and leaned in wrapping my arms around him tightly.

He kissed my neck softly and whispered, "I think we both could use a breather."

I nodded and placed my hands on his shoulders once more for balance as I slid my legs back towards the side of the bed hoping it was not far. Once they were safely to the side and then onto the floor I stood. Of course, seeing how my legs were bent in such a way for so long I wobbled a wee bit at first, but soon regained my footing. Once I was steady, I reached for Tyler and pulled him up towards me. He stood with ease, gave me a peck on the cheek and then took my hand before walking towards the door.

As we started walking down the hall, hand in hand, the thought entered my mind of what if this was where I was supposed to be all along? If this mess would have never happened, would I have even met Tyler? Could he have been the reason for it all? Like many, I do not believe our lives are predestined, but I do believe that critical events in our lives do not occur without a purpose behind them. Sometimes it's to help learn a lesson, whether large or small, and other times it's to help give us direction. Thinking back to the passing of Tyler's mum, practicing medicine may not have ever occurred to him and I couldn't think of anyone more suited for that line of work.

I was still focused on this thought when we entered the living room. In the midst of our distractions, I failed to notice how dark it had become outside. It's must have been at least six or seven o'clock by now. By now they would more than likely have sent out a search party, but I felt safe in the confines of the Hale house.

"I know it's probably improper to ask the guest to assist with cooking, but would you like to help me make dinner?" Tyler said softly.

"It would be my pleasure."

We strolled into the kitchen and where Tyler began pulling items from the fridge and cupboard. Flatware and utensils were handed to me, and I quickly began work on setting the table. Tyler didn't seem the least bit phased by my presence just continued on business as usual. Once the table was set, he had me help make the sauce. I stepped in front of him and slowly stirred the steaming pot as Tyler leaned over my shoulder adding bits of herbs and spices until the scent was nearly perfect while showering me with kisses along the way. His dad had apparently stepped into the room without our knowledge and caught us both off guard.

"I apologize, did we disturb you?" I said softly feeling like a deer in headlights.

He smiled and shook his head, "Not at all. It's nice to have a lady in the house again."

I smiled.

"Dad, would you mind if Izz stays with us tonight? There are some things going on at home and it's not safe forher to be there right now."

"Of course, I'll make up the guest room," he sounded rather hesitant about what he had just agreed to but proceeded to return to business as usual.

Dinner was relatively quiet, but it wasn't an uncomfortable silence by any means. Mr. Hale and I continued to pick up from where we left off earlier which was really a surprise. Part of me thought he was trying to get to know me, and the other part seemed like he was just filling the void. I probably shouldn't have been surprised at all considering his reaction to my presence and that Tyler doesn't bring women home very often, or possibly ever. That thought comforted me considerably. Feeling like a notch in someone's bedpost, so to speak, can never be comforting no matter who it is.

We finished eating and it was fantastic. He either has had years of practice or sheer dumb luck with winging it. I took the opportunity to clean up as a form of thanks while Tyler and his dad sat at the table talking quietly. It wasn't long before I was finished, and I did what I could to slip away giving them more privacy. Unfortunately, neither appeared to want privacy and they invited me back to the table where I sat comfortably next to Tyler. I may have folded my hands in my lap, but that didn't stop Tyler's hand from finding mine. I watched the two of them go back and forth on several different topics as if this was once again normal business for them. I was started to drift off in thought when I heard Mr. Hale speak to me.

"Isolde, are you alright?"

I tried to shake off the pain that was rapidly coming back, but I didn't know how to explain what was going on since I didn't know what he may have already known.

"I apologize. Yes, of course. Just a bit tired that's all," I gave an awkward smile then turned away.

Tyler leaned in and whispered, "It will be alright."

"How do you know that?" I whispered back.

"Because it has to be," he sighed. "I have faith and that's what gets me through."

He squeezed my hand gently in an attempt to calm my nerves or at the very least distract me from my pain. I couldn't prolong the inevitable and it wasn't fair to him to be placed in the middle of a battle he wasn't a part of.

However, he puts my mind and body at ease. There was no price I wouldn't be willing to pay to hold onto that feeling. I leaned over and kissed his cheek. I turned in my seat and stood quickly when I felt his hand still touching my hand. I glanced over my shoulder towards him.

"Would it be alright if I excuse myself to freshen up a bit?"

They both nodded just before I began heading my way towards the hall. While my prior sanctuary was filled with foliage my new comfort came from blistering hot water and I desperately wanted to get lost in a sea of bubbles or steam. I made it nearly halfway down the hall when I realized I had nothing to change into. I stopped frozen in the hall not sure whether or not to say something and if so, to whom? I decided I had no better course of action than to just head back and hope Tyler could rescue me from yet another awkward situation. I reached the opening and did my best to get Tyler's attention while lurking in the shadows. When that didn't work, I was left with no choice, but to step back into the light.

"Ty, would you be able to help me for a moment."

"Oh yes, I'm sorry," he quickly pushed his chair back and rushed over towards me. "Here, let me pullsome things out for you."

It wasn't long before we reached the family bath. As the lights came on, I noticed it appeared larger than anticipated with the lights on. When I entered this room earlier, I didn't even bother turning the lights on for fear of seeing my own dreadful reflection. Standing only a step away from the mirror I couldsee my face in vibrant detail. It was still badly bruised and just the site of it caused me additional embarrassment. I turned away from the mirror and tried to keep my focus onwhat he was telling me about the bath.

"Izz, why don't you take a seat here?" he placed his hand down on the counter.

"No, that's alright, I'm alright."

Without another word he picked me up and gently set me down on the counter. I felt like a child that just skinned her knee on the playground and needed my mum to kiss it better. He brushed my hair back and turned my cheek towards the light.

"Please don't, I look like some stinking awful rightnow," I scoffed.

"You're beautiful and this will heal," he kissed my cheek softly. "Just relax while I draw you a bath."

I watched him move around the room in a very systematic manner. Every movement appeared to be deliberate and carried out with precision. Nothing seemed to faze him, and that kind of strength couldn't have come easily. This wasn't the first time he had cared for someone, but without siblings could it have been his ill mother he cared for or someone else? I wanted to think on it more, but my attention was drawn to the steam that was now filling the room. Its warmth wrapped around me like a warm blanket, and I longed to be greeted by the source of itsheat.

Tyler came over to me and touched me lightly on the shoulder. "It's all yours. Please take all the time you need."

I smiled and began slowly sliding off of the counter as Tyler opened the door.

"Ty," he glanced over his shoulder towards me, "thank you."

He smiled and closed the door behind himself. Sliding out of the scrubs proved to be more difficult than I anticipated and if I wouldn't have died of embarrassment, I would have requested assistance. Fortunately, the bath water was still piping hot despite my struggles. I climbed in allowing the hot water to rush over my skin quickly putting me at ease. This had become my new happy place, well, one of them. Wrapped in Tyler's arms superseded a hot bath any day.

As I lay there wrapped in warmth and steam, I felt myself start to drift off. However, I wasn't so much as falling asleep as daydreaming. I fantasized about what it would be like to be with Tyler out in the open, being able to take a walk in the park, go to homecoming together, or see a movie together, anything really. I know the age difference concerns him, but I wasn't sure how to put his mind as ease about it. His dad seems remarkably at peace with our situation, but maybe that is just an illusion of my overworked mind. Regardless, it got me thinking and at least this time it was positive thinking.

24

I emerged from the bath a short time later realizing that I had nothing to wear other than the towels Tyler provided to me. I wasn't sure how to properly broach this with him but walking around with no more than a towel didn't seem proper either. I picked up the scrubs I had worn before quietly opening the bathroom door. I glanced down the hall hoping for a subtle exit. All clear. I scurried my way back into Tyler's bedroom where I quickly closed the door behind me. Unfortunately, I failed to scan the room after I entered and now noticed Tyler was taken aback by my entrance and was now staring at me.

"Umm, wow, I mean, I didn't expect you so soon."

He stumbled over his words as if he had just walked in on me naked. Clearly, outside of the confines of the hospital he was slightly awkward around the human form, no more than I probably should have expected, but nevertheless I was flattered.

"Ty, I'm alright. I just don't know how to say this."

He stumbled to his feet and began advancing in my direction. "Izz, are you alright? Are you in any pain? Can I get you anything?"

The questions came at me like a barrage of missiles set to rapid fire. I didn't even have a chance to answer before another one was fired upon me.

"Ty, I'm alright. I just don't have anything to wear." I gave an awkward smile before biting my lower lip.

"Oh, I think I have something that will work. At the very least it will keep you warm."

"I was actually hoping you'd keep me warm."

Based on the look upon his face this thought hadn't even crossed his mind, but he was clearly a quick thinker. Before I even had a chance to say anything more, he kissed me giving me exactly what I needed to warm this shivering body up. This time however he didn't linger and when he broke off the kiss, he winked at me as he took the worn scrubs from my hands. Stepping over towards a dresser on the far side of the room next to his desk he began rummaging through the drawers until he appeared to find what he was looking for. He held up what appeared to be a large sweatshirt, but he wasn't so much as looking to see if it was appropriate as he was sizing it up to me. Glancing back and forth between the shirt and me was causing the little insecure monster in me to stir.

"This should help." He held it out for me to grab and I stepped towards him. "Or would you prefer something else?"

"Whatever you decide will be fine," I said, "part of me was hoping for nothing."

As soon as the words passed my lips, I instantly regretted them, and I could feel my face becoming heated. I quickly looked away out of sheer embarrassment and hoped he would see it more as a joke than actual pass at him. Thankfully, when I glanced back, he was blushing too.

"I apologize, I shouldn't have said that," I uttered in hopes of diffusing any offense he might have taken at that off handed comment.

"Please don't apologize," he turned towards me, "I wasn't offended."

I felt like this was too soon and even though I wanted to share that closeness with him I didn't want it to be like this. I was confident he could restrain himself, but I wasn't entirely sure if I had enough willpower to stop myself if we started down that path. It wasn't about trusting him, so much as myself. While there have been moments when I exhibited signs of great strength, I knew I was weak to his touch. We both deserved to be more than a moment of weakness and I think if given the choice he would agree with me.

I took the sweatshirt from his hand and stepped back towards the bed where I sat waiting patiently for him to find whatever he was seeking. I was really starting to shiver when I decided this towel needed to come off. Rather than completely drop the towel and make us both uncomfortable I slid my arms into the sweatshirt before bringing it over my head. The action caused a slight groan to escape my body, but hopefully nothing that couldn't havebeen overlooked. I glanced over towards Tyler and noticedhe was still rummaging only this time in a different drawer.I did my best to stand while pulling the sweatshirt down, allowing me to drop the towel to the floor. Standing there in his baggy shirt I actually felt more naked than when I was wearing nothing but a towel, making me very aware ofeverything I was feeling.

As the towel struck the floor his attention was drawn back to me. The shirt more than covered me, but something about the way he was now looking at me was different. It wasn't an awkward silence but standing there still nearly naked with both of us very aware of it was causing desire to stir. It was taking all of my restraint not to act on it, and it appeared Tyler was fighting a similar battle on the matter.

"I'm sorry, I didn't mean to stare," he mumbled.

I smiled, "I was thinking about it too."

His concentration was breaking, and that comment jolted him back to reality. I don't think he was prepared to acknowledge what he was thinking let alone have to embrace the fact I was thinking the same thing.

"I'm sorry again. I know this is something we shouldn't be thinking about," he said softly.

"Then why do we both want to?" I quietly added.

He remained quiet more than likely unsure how to answer a question of such delicate subject matter. I remained quiet as well. Our silence closed the matter at least for now and he turned back to locate something appropriate for me to wear. It wasn't much longer before he located what he needed and stepped towards me.

"It's a bit large but should fit."

"Wait, what?"

"The sweatpants," he held them up.

Clearly, my mind was still somewhere else.

"Oh, right." My face once more flushed with embarrassment. "Thank you."

He smiled, "I'll just give you a moment to get dressed."

He knelt to pick up the towel I had dropped earlier but lingered a bit longer than I expected. Just as I was beginning to wonder what was keeping him, I felt his hand sliding up my one leg and stopping just above my knee.

"You're shivering," he held up the sweatpants for me to grab just before rising to my level. "Please put these on."

I reached out to grab them, but something stopped me. Lately, I've broken more rules and principles than I care to count, but what of matters of the heart? I truly believed I was falling in love with him, and shouldn't that count for something? There was a line it seemed that both of us were uncomfortable crossing, but what about everything else before that line? It may not have been the right thing or even the proper thing, but I wanted to share that closeness with him. I stepped back from him and pulled the comforter on his bed down just enough that I was able to slide inside. I placed my hand on the bed next to me unsure what to say.

"Izz," he reached up and began rubbing the back of his neck trying to relieve the tension that was beginning to build up. "I don't want to hurt you, in any way."

"Ty," he didn't look at me, "please," I said softly as I outstretched my one hand towards him.

He stepped closer to the bed but did not take my hand. Instead, he braced his legs against the side and continued to divert his gaze from mine. Generally, my timid personality would have forced me to drop the matter, but this time I wasn't going to let the matter go. I leaned in closer to him forcing myself into his view as I grabbed part of his shirt pulling him towards me. In doing so, it drew me up and towards him like a moth to a flame. I relaxed my grip and slid my hands just under the base of his shirt. His warmth radiated onto my hands and began warming the chill that had set in my bones. In that moment I knew just what to say.

"Will you lay with me if only for tonight?" I said softly as I leaned in further hoping at the very least for one of his sweet kisses.

He nodded just before swooping me up with one arm and sliding us both down onto the bed in mere seconds. I don't think I'd even need the comforter tonight with him by my side. Just being near him made me feel like we had been transported back to that night at the hospital when he laid beside me calming my uneasy mind and body. I longed for security that night, but I received more than a watchful bodyguard. I received something more. I tried reliving the moment in my mind and I could feel tonight was different. I wasn't afraid and while I was in pain it seemed to subside considerably when I'm in his presence.

I drew myself closer to him allowing my fingers to caress different parts of his back as he leaned in and began kissing my neck. I was completely taken in by him in that moment. I began tugging at his shirt as the kisses intensified. It didn't take him long to take the hint and he pulled back briefly to remove it revealing a remarkably toned body underneath. Could working at the hospital really keep him in this kind of shape or could he have been an athlete masquerading? As his attention and kisses were drawn back to me, I decided that debating the matter further would have distracted me more than I would like from my present situation. So, I decided to let the matter rest and enjoy what I could while it lasted.

Our kisses were so intense that I thought my lips were going to go numb, but I still wanted more. I brought my leg up and placed it over his hip pulling him towards me. His hand quickly found my thigh and began caressing it. Gentle, but firm like a massage as I expected. As his hand began to move up my thigh and onto my bottom, we both suddenly became very aware that I wasn't wearing any knickers. I felt his hand quickly pull away in surprise and our kiss broken. I must admit that I actually had forgotten about that, but I didn't expect him to be so taken back by the situation. He seemed reluctant once more and I can only assume the internal debate had resumed.

"Ty," I whispered.

"Yea," he whispered back.

"Are you alright?" I looked up at him, "just now you went somewhere else."

"I'm sorry. I just forgot you were so—"

"Naked?" I interjected.

"Yea," he smirked, "I just don't want you to feel pressured."

"You're not pressuring me. If anything, I feel like it is quite the opposite."

"I'm willing to wait, however long it takes," he whispered softly.

"I know you are, and I feel the same way."

"So, where does that leave us?"

"Kiss me again and I'll let you know," I smirked.

"Gladly," he smirked.

His kiss melted me like butter on a hot day and if asked in that very moment I would have sold my soul for another taste. I could feel his hands rushing over my body. As they found their way under the shirt and up onto my back the thought crossed my mind of removing it. I was already overheating from his warmth and my very own, so what could be the harm? I did what I could to persuade him to turn onto his back and, as he turned over, I climbed on top of him straddling his body. Unfortunately, once I was there, I sort of lost my nerve and wasn't sure what to do. I could feel Tyler watching me and that only made it worse. Maybe I should have invested slightly more time into researching this before jumping in at the expert level.

I think he could sense something was amiss and sat up as best as he could. After a few moments when I still didn't say anything, he reached for my arms and placed them on his chest just before wrapping his arms around me. I didn't particularly want to be hugged at the present moment, but sometimes we get what we need instead of what we want. As the nerves started to settle, I began to feel better. I began to peel my upper body away from his by giving him a slight nudge. He propped himself up as I began reaching for the bottom of the shirt and his eyes widened. He opened his mouth as if to speak, but I did not hear a word.

When my gaze returned from watching the shirt fall to his bedroom floor his eyes were fixed on me. Part of his chest and face had become flushed and his breathing had changed much like my own. I glanced down to find my hair nearly dry now and had fallen perfectly providing a good bit of coverage over my stark-naked body.

He raised one of his eyebrows, "Izz, are you sure this is what you want? I don't want to hurt you?"

I cut him off. "You won't."

He nodded and exhaled, "As long as you're sure."

"I am."

He sat up fully and wrapped his arms around me pulling me tightly against him. I wrapped my legs around his torso just in time to be flipped onto my back causing me to now let out a giggle. We kissed again and again until our lips were swollen and tingling then we kissed some more. There wasn't any part of my body his hands hadn't touched and our passion for each other only accelerated with each passing moment. I was floating on a cloud of ecstasy, and I didn't want to wait any longer. We conceded to our desires off and on all night long until we collapsed from exhaustion. It may have been slightly awkward the first time, but we quickly learned what the other one wanted or needed and that only heightened the passion between us. This was one of the single most exhilarating experiences of my life and given the chance I wanted to experience it again with him.

We fell asleep naked in each other's arms and that is where I awoke the next morning. He'd been awake at least for a few moments based on his breathing, but I couldn't venture to guess longer than that. His arms were wrapped tightly around me pressing me to his chest keeping me warm. While there were parts of me that felt tender, I woke elated at the sheer sight of him. I could feelhim lean down and lightly kiss my forehead.

"You're awake," he whispered.

I nodded and began tracing the muscles in his chest with my fingertips. Just watching the slow rise and fall of his chest comforted me. There were so many things that I wanted to say to him, but I didn't want to spoil the moment. I kissed his chest and drew in a deep breath. I pulled my one leg up onto his hip squeezing him ever so gently. I felt his hand slide down my side and began gently massaging my thigh. His hands felt incredible and once again drew me in. Physically I didn't think that my body would allow for any more passion right now, but there was a part of me that couldn't resist him.

Unfortunately, as I began to shift my weight about, I was reminded that I was in fact human and without pain meds or the adrenaline that came from sexual arousal it was exhausting just to hold my head up. Of course, the desire was there, but some pain the brain cannot trick away. I wanted to look at him, but just blinking seemed to cause me discomfort. As all my senses awakened the pain worsened causing me to grimace. Thankfully, while he may not be able to see my pain, I'm certain he would be able to feel my discomfort as my body was tightening up.

"Did I hurt you?" he whispered.

When I didn't respond right away, he began to shift his weight out from under me and fully onto his side. I wouldn't be able to hide from his gaze in this position. I closed my eyes tightly and tried to bring myself back into the memory of last night. Then I felt his lips on mine and I didn't want to hold onto the memory when he was here with me right now. When I opened my eyes again, he was laying there just watching me. One arm tucked behind his head and the other caressing my arm.

"Is it always like this?" I whispered.

"Recovery?" he sounded perplexed.

I shook my head, "Being with someone like we were last night."

"I don't know what you mean."

"So, electrifying, exhilarating. If I wouldn't have collapsed from exhaustion I don't know if I would have ever wanted to stop."

He snickered, "No, at least not from my experience."

I swallowed hard, "Umm, how much experience do you have exactly?"

He smiled, "The same as you," he paused and turned over on his back. "However, my first time was with my high school sweetheart. We had been dating for a while and I think the pressure was getting to us to take that next step. When we did it filled us both with regret turning our hearts sour," he paused again, "so, you can understand why I was hesitant last night."

I reached over and touched the side of his face causing him to look in my direction.

"I regret nothing," I assured him.

He brushed my hair back and began kissing my neck and shoulder. This feeling is so overwhelming and all-consuming it has become worse than a heroin addiction. He's become like oxygen to me and while I know I will have to learn to be without him, I'm not sure I want to. My mind began to race with the possibilities of a future with him. Just the thought filled my heart with warmth, and I knew then the lady I thought was gone had been found.

Something about Tyler had brought me back to life and I could never express to him what that meant to me.

He smiled and kissed both of my cheeks. "I'm going to get up and make some coffee. Can I get you anything?"

"A cup of coffee would be lovely."

He winked at me just before standing and sliding into his pants from the night before. He exuded confidence with each step and watching his strut off made me a tad envious of his confidence. After his exit I noticed he did not close the door, so I was hoping that meant his father was not home or this could become terribly awkward. I propped myself up on one elbow and scanned the room. There were pillows on the floor along with clothes and what appeared to be an array of condom wrappers scattered about. I said a silent prayer for Tyler's good sense as I didn't even think about that until now.

I sat up slowly and let my legs dangle off the side of the bed. They felt like rubber, and I wasn't sure if I could walk, but I desperately needed to use the bathroom. I leaned forward and picked up Tyler's shirt with my toes and brought it towards me. Once it was within my reach, I snatched it up and slid into it. I gathered my strength to stand and did my best to balance on my now rubber legs. It took a moment or two to get my bearings, but with assistance of the furniture and the walls I was able to make my way into the bathroom. I closed the door quietly behind me.

I let out a gasp of air once inside that I didn't realize I was holding in during my journey here and knew I needed something to dull the pain. I quickly flipped the shower on and sat down. This time my insides didn't feel as if they were on fire, but I was extremely sensitive and swollen. My entire body ached and just bearing down to void was agony. I could hear a cry starting to escape my body and I quickly covered my mouth. I did what I could to calm myself as I didn't want to alarm him should he pass by. I was hurting, but he didn't hurt me. I just think that my body wasn't ready for what I pushed it to do and now I was going to need some time to recover.

The knock at the door startled me and I quickly rose up in a panic wiping the tears from my eyes. He clearly thought I was in the shower and was just dropping off a cup of coffee for when I was ready, but when he saw me, his behavior changed.

"Izz, do you mind if I come in?"

I moved closer to the shower just shy of his line of sight.

"I was just about to shower actually," I sniffled.

I could hear him sigh, "Please just call me if you need me."

"Yes, of course."

I held my breath until I heard the door click and then stepped into the shower. I know being honest with the person you're seeing is important, but I've been so vulnerable around him for so long I was worried he wouldn't be able to see me as anything other than that. The hot water washed over me nearly scalding every inch of me. At first it was painful, but then it began to relieve some of my more basic aches and pains. I doubt overnight some of my wounds would have healed, but I was holding out on a hope. I wanted him to see me how I used to look, not like this beat up old rag doll I had become.

I reached over and swatted the handle to the shower just enough for it to click off. I didn't really want to take a shower, but I needed a few private moments to myself. I was no longer a child and while last night was by far one of the best nights of my life it was not without consequence. That was a moment meant to be reserved for the husband I might one day have, but I was weak. As I stood there against the shower wall I prayed for forgiveness and mercy. Unfortunately, the cry that was being released from my body deafened my ability to hear a response. Maybe tomorrow I would try again.

I stepped out of the shower and grabbed the nearest towel. I noticed the cup Tyler set on the counter was still steaming, so I must not have been in there too long. Taking the cup in one hand I opened the door and stepped out to return to his bedroom. After a few moments of silence, I felt better and as the warm coffee began coating the lining of my stomach I felt even better. I was in need of nourishment and rest if I was going to get through this, and I was determined to make it through this.

As I entered the room, I found Tyler sitting on the side of the bed with his head lowered in his hands.

"Ty, is everything alright?" I stepped carefully towards him.

He nodded and slowly looked up towards me. "I need to go take my exam soon. Are you comfortable staying here alone or would you like to come with me?"

"I don't want you to leave, but would it really be safe for me to go with you?"

"Probably not." He picked up something from his nightstand and held it out for me to grab. "Please take these. They will help with the pain and allow you to sleep."

"What makes you think I'm in pain?" I said quizzically.

"Let's just call it a hunch," he smirked.

I took the pills out of his hand and swallowed them with a swig of coffee. The warmth of the coffee caused them to start dissolving a bit sooner than I would have liked resulting in a bitter aftertaste. A few more swigs of coffee are definitely in order now. As I continued to sip my coffee, I felt Tyler grab my hand and pull me closer to him. He reached up and brushed his hand along my cheek then down my neck.

"You know you can tell me anything, right?"

"I know."

He stood and kissed my cheek before pointing to a stack of clothes on the bed. "I thought you might like to get dressed. When you're ready of course." He stepped towards the door. "I'll be in the shower if you need me."

I nodded and turned to sit on the side of the bed. He closed the door behind himself, and I sat there in silence justscanning the room. In what little time I was absent from his presence he had picked up his room, made his bed, made coffee, and had time to rest. I admired his efficiency in everything he did and now knew that little time would ever be wasted with him. I tried to take a page out of his book and got dressed. The clothes appeared to be the sweats pulled out last night, but neatly folded while waitingfor me. I slipped into them and then finished my

coffee. I laid back down on the bed unsure what to do, but as I laid there, I could feel myself getting sleepy. I'm not sure what medication Tyler gave me were, but they were already taking effect.

25

As I opened my eyes, I could see the evening light through a window in Tyler's room. Was it possible that I slept all morning and afternoon? I sat up slowly to find a glass of water on the nightstand and I quickly devoured it. It filled my stomach, and I almost instantly felt better. However, for the first time in hours I thought of Rhys. Staying here satisfied my selfish needs, but it kept me at a great distance from him. I couldn't stay here any longer. I needed to go back even if it wasn't safe.

I climbed out of bed and headed towards the living room. As I moved closer, I could hear some talking, but the conversation appeared to be very one sided. Whoever it was they must have either been on the phone or the other party spoke quieter than a mouse. As I drew close, I could hear them clearer now and the conversation was occurring at the main door. I slowed my pace and stopped just shy of the mouth to the living room. I clung to the wall and listened carefully trying not to make a sound.

By the sounds of it there were officers here and they were inquiring after me. What would make them think to come here? They couldn't have followed me here or they would have arrived shortly after we did yesterday, so why now? I plastered myself against the wall while holding my breath hoping to get a better listen. Tyler wasn't speaking, but I could hear his father clearly as I was standing next to him. I didn't know how long they had been there, but I knew they couldn't find me here. Based on what I've heard Mr. Hale wasn't providing them with any information only confirming what little he knew of Tyler's position. While I'm certain he knew more than he was saying by choosing to keep quiet he wasn't just protecting me.

During this time, I did not see or hear Tyler, but I knew he couldn't have been far. More than likely, it was too early for his shift to have begun, but for him to still be at university would be highly unlikely as well. I needed to find him and get out of here before we were found out. I crept along the wall while making my way back towards Tyler's room. I did not fully close the door behind me for fear of someone hearing it, but once inside I scrambled to find anything that would lead them to believe I was here should they insist on coming inside. I found the shoes from the day before and put them on. I didn't have time to wipe everything down, but I hoped it wouldn't come to that.

I made my way towards the window on the backside of the room and lifted it open. The bitter cold from outside rushed in and I was terrified of going outside like this, but my options were limited. Someone else knew I would be here. Just as I had one leg out the door, I felt someone grasp my shoulder. It was Mr. Hale and just as he entered my view, he placed a hand over his mouth signaling the need for silence.

"Quickly now," he whispered, "take this and make your way to the tree line. They will be gone soon and then he can take you home."

He handed me a winter coat and a book bag although I'm not sure why he was insistent on helping me. Unfortunately, while I wanted to dwell on the reasoning now wasn't the time. I quickly took what he had to offer and slid the rest of the way out the window. I saw the window slide closed just shortly after my exit. While donning the coat and bag I scanned my surroundings. There was nothing for what appeared to be miles behind the Hale's home making a grab and snatch highly unlikely from that side. I crouched down keeping as low to the ground as possible. In the event they were inside there may be a chance that they glance out the window just to be thorough.

I reached the side of the home and peered around the corner towards the driveway. I could see the top of the officer's cruiser in the drive, but not much else. It wasn't far to the nearest tree line, only about thirty meters or so, and soon I would need to make a break for it. I glanced back once more and then again towards the drive. All clear. I rose out of the crouch just before bolting towards the tree line with as much ferocity as I could muster. In just a few short breaths later I blew through the tree line and continued on for an additional ten to fifteen meters just to ensure I was out of sight. When I finally stopped, I dropped to the ground panting like a whipped pooch.

This was far from over, but hopefully not being found in the bed of my caregiver would offer more protection than if I would have stayed. As I waited patiently for the officers to finish with their interrogation my mind was plagued by questions. Who else knew I was here? Was I so consumed by my selfishness and desire I failed to see someone watching me? The thought made my skin crawl and forced me to acknowledge I may not have out witted my foe just merely delayed him. What if this same person was watching me right now and my escape from their grasp was a mere illusion? I was starting to believe I was a key player in an elaborate game of cat and mouse.

I was still deep in thought when I heard a car door slam shut drawing my attention back to the police cruiser in the drive. Through the tinted windows it was difficult to discern the contents, but it appeared only one officer was hidden within. I crouched behind a nearby tree hoping to shield my presence from his sight as I searched for the remaining officer. I couldn't hear his voice as I once did, meaning he was still inside, or he was alone and searching. The internal battle of fight versus flight was underway, but I knew there was a good chance if I fled now, I would be caught. I couldn't risk it.

I sat there unsure as to the amount of time passing and just waited. Then I heard the final door open and close. The final officer was in the car and soon I would be able to seek refuge in Tyler's Jeep until we were able to depart. Unfortunately for us if the police were asking questions, they would more than likely be watching him as well. We both would need to be mindful of our steps until this was over.

As the cruiser backed out, I noticed that Mr. Hale was walking towards the Jeep with Tyler nearly chomping at the bit behind him. Mr. Hale had a few bags in tow and Tyler appeared to be carrying a crate of some sort, but why? None of it made any sense. If anything, I would have thought they would have been trying to keep a low profile, but this looked suspicious even to me. My curiosity drew me away from the tree I was hiding behind and towards the edge. I could hear them talking now and even though their voices were just above a whisper their voices carried towards me. They weren't speaking English causing part of my confusion, but more importantly why weren't they speaking English?

I hadn't realized that my curiosity had brought me a few steps out from the tree line leaving me exposed. Tyler's eyes noticed me seconds after I realized my mistake and hewaved me towards the Jeep door that was now ajar. I said nothing, but quickly scurried towards them. Upon my arrival I opened the door just enough for me to climb insidebefore falling into the floorboard of the backseat. With thetailgate open I could hear them more clearly now.

"Izz," Tyler whispered, "someone knows you were here. We need to go and quickly before they come back."

I didn't respond, but I now felt like a fugitive. I didn't know who could have told the police about my personal involvement with Tyler, but I was clearly being weeded out of the tall grass that was protecting me.

"Isolde," Mr. Hale whispered, "I hope to see you again when this is all over."

I heard the tailgate latch closed just before Tyler climbed into the front seat. Even though worry had now taken a foothold upon his brow causing him to age slightly he was still better looking than I remembered. I leaned myself against the passenger seat to see him better and as he turned to back out of the drive our eyes met. I knew in that moment that I was irrevocably and irrefutably in love with him.

"Where are we going?" I whispered.

His eyes were drawn back to the road, "I'm taking you home or as close to home as I can safely get you."

"No, you can't," the words caught in my throat, "he will find me there."

"Izz, I don't know how he did it, but he already has found you and that's why I need to get you somewhere safe."

I could already feel my blood pressure rising. I hadn't seen my parents since I left fuming and I wasn't sure what kind of a mess I was going to arrive home to find especially with Rhys in critical care. I think he could sense something was amiss with me and reached back for his hand to find mine. He squeezed my hand gently in his as we made our way back towards town. Just after entering the city limits, he turned off on a road I did not recognize causing unrest within me. I felt the urgency to demand where we were going, but part of me believed I already knew. Maybe this was a shortcut or his way of being cautious, but I was already dreading my arrival home. Several turns later I started seeing familiar surroundings again. While it was comforting to be near home again that meant my time with him was nearly up.

"Can you drive around a bit longer? I'm not ready to let go just yet."

He nodded and gave my hand another squeeze as he continued down the road. He drove down several streets in an attempt to pass the time or at least until my nerves were calmed a bit. I couldn't prolong the inevitable, but I knew it wasn't safe for him either if Derek knew we were involved in any way.

"I have brought something in case you need to get out quickly. Is there a place that you might store them until they are needed?"

"We have a storage shed out back. It's rarely used outside of summer, so that should work," I blurted out a bit louder than intended. "Although, I'm not sure how to get things from your Jeep to the shed."

He smiled, "I'll take care of it."

I noticed we began to slow down, but I wasn't confident where we were. I sat up slowly and quickly glanced outside. I noticed we were in what appeared to be a vacant lot, but with my quick scan I could not discern much else. I reached forward to turn the key to the ignition back quieting the engine and allowing the lights to fade away. Drawing additional attention to ourselves at this point wouldn't have been helpful. Upon further inspection I noticed we were near the school board office. I cannot recall being here before, but I knew my family home wasn't far. We sat in silence for a few moments just staring out the window when finally, he spoke.

"Head out behind that building and take the long way around using the trees for coverage. I'll be right behind you to make sure you're not followed."

I nodded, "Please be careful. I don't know what I would do without you."

He smiled before leaning in to kiss me softly, "I hope you never have to find out."

We opened our doors in unison hoping that if someone was listening, they wouldn't notice the sound of a second door being opened or closed. I scurried towards the school board office and upon my arrival did my best to slink into the shadows. Night was beginning to fall upon us, anI knew we didn't have much time. The forest can be difficult to navigate in the dark and if were truly going to attempt to be unseen we would need to hurry. Sliding along the brick wall I managed to reach the far side unseen, but now I could no longer see Tyler. I had to keep moving. I wasn't sure whether to slink across the ground or just run, but I didn't have long to decide. There were homes nearby and anyone of them could have already seen meor grown suspicious of the shadow lurking nearby.

I made a run for it and soon reached the trees where I was quickly masked in the foliage. I heard some noise to the rear of me causing me to hesitate, but when I heard nothing further, I pressed onward. This wasn't a path I had taken before, so while at first, I was disoriented soon my keen sense of direction kicked in. Rather than opt for speed I opted for stealth slowly making my way through the brush. I hadn't heard anything other than my own fumbling in what felt like ages, so I can't even assume Tyler was behind me any longer.

After several freaked-out minutes I saw something bright in the distance drawing me closer. It wasn't a light source of any kind, but bright in color. It was clearly larger than a plant, but smaller than the majority of trees that would have been found here. As I stepped closer and closer towards it, I noticed it appeared to be more like debris left to float in the breeze rather than anything else. Regardless I couldn't take my eyes off of it. It soon came into focus and then I realized it wasn't just any debris. It was caution tape that had clearly been left behind as it was no longer curtaining off any particular area that I could see.

I rushed towards it and placed my fingers upon it. I wasn't sure what I was hoping to feel or to find, but I just had to touch it. There was nothing other than the cool sensation of plastic touching my skin. As I turned, I noticed there were several pieces of caution tape draped around the area and then I finally realized what this place was. This was where I was found or so they say. The area was heavily trampled, but I recognized it almost immediately. What once was my sanctuary was now no better than your average vacant lot. Beaten down earth forgotten by most, but the memory of what happened here I feared would forever haunt me. I always believed I was a strong individual and could persevere even in the more dire of circumstances but standing here now brought to light a frightened little girl I desperately wanted to hide.

I stepped towards the tree where it all started and placed my hand upon it. Like a bolt of lightning striking me, the image of him pinning me to the tree rushed through my mind. I quickly removed my hand from the tree and stepped backward. Lingering here would only cause more pain. I turned sharply and began making my way back towards the path I had veered from. However, at only a few steps into my journey I heard leaves rustling, but there wasn't any sort of breeze presently blowing through. I wasn't alone, but whether friend or foe that stumbled upon me I wasn't entirely confident I wished to stay for the reveal.

I may not have always listened to my body previously, but I was learning to trust it. It was telling me to run. In a burst of fury, I quickly dug my toes into the soft earth before pressing against it with all of my might. Trees were no more than a blur in my peripheral vision now and what once nearly consumed me was rapidly vanishing in the distance. I didn't look back, but as the pain increased, I felt the need to slow down. My family home was now visible through the trees giving me a false sense of relief. I was being forced to slow down but stopping was not an option. Keep moving I told myself. Keep moving. I no longer heard rustling in the distance, but that didn't mean someone, or something wasn't there.

I reached the boundaries of our backyard and moved quickly towards the shed. Upon my arrival I noticed it was already unlocked, but how could that be? My folks have never been the type to leave their things unattended or unprotected. I felt like I was being played or something. Like I had already been here and unlocked it, but somehow it was forgotten. I stood there for a moment taking in the full view of the house in the dark light. It seemed enraged and eerie looking in its current light or maybe that was just my subconscious playing tricks on me. I walked towards the drive and noticed Rhys's truck was there. I paused in a moment of reflection before turning back towards the shed. Still no Tyler.

I waited near the backside of the property a bit longer in hoping he would show, but he never did. My time was up, and I needed to seek refuge wherever I could.I gave a little sigh and then pressed onward towards the backdoor. I placed my hand on the door, but something stopped me from opening it. We were a lively family, so a lit house without any sound coming from it seemed a bit unusual. I glanced to both sides of me just to make sure I wastruly alone. When I was sure I was I slowly turned the knob and pushed the door open. I just needed to get upstairs. I tried not to creep, but I think it's a natural reaction in this case. My father was in the den reading and didn't seem to notice my presence or so I thought.

"Isolde, come and have a seat."

His voice boomed through the quiet kitchen despite his casual tone. His tone forced me to let out another heavy sigh before stepping towards the den. I lingered in the doorway hoping that would be far enough, but his focus didn't falter from what he was reading. More term papers I assume, but he is always in the den working on something. He only raised a hand and pointed towards the sofa resting across the way from him demanding I sit. I was smart enough to know that bolting right now wouldn't be a good idea, so I sat down and did my best to appear reformed. He lowered the paperwork he was holding and folded his hands.

"Are you feeling better?"

"A little, thank you for asking," I replied still with a fair amount of confidence in my voice.

"I'm pleased to hear that," he paused, "Care to tell me where you have been!" he shouted.

"I was with a friend."

I felt my voice catch as the lie crossed my lips. However, lying at this point seemed like a moot point considering everything else that has happened and starting off my return by telling my father that I was with my *boyfriend* or lover that just happened to be an adult seemed like a very poor choice to go with.

"A friend?" he glanced at my appearance. "You expect me to believe that."

"I'm not sure what you mean." My voice didn't falter this time, but I could feel myself becoming jittery.

"And who brought you home tonight?"

"I ran."

He leaned forward slightly, "I'm disappointed in you. You're lying to me and that's beneath you."

I pursed my lips and knew I was beat. I couldn't say anything to throw him off the scent, but I didn't want to go down without a fight.

"It's not what you think," I urged.

He stood and stepped towards me. He was infuriated at my boldness. "My eldest son is laying in a hospital with machines keeping him alive! My only daughter disappears without a trace from the same hospital only to return wearing a man's clothes, but claims she was just with a friend!"

"I ran away to save Rhys!" I jumped up and shouted back at him.

"This could have all been prevented if you just told the truth from the beginning!" he paused for quite some time before turning away from me. "What happened to you I cannot begin to understand, but the young woman that emerged from that trauma isn't my daughter."

I desperately wanted to say something to him, but his words cut through me like knives. I began walking and doing my best not to completely breakdown in tears. I felt my body begin to shiver and I knew the rush was fading away only to be replaced by disappointment. I tried to hold my breath as I walked knowing I would walk quicker if I did. I hurried my way through the living room just before beginning my ascent up the stairs nearly running into Liam along the way.

"Whoa, where's the fire?" he threw his hands up in defense.

"Just get out of my way," I spat while trying to push past him.

"I'd watch your step if I were you," he smirked and raised one of his eyebrows. "Wouldn't want you to have another accident."

His response took me by surprise, and I turned towards him, my brow furrowed and my eyes narrowing. "What did you just say to me?"

"I said you should be careful," he continued walking down the steps before uttering, "Based on how you look one of your lover's has clearly already worked you over today."

I couldn't even believe what I just heard, and I became enraged. I rushed back down the steps towards him and jumped on his back taking him to the floor. He wasn't expecting it and when he hit, he hit hard. I started to gather my footing in an attempt to stand, but I was unable to do so quick enough. It took only a few seconds, but without difficulty he managed to knock me back. My head was pounding, and my vision blurred. The scuffle clearly caught the attention of our father, and he was now inbetween the two of us.

"What in God's name is wrong with the two of you!?" our father demanded.

I shook my head not sure how to respond.

"Izzy has clearly gone mental." I saw Liam jump to his feet.

"Calm down Liam," our father insisted. "Let's get you up." He helped me stand and walk over to the couch.

"What the hell Pops?! She jumps me and now you're on her side?!" Liam roared.

"Sit down Liam!" he demanded, and Liam quicklyheeded his request.

Our father turned towards me and began to give me the once over. I already felt out of sorts, so I didn't notice any one particular thing to be out of the ordinary. I attempted to gather my wits about me, but the fury that once overcame me was coming back as I turned towards Liam. I lunged towards him hoping to get another good hit in, but unfortunately our father was able to intervene before my hand could connect with his face.

"What the hell is wrong with you?!" I shouted at Liam.

"You jumped me remember!"

"Only after you provoked me!" I shouted back.

"Maybe you deserved everything you got, you little trollop!"

I reached for him again, but I felt our father grasp my wrist firmly to get my attention.

"This ends now," our father bellowed, "we do not attack our own!"

He glared at both of us and that was a remarkably sobering effect. I took a few deep breaths and was able to slightly calm my nerves. I glanced over at Liam, and he was still far from calm. I couldn't see smoke pouring from his nostrils, but with any kind of imagination I believed it was there. In minutes, the room was filled with so much tension that we would need a knife in order to cut our way out. Something wasn't adding up and now it was out in the open. Liam knew something and I wasn't going to let that go.

I stormed up the steps and slammed my bedroom door behind me. I now had something new to focus on. During the week or so that followed my attack Liam has been remarkably quiet about everything. While he appeared to be concerned and feeling guilty according to Rhys, I can't say that I've witnessed this behavior. If I didn't know any better, I would assume tonight's actions were in an attempt to provoke me, but why? If we weren't careful this house was going to need supernatural protection to keep us from destroying one another.

26

When I spun around, I felt relief as the room was quiet and closed off. It wasn't exactly as I remembered, but it had been a few days since I'd been there. I turned briefly to flip the lock on my door before walking over to my bed. There the photographs were from days before when my mum and I spat over their meaning. Looking at them now just made me ill, but unfortunately as I turned to shy away from them, I noticed the others still on the back of my mirror along with the evening gown that once so captivated me. I longed to be relieved of them.

I quickly tore off the photos from the back of the mirror and threw them to the ground followed by the ones on my bed. Where I once looked at them with curiosity, they now only brought me disdain and torment. I decided that wasn't enough. I picked them up again and, in a fury, tore them into as many pieces as possible before chucking them out the window. The pieces fell to the ground like a cloud of confetti and reminded me of watching snow fall in the early winter months. They would twirl about swaying back and forth giving the illusion of an elaborate waltz in the evening light. It's a shame that something so monstrous could be so beautiful in the right light.

As the pieces continued to fall, I noticed that there was something near the base of the tree. From this angle I couldn't get a clear shot, but I knew there was something other than shadow to be found there. I opened my window as far as it would go before leaning out in hopes of getting a better view, but alas still nothing clear. I glanced around the room quickly and began to climb out onto the large branches. Unsteady at first, but I quickly regained my balance slowly making my way towards the tree's large trunk. When I arrived, I took another glance downward and this time the object became clear. It was someone's arm, but who?

Unfortunately, as I drew closer the arm came into focus and I realized it was Tyler's arm laying there lifeless. In a panic, I scurried my way down the remaining branches causing several more scrapes and bruises that I would surelyfeel in the morning. As I rounded the base of the tree his body was brought into view. His once bright smile now appeared terrifyingly cold and lifeless. In that moment, I felt severe pain starting in my back then searing through my insides. While I could feel my heart was breaking seeing him in this light, this pain was different.

I stood there for several moments trying to piece together what had just happened and in my hastened attempt to reach Tyler I failed to take in my surroundings. We weren't alone. I tried to step towards Tyler but was met with resistance. With each attempt to pull away the pain grew stronger. This pain while excruciating felt like only the beginning. As the seconds ticked by, I felt the pain grow stronger and more widespread. I wasn't sure what was locking me in place, but I felt my legs start to give way. I collapsed onto the ground with only a matter of inches now between Tyler and I. As I reached for him, I felt that same searing pain strike me just beneath my ribs.

I attempted to turn slightly to reveal the source of my torment, but as I did the pain only intensified forcing my body to recoil. Every movement now seemed to take great effort and just breathing was becoming strenuous. I lay there clinging to life when I felt a firm hand grasp my shoulder followed by a sudden urge to cough. Kind of like when fluid accidentally spills over into your windpipe. I was beginning to feel as if I was drowning. Whether or notI wanted to exert the energy or not my body forced me to cough violently. I turned slightly towards the ground hoping to seek some comfort and calm my tense body. While the coughing continued it wasn't nearly as violent as it began, but I could feel something running down my chin. I picked up my hand and quickly brushed it away, but even in darkness I could see this wasn't just some ordinary saliva that escaped my body, it was blood. Thick and red. Then it struck me like lightening, I had been stabbed.

As I lay there clinging to life, I felt a glimmer of hope as I saw Tyler move ever so slightly. He was alive. I think part of me knew that all along, but I didn't want to give myself false hope. It gave me a brief sense of security that I knew would not last, but it may have given me the positive energy I needed to pass into the light. Moments later my assailant came into view, and I knew then that there was no escaping his wrath. The monster hadfound us. Unfortunately, I think he saw what I did and intended to rectify the situation. He stepped over towards him and began hovering over his body. With a blood-soaked knife in one hand he turned Tyler's face towards meand held the knife dangerously close to Tyler's throat.

"Tell me Izzy, what is his life worth to you?" Derek hissed.

I focused heavily on Tyler's face and then Derek's. I don't believe anything I said at this point would cause the tide to sway in my favor, so maybe saying nothing was the answer. I could feel myself fading and I desperately wanted to close my eyes. I was now terribly cold, but I wasn't shivering. As my eyes fluttered open then closed, I could see Derek shaking Tyler more than likely in an attempt to wake him, but why I cannot say for sure. I curled up into the fetal position for warmth and held out on a hope. Just as I believed my eyes were determined to close forever, I heard his voice ever so faint.

"Izz, open your eyes. I'm here with you," Tyler whispered.

Unfortunately, as I opened my eyes, I could see he was being restrained with a knife to his throat. My eyes began darting between the knife and Derek. What did he hope to accomplish by all of this? By this point, fear and I had become best friends, so attempting to frighten me more than he had already done would be frivolous. At one time I really believed I would be able to get through all of this, but it seems there was another plan for me.

"Izz, look at me. You've lost a lot of blood-"

Derek clinched Tyler's neck tighter cutting him off. "Stop trying to comfort her," he growled, "I just need her to stay awake long enough to watch you die."

Tyler mouthed something to me, but I didn't quite catch it all and I think he knew that. I did my best not to alert Derek what was going on as he mouthed the words to me again. *I'll hold the door for you.* Somehow, he knew what was about to happen and rather than panic over his own predicament he took his final moments to reassure me. These would be our last moments together and I didn't have time to think long or second guess a reply. I replied by mouthing *my heart goes with you.* It wasn't poetic, but it was the truth. While I was afraid of what would come next, I couldn't bring myself to close my eyes. He needed to see my strength not my self-preservation.

Within seconds Tyler's body hung lifeless in Derek's hands as the blood began rushing from his body. It was over. My eyes fell closed, and tears began streaming down my cheeks. I tried to bringback the memory of the first time I woke up next to him. I was happy and at peace wrapped in his arms. I didn't knowhim then, but the comfort his presence brought was something money couldn't buy. I remembered his smell and the warmth of his breath upon my skin. The memory flooded my senses, and I said a silent prayer that I would one day see him again.

27

I cannot recall seeing a white light or even a slideshow from the memories of my life as I passed through, but to my surprise I awoke once more in a strange room. It was remarkably clean and tidy but didn't appear to be a hospital room. Well, if it was it wasn't like any, I hadthe pleasure of staying in. There was a sofa and armchair at one end of the room accompanied by what appeared to be a kitchenette. If I didn't know any better, I would say I was in a hotel, but why? I attempted to turn my head slightly to get a better view of the room but was met with resistance. There was something stuck on my face and while I desperately wanted to remove whatever it was, I couldn't seem to move my arms. Why won't my arms move?

I tried to toss myself about in the bed, but while internally I felt like I was in a mosh pit at a concert what I witnessed was very little to no movement. I tried to call for help, but something was caught in my throat muffling the sound. The sound reverberated from my body like sound pushing its way through a French horn. Low at first, but then grew louder with each passing second. The strain from it was exhausting and I nearly fainted from the exertion. Please let someone hear me. Something isn't right. I attempted to breathe in once more, but clearly something was caught in my throat.

The sensation was beginning to make me gag and the more I gagged the more it was beginning to turn my stomach. In my struggle, there must have been a sensor or something that I set off because the entry door flung open. I couldn't tell who entered the room as I was distracted by my current state, but I was grateful for their attention. I couldn't make out what they were saying, but one of them pushed my head back while shouting at me. It took a moment to focus my attention on them, but when I did, I could hear one word distinctly now. Exhale. I exhaled as best as I could and watched a long tube being extracted from my body. As it slid up and out of my body it felt like someone was dragging sandpaper along my windpipe making me gag even more.

They dropped it quickly onto my chest and offered me some water to help soothe the discomfort. I tried to speak, but it just came out as a croak. Everything seemed to ache now, and I felt drier than the Sahara. I took in a few more sips and tried again.

"Where am I?" It came out as a whisper, but it was much clearer now.

"My name is Dr. Kelly, and you are a patient at St. James Hospital. Can you tell me your name?"

"Isolde Walsh," I croaked again, "how long have I been here?"

The nurse handed me a glass of water and I sipped it slowly while waiting for a reply.

"Can you tell me how old you are?"

"Seventeen."

Both looked at each other perplexedand then back at me. "Is my brother still alive? What about the man I was with? Did he live? Was Derek ever caught?" I fired the questions in rapid succession causing me to feel the strain clear down into my chest rather than just in my throat.

They both still looked confused, and I wasn't surehow I was supposed to take that. I continued to sip the water as my throat was incredibly dry.

"Do you remember what happened?" Dr. Kelly inquired.

I nodded.

"Would you mind telling me or writing it down for me?"

Again, I nodded.

I began retelling my tragic tale for what I hoped would be the last time in as little detail as possible. Honestly, they should have all heard this before, so I'm not even sure why she was asking. Either way, I felt obligated to oblige her. I stopped in places or used the paper notebook provided to get me through. The entire time the nurse and Dr. Kelly were watching over me with increasing curiosity and confusion.

"Isolde, do you think you would be able to identify these men if shown photographs or would be able to describe them to me in greater detail?"

I was confused. What did she mean by identify these men?

"Yes, of course," I whispered.

She turned towards the nurse and whispered something my exhausted mind wouldn't allow me to decipher. The nurse soon exited the room and returned with two others along with a large manila envelope. I quickly took in some more water, but while I was quite parched other forms of nourishment never crossed my mind. At this time Dr. Kelly was still sifting through the contents of the envelope. Clearly these weren't mugshots, but I'm not sure what photos she could possibly have for me to review. However, before I was able to give it too much thought a photo was held out for me to see.

"Do you recognize this photo?"

I looked upon it carefully. It was a family photo of us taken at a local pub in Dublin.

"Yes."

"Do you recall when this photo was taken?"

"Probably over a year ago just before we moved. Why are you asking me about this photo?"

She pulled out another photo, "Do you recognize this photo?"

I glanced at the photo, but just as I was about to speak, I glanced at it again. I was standing in front of my Gran's house clearly much older, but I haven't been to my Gran's house in years. The last photo taken there would have been prior to us moving and that photo is currently in my bedroom, but this was not the same photo or even taken on the same day.

"No, I don't," I mumbled, "I mean, I know that's me in the photo and the location, but I do not recognize the photo or recall it being taken."

She nodded and exhaled before pulling the next photo out of the envelope, "Do you recognize this man?"

I grasped the photo and pulled it towards myself to get a better view. It was a photo of Derek at graduation, but he couldn't have graduated just yet. It was still autumn.

"How is this possible?" I said sharply.

"Do you recognize this man?"

"Of course, this is the monster who…," I scoffed. "How long have I been here?"

She snapped her fingers at the nurse that entered the room with her originally and she quickly began fumbling through drawers in an attempt to find something. While my attention was originally drawn to her, I needed to focus on Dr. Kelly.

"Approximately six months," she replied.

I gasped, "Where's Rhys? Does he live? What about Tyler? Were you able to save Tyler?"

Dr. Kelly snapped her fingers at the nurse once more and the nurse placed her hand upon one of my shoulders. Just the weight of her hand felt heavy, but her prompt attention quickly caused my blood pressure to rise.

"Tell me the last thing you remember about your brother, Rhys?"

"I already told you. He was laying in an ICU bed barely alive."

"Before that. Try to remember," she insisted.

"I already told you..." I attempted to shout but was met with an unfortunate frog in my throat. "Derek stabbed him because he saved me."

"Did you witness this?"

"Not him being stabbed," I muttered.

"Do you remember where you were?"

"We were at…" I stopped myself as I now realized that St. James hospital is nowhere near where we lived. "Where am I again?"

Dr. Kelly turned slightly to one of the other staff members standing behind her and whispered something once more before they vacated the room.

"Isolde, I'm about to discuss a series of traumatic events with you. This will be difficult, but I need you to try btake a deep breath." I nodded. "Six months ago, you were in a motor vehicle accident. Your brother, Rhys, and your husband were, also, in the same accident."

"Wait, what?" I could feel my body tensing up. "How could I be married? I'm seventeen years old," I spouted out in confusion.

"Isolde, I need you to take a deep breath." She stood and stepped closer to me giving a nod to the nurse standing on my right. "You're not seventeen, you're twenty-seven and up until this accident you and your husband, Derek, have been happily married and living in Dublin. Which is where you are now."

"We can't be in Dublin! We moved to the United States just shy of a year ago. Where is Tyler? I need to see him now! Right now!" I urged. "I could never be with Derek, he's a monster."

"Isolde, look at me." She held a photo up in front of me. There I stood with Derek, hand in hand, looking stunning and happy in the deep red gown.

"No, no, no, that's not true. I would never," I insisted.

She held up another photo in front of me. I was wearing a white gown with soft white jewels in my hair as

Derek kissed my cheek in the evening light. My eyes darted between her and the photos.

"This can't be. I don't believe you. Where is Tyler? Where is Rhys?"

I was starting to cry. My frustration was at an all-time high and it had nowhere to go, but out my eyes. Dr. Kelly said nothing but reached back into the envelope for something a bit larger than a photograph. She held it out for me to grab. It was a newspaper clipping. I did what I could to focus on the written word while attempting to maintain my composure. Unfortunately, about two lines in I couldn't bear to read anymore.

"This can't be real," I mumbled.

"Isolde, this is real. You've been a patient at this facility for nearly six months. I cannot explain what you experienced while you were in a coma, but I assure you this is quite real." She picked up my hand and grasped it in hers. "We are giving you something to calm your nerves. Please just try to breathe with me."

Moments later the door clicked open, and two menentered the room. I recognized them both instantly. Unfortunately for me, with their presence I could feel relief accompanied by extreme terror. Derek rushed towards my side, and I did what I could to recoil from him. My strength was not what it used to be, and it failed me as Iattempted to turn away from him. His soft lips landed on my cheek, and he whispered something to me.

"Thank you for coming back to me."

I looked at him completely frightened hoping Tyler would save me from this monster, but he never did. He stood tall with hands tucked neatly behind his back.

"Mrs. Strom—"

"Please don't call me that," I interrupted.

She gave a brief look of shock before continuing, "This is Tyler. He was one of the medics on scene after the accident. He assisted in your extraction from the vehicle and stayed with you per Mr. Strom's request. They didn't want you to ever be alone."

Tyler stepped forward and bowed slightly just as Dr. Kelly stepped back. "Mrs. Strom, I'm glad to see you've awoken. I know everyone has been anxiously waiting to see if you would," he looked down at the ground briefly before continuing. "I was with your brother when he passed, and I wanted to say how sorry I am for your loss. Through the last several months I've gotten to know him quite well through the eyes of others and he will be missed."

He smiled politely and stepped back. I attempted to reach for him, but instead of his hand finding mine Derek cupped mine in his.

"Don't touch me," I growled and watched as a look of shock flushed over his face.

His touch caused a chill to wash over me and made my heart ache for my long-lost love. I prayed we would meet again, but maybe I should have been more specific in my request. Dr. Kelly nodded him off and just quickly as he appeared, he was gone again. I felt like I couldn't breathe. How could this be? I was in high school and now I was married. I tried to piece together everything in my mind, and I realized I couldn't remember anything really before that night at the football game. I felt like my life had been stolen from me with no way of getting it back.

My eyes were darting around the room at all the people and faces trying to find something that made sense to me. I found nothing. I closed my eyes and tried to focus on the details when I heard Dr. Kelly speak again only much softer this time.

"Mr. Strom, this is what we had talked about. With the type of head injury your wife sustained there is no way of knowing what she may or may not remember. Right now, she believes that you attacked her and her brother causing an unrelenting desire to flee when in your presence. While we can work with both of you to alleviate some ofthe strain it will take time."

He nodded, but the look of disappointment was written all over his face.

"You can't leave me alone with him," I demanded.

"Mrs. Strom, you are in a controlled environment here and until you are comfortable, I will have a nurse stay with you."

She nodded to the nurse directly beside me and went to hand her the manila envelope.

"Can you leave that with me?" I asked softly.

She smiled, "I was hoping you'd say that."

Derek turned and walked towards a closet in the room. He returned a short time later with a box and pulled a chair up next to my bedside. I know physically I couldn't scream, but every fiber of my being desperately wanted to. He inched towards me and began rambling. I waved my hand up hoping it would silence him and to my surprise he quickly heeded to my request. I glanced towards the nurse and was about to ask for a cup of tea when I noticed the door was opening again. A visitor was carrying several items and quickly entered the room.

"I heard Mrs. Strom was awake and I didn't know what you might need or what she might like."

I gave a brief smile and then returned my attention to Derek still sitting patiently at my bedside.

"I'm sorry, I just," I paused. I could hardly believe those words just came out of my mouth. What exactly was I sorry about?

"Izzy, you're my whole world. I'll wait for you no matter how long it takes." He tried to smile, but something about him seemed broken. Very different from the man in my nightmare. "I brought you a few things from home."

I wanted to lean over and glance in the box, but realistically I may have fallen over if I did. The nurse continued to move about the room keeping busy, but I was thankful for her presence. Not to mention whatever they gave me to help relax me was really kicking in. I felt like I was floating at this point. I watched attentively as Derek began removing items from the box, but before he was finished, I stopped him.

"I need time," I whispered.

He nodded, but I could tell it wasn't what he wanted to hear. Moments later the nurse escorted him out and came back to my bedside.

"What's wrong with me?" I whispered.

She gave a smile, "You've been through so much that we don't understand. It will take time, but he's a good man. He's rarely left your side and he's never given up on you. He always knew you'd wake." She picked up the manila envelope pouring out the contents onto my lap. "Ready to begin?"

Epilogue

It's been nearly a year now since I woke from my nightmare. While we may never fully understand what happened while I was in a coma, my team of medical doctors believe there isn't one theory that could explain everything that happened, but maybe a combination of theories. After talking with several physicians and recovered coma patients, what I experienced was uncommon but not entirely unheard of. Depending on the illness or the portion of the brain that has been injured, the results and experiences vary. There have been reports of patients dreaming with pieces of the outside world penetrating through while others recall only terrible nightmares.

After several research studies, the fuzzy trace theory has provided the most valuable insight to the terror I experienced while in a coma. It was one of several theories mentioned during my recovery. This theory is founded on our just memory with the understanding that our memories our coded in our brain as simply fuzzy traces. These traces or fragments of a memory are what remains of an event rather than the entire memory. Unfortunately, as we age, we are more likely to create or have false memories stemming from these traces. This explains how two people who experienced the same event can essentially provide two very different accounts when asked days or even years later. The same response occurs in conversation. The more time that passes after a conversation occurs the less likely someone will remember it accurately. This could explain why members of law enforcement are so quick to take a statement when an incident occurs.

As a secondary theory, one research team believed transference was to blame. While Derek was driving the vehicle the afternoon of the crash, I painted him as the villain because subconsciously I blamed him for my brother's death. I do not believe he wrecked the vehicle that afternoon on purpose, but on some level, I needed to blame someone. While I can see validity to their conclusion, I believe there was more to it than that. Rhys was a good man and I still have a difficult time seeing the reason behind his sudden departure. I still cannot fully remember the events of that afternoon, but it is my understanding this is common with retrograde amnesia. In truth, I'm not sure I want to remember it as reliving it could possibly be more painful than just blocking it from my memory altogether. With help, I've been able to move on from the accident and make peace with my brother's passing.

After the day I woke, I never saw Tyler again. I attempted to inquire as to his well-being once or twice, but the mere suggestion only caused me more pain. There was a time where I gave a great deal of thought to how his presence entered my mind, but after many exhausting hours I decided that to heal I needed to give up the search. The person or spirit that helped me wade through the storm

356

while my body healed had since died and we were both reborn. I hope wherever he is, he is happy and well.

Many days and nights were spent with family and friends combing over old photo albums and trinkets from the past in order to help me recover. It was difficult to be with Derek at first especially once we returned home, but we worked through my fear and apprehension faster than I anticipated. I do my best not to think of the nightmare these days as I now know it was nothing more than a bad dream and dreams are meant to be forgotten. However, when I do think of it now, I know that all the things that didn't make sense then were bits of my life trying to push their way inside. From the red gown, the notes in my book bag, the photos behind my bedroom mirror and so on. These amongst other things were truly part of Derek's and my story. Unfortunately, in my weakened state of mind, the events became distorted.

Shortly after my high school graduation, my family and I returned to Ireland. It was as if we'd never left, and I was comforted to be home again. Derek relocated to Ireland as well where we attended and graduated from the university together. There may have been secret kisses in our past, but my honor remained intact until we were wed the autumn after graduation. Rhys was his best man and Liam was our photographer. He became an artist after all.

Throughout the last year, Derek's will to conquer my nightmare was more inspiring than my own desire. Despite the struggle we encountered at first, we were able to reconnect and find happiness again. Love isn't a fairy tale or about venturing down a smooth path, it's about weathering the storm with someone who refuses to give up on you even when you believed you were already gone.